THE LINE BETWEEN LOVE AND HATE

Charli Gillies

Copyright © 2023 by Charli Gillies

All rights reserved.

No portion of this book may be reproduced in any form without written permission from the publisher or author, except as permitted by U.S. copyright law.

Contents

1. The News

After leaving the attorney's office, I nearly got hit by a car as I floated across the street in a daze. After all these years, I'd tried so hard not to think about her. But now, she was all I could think about.

Lisa.Oh god.

Flashes of her flooded my mind - her soft black hair, her excitement, the strum of her guitar, and the deep sadness and heartbreak in her beautiful big brown eyes the last time I saw her fifteen years ago.

I wasn't supposed to see her again. Living with Lalisa Manoban, even if only for the summer, was not an option. It was probably more like there was no way in hell Lalisa Manoban was going to agree to share a house with me. Whether we liked it or not, the beach house in Newport was now ours. It's not my mine. It's not hers. But ours. Fifty-fifty.

What the hell was my grandma thinking?

I'd always known she clearly cared about her, but nothing could have prepared me for the extent of her generosity. She wasn't even related to us, but she'd always thought of her as her granddaughter, and now-fuck off, I need to share a house with her.

I took up my phone and scrolled down until I found Jennie's name. I breathed a sigh of relief when she answered the phone.

"Where are you, Jen?"

"The East Side, why?"

"Are you free to meet up? I really need to talk with someone, Jen..."

"Are you okay?"

My mind went blank before gradually filling up with fragmented memories of Lisa. My chest constricted. She hated me. I'd avoided her for so long, but I was about to have to confront her.

Jennie's voice jolted me out of my reverie.

"Rosie? Are you still there?"

"Um..yeah, sorry. Everything is fine. Uh...where are you again?"

"Meet me on Thayer Street at the falafel shop. We'll eat early and talk about whatever is on your minds."

"Okay. I'll see you in ten."

Jennie was a new-but not-so-new-friend, and she didn't know much about my teen years. We worked together at a Providence charter school. I had scheduled a meeting with my grandmother's attorney for today.

The aromas of cumin and dried mint filled the air inside the Middle Eastern fast food restaurant. Jennie waved from a corner booth, a Styrofoam container piled high with tahini-covered chicken kabobs and rice already served in front of her.

"Are you going to get anything to eat?" She inquired, her mouth full. Her mouth was coated with a dollop of yoghurt sauce.

"No. I'm not hungry. But maybe I'll take something to go on the way out. I just needed to talk." I bit on my bottom lip.

"What's going on?"

My throat had become parched. "Actually, I need to drink something first. Hold on."

As I made my way to the refrigerator by the counter, the room seemed to sway. I sat down and took a deep breath after returning from buying a bottle of water.

"At the lawyer's office today, I got some pretty crazy news."

"Okay..." Jennie's brow furrowed.

"So, clearly, you know that I went there because my grandmother died a month ago..."

"Yes, and I'm still sorry for your loss." Jennie nodded, a sad smile on her face.

"Well, that's not the issue anyway, but thank you Jen. And, well, I was just meeting with her estate attorney to go over her will. She apparently left me all of her jewellery... and half of her summer home on Aquidneck Island."

"What? Is that the beautiful house in the picture on your desk?"

"Yeah. That's the right one. We used to go there a lot in the summer when I was younger, but she'd rented it out in recent years. Her family had owned the property for generation after generation. It's a little older, but it's beautiful and overlooks the water."

"Wow, that's cool! So what's the deal with you being so upset and looks the same like a broken sad engine face?"

"Jen...can you not?" I groaned and tilted my head back in frustration. I slapped her on her hand and she whined.

"Ow! I was just kidding. Now what is it, little princess?" Jennie smiled and sometimes I just wanna give a bite on her fluffy cheeks.

"Well...she gave the other half to a woman named Lalisa Manoban, where's the fun? I'm not complaining about my late grandmother, but after she died, she should have made my life easier rather than otherwis e...ugh!" I dropped my forehead on the table and deliberately hit the table with my fist. Then I sat still again and looked at Jennie with frustration.

"Who is she?"

The only person I've ever loved.

"She was likely a girl with whom I grew up. My grandmother looked after her while her parents were at work. My house was on one side, Lisa's on the other, and my grandmother's in the middle."

"Did she feel like a sister to you?"

I wish.

"For many years, we were close." I exhaled a sigh.

"Uh well, from the expression on your face, I get the feeling that something has...uh changed?" Jennie raised her brow and made a guessing expression.

"You'd be right."

"What happened?" Jennie moved forward and a little closer to me, her face filled with questions. I can sense it.

I couldn't bear the thought of going over everything again. It had already been too much for me to take in today. I'd give her a condensed version. The shorter it was, the better, and the easier it was for her to understand, as she was always a little slow in understanding things.

"Basically, I found out that she was hiding something from me. And then I freaked out. I'd rather not get into it. But let's just say I was fifteen at the time and struggling with my hormones and issues with my mother. I made a hasty decision to leave and live with my dad." I said, swallowing the pain.

"I left it all behind in Providence and moved to New Hampshire." I continued.

Fortunately, Jennie did not pry about the secret since that wasn't the problem I needed to talk today. It was more important for her to help me in determining my next step than for me to reopen old wounds.

"So, instead of dealing with it, you basically ran away from it all."

"Yeah. I ran away from my problems...and Lisa."

"You haven't spoken to her since?"

"There was no contact for several months after I left. I felt terrible about how I handled things. I did eventually try to see her and apologise once I realised what I had done, but it was too late. She didn't want to see or speak with me. I can't say I blamed her. She'd moved on, joined a different crowd, and eventually relocated to New York shortly after graduating from high school. We lost contact, but she apparently maintained contact with Grandma. She regarded her as a second mother."

"Do you know what happened to her?"

"I haven't looked her up. I've always been too afraid to ask."

"Well, we need to take care of that right now." She set down her fork and reached into her purse for her phone.

"Whoa...What are you doing?"

"You know that I am a self-proclaimed professional stalker." Jennie grinned. "I'm going to look her up on Twitter, Facebook or something, you know...Laliiii...what was her name again? And she resides in New York?"

"I can't look," I said, covering my eyes. "And I won't look. There are probably hundreds of girls out there named Lalisa Manoban. You're not going to find her."

"Oh, cool bestie. Nothing is impossible if you didn't give a try on it. So, how does she look?"

"I last saw her when she was sixteen, so I'm sure she doesn't look the same. She does, however, have shiny and soft black hair."

She was adorable and strikingly beautiful. I can still see her face as if it were yesterday. It was something I'd never forget.

Jennie was reading aloud information for the various Lalisa Manoban that were appearing. Nothing stood out until she said, "Lalisa Manoban, New York, New York, musician at Just In Time Acoustic Guitar."

My heart rate dropped, and to my surprise, I could feel tears trying to escape through my eyelids. The intensity of the emotions that bubbled to the surface was unsettling. It was as if she'd risen from the dead. "What did you just say? Works at where?"

"Acoustic Guitar Just in Time? Is that her?"

I remained silent, pondering the name; it was the same one she'd always used, even as a kid playing guitar on our public street.

Just in time.

"That's her!" I finally gave in.

"Oh. My. Fucking. God. Roseanne!"

My heart began to beat faster. "What?"

"This woman is..."

"What? Tell me," I practically yelled before finishing my water.

"She's...gorgeous. Absofuckinglutely gorgeous."

"Jesus," I said, covering my face. "Please don't tell me that."

"Look at it."

"I can't."

Jennie shoved the phone in front of my face before I could say anything else. As I took it, it shook in my hands.

Jesus, sweet baby Jesus.

Why did I even dare to look?

From what I could see in the one photo, she was stunning-just like I remembered her, but also very different.

Grown up.

She wore a grey beanie and black-looking-expensive-glasses. She was leaning into a guitar and looking like she was about to sing into a microphone in her profile photo. Her expression was intense, and it gave me chills.

When I tried to access the other photos, I was disallowed because her profile was set to private.

Jennie reached for the phone. "Is she a musician?"

"I assume so," I said as I handed it back to her.

She used to write songs for me.

"Are you planning on contacting her?"

"No."

"Lol why no?"

"I guess I don't know what to say is all. Whatever is meant to happen is going to happen. I'll have to talk to her eventually. I'm sorry, but I'm not going to be the one to make the first move. Why would she agree to this agreement in the first place!?"

"How exactly is this housing arrangement supposed to work?" "

"Well, the attorney handed me a set of keys and informed me that another set had been sent to Rosie. The deed will have both of our names on it. Grandma also set aside money for house repairs and property maintenance during the off season. I'm assuming she's been given all of the same information."

"Are you sure you don't want to sell the house?"

"Nah, of course no. There are far too many memories, and it meant a great deal to Grandma. I'm going to use it this summer and then possibly rent it out if Lisa agrees."

"So, you have no idea how she plans to use her half? You're just going to show up there in a few weeks, and if she's there, she's there, and if she's not then she's not eh?"

"Well, pretty much"

"Oh, this is going to be very interesting." Jennie smirked and let out a small chuckled.

Fifteen years ago.

Grandma was sitting outside her house, watching the girl she had started watching this summer. I couldn't bear the thought of her seeing me the way I was right now. I wanted to watch her through the curtains of my bedroom window without her knowing I was there.

I didn't know much about her. Lisa was her name. She was ten years old, a year or two older than me, possibly eleven. She'd recently relocated to Rhode Island from Cincinnati. Her parents had money; they had to if they were going to buy the large Victorian house next door to Grandma's. They both worked in downtown Providence and paid grandma to look after Lisa after school.

I could now see what she looked like. She had shaggy dark hair and appeared to be learning how to play the guitar. I must have stood at the window for nearly an hour just watching her strumming the strings.

Then god, my sneeze came out of nowhere. Her head shot up toward the window. We exchanged glances for a few seconds before I ducked. My heart was racing because she'd discovered I'd been spying on her.

"Hey. Where have you gone?" I could hear her inquire.

I remained crouched and silent.

"Roseanne...I know you're there."

She knew my name?

"What's the deal with hiding from me?"

I finally responded, "I have a lazy eye," as I slowly stood up with my back to the window.

"Uh..a lazy eye? Is that like a wandering eye?"

"What is a wandering eye?"

"I'm actually not sure. My mother always says that my father has a wandering eye."

"A lazy eye implies that I'm cross-eyed."

"Like cock-eyed?" She burst out laughing. "No way. That must be so cool! Let me see!"

"Do you think it's cool to have an inward-facing eyeball?"

"Yeah. That would be cool! You could look at people and they wouldn't even realise you were looking at them." She was beginning to make me laugh.

"Well, mine isn't all that bad...yet."

"Come on, kiddo. Turn around. I'd like to see it."

"No."

"Please?"

Unsure of what had happened to me, I decided to let her see me. I couldn't put it off forever.

She flinched when I turned around. "Can you tell me what happened to your other eye?"

"It's still standing." I indicated my right eye. "This is just a band-aid over it."

"How come it's the same colour as your skin? From where I was standing, you seemed to be blind. It scared the crap out of me for a second!"

"It's hidden under the patch. My eye doctor is going to make me wear this for four days a week. Today is the first day and that's why I didn't want you to see me!"

"There's nothing to be embarrassed about. I was taken aback at first because I had no idea what was going to happen. So, your cockeye is down there? I'd like to see it."

"No, actually, my good eye is the one with the covered eye. According to the doctor, if I don't use my good eye, my lazy eye will strengthen and straighten out over time."

"Oh...I understand. So, are you free to go outside now? Since you no longer have to hide from me?"

"No. I don't want anyone else to see me."

"What are you going to do when you have to go back to school the next day?"

"I'm not sure."

"So you're going to stay inside all day?"

"For the time being. Yes..."

Lisa remained silent. She simply set down her guitar, stood up, and ran over to her house. Maybe I really did scare her away after all.

She came running back to her spot in front of Grandma's five minutes later.

I couldn't believe my eyes when she looked up into my window again. Well, "eye," to be precise. A massive black patch covered her right eye. Lisa closely resembles a pirate.

She sat down, picked up her guitar, and began strumming. She then began to sing a song, which surprised me. It was a cover of Brown Eyed Girl, but with the lyrics changed to One Eyed Girl.

That's when I realised Lalisa Manoban was equal parts insane and adorable.

She took a black Sharpie marker from her pocket after she finished singing.

"I'll colour in yours as well. Will you please come outside now?"

My heart was filled with a warmth I'd never felt before. Thinking back, I believe that was the exact moment Lalisa Manoban became my best friend. That was also the day she gave me a nickname that would stick with me throughout our teenage years: Patch.

End of flashback.

2. THE MEET UP

Humans are like jigsaw pieces and they have to keep finding a spot where they could fit in and feel complete. It's gonna be hard but in the end, there would always be a place where other pieces would be connected to you.

The day has finally came.

It was unmistakably the calm before the storm; I just didn't realise it at the time. The property was in good condition because the neighbour, Naddy, who was also Grandma's close friend, had taken care of it.

I was knocking on wood two weeks into my stay at grandma's summer house—my summer house—hoping that the peace and quiet would last.

Lisa hasn't said anything. Nobody has said anything. Just me, myself, and my books as I began the summer in peace amidst the salty ocean air that surrounded me on the island.

Never in my life had I been more grateful for such tranquillity. It was only a little more than a month ago that I felt as if my world had come to an end. Not only had Grandma died, but I'd also recently discovered that Shawn, my two-year boyfriend, had been cheating on me.

We'd just had sex when he went to the bathroom to dispose of the condom and to take a shower the night I found out. He'd left his phone by the bedside, and that's when I discovered all of the messages from this bitch named Dina.

He usually carried his phone with him everywhere, including the bathroom, but he made a mistake that night. I later found Dina on Facebook and discovered that half of the photos she posted were of the two of them. I'd had a feeling something was wrong with him for the previous six months. That was the final confirmation I needed. I found out just before I left for the summer house that Shawn had moved to Boston to live with her.

As a result, this was a significant period of transition for me. I was twenty-four years old, single again, and embarking on a new adventure in Newport for the summer.

Summers were free for me because of my teaching job in Providence. My hope was to find a temporary job for the season, but for the time being, I just wanted to relax for a few weeks.

My day would begin with a cup of coffee on the upper deck, which overlooked Easton's Beach. While listening to the seagulls, I would check Facebook, read In Style, or simply meditate. I'd then soak in the tub upstairs for as long as I wanted before getting dressed and starting my day, which would entail curling up on the couch with a book.

I'd make lunch and bring it back out to the upper deck by mid-afternoon. I used to drive down to Thames Street in Newport before dark and browse the shops, looking at blown glass, trinkets, and nautical artwork. Then I'd make a pit stop for gelato or coffee.

The day would usually end with a trip down to the dock for some freshly caught lobster or quahogs. I'd bring them home in a bag and steam them in a pot in the backyard.Then, while watching the sunset over the Atlantic, I'd sit down to dinner with a bottle of chilled white wine.

This was the way of life.

Just no matter how beautiful something is,It may end up with tragedy someday or another,Just like humans—

Beauty hurts more when no one expects the most.

What matters is the heart.

For a few weeks, my daily routine remained the same until my rude awakening.

—

One night, on my way back from downtown Newport with my bag of crustaceans, I noticed that the front door to the house was wide open.

Is it possible that I forgot to lock it? Was it because of the wind?

When I walked into the kitchen, I was greeted by a tall, leggy woman with short, cropped platinum blonde hair. She was stocking the cabinets and looked like a young Kim Taeyeon.

I swallowed and cleared my throat. "Hello?"

She turned around and covered her chest. "Oh my goodness. You scared me." She smiled as she walked over to me and extended her hand.

"Hello, my name is Winter."

Winter could have been a model with her fine features, high cheekbones, and pixie cut. She's beautiful.

"My name is Park Roseanne. W-who are you?"

"I'm Lisa's girlfriend."

My stomach churned. "Oh... Yes, I see. Where is she?"

"She only went to the grocery store and the liquor store." Winter said and I just nodded my head, feeling glad that she wasn't here at the moment.

"Anyway, how long you've been here?"

"We only arrived an hour ago."

"How long will you be here?" I asked again, to feed my curiosity the best tea.

"I'm not sure. We'll just have to wait and see where the summer takes us. Neither of us had anticipated this development...you know, the house."

"Yeah...I know." I looked down at her French-manicured toes peeking out from beneath her heels. "Do you have any job?"

"Actually, I'm a Broadway actress. For the time being, it's off Broadway. I'm between jobs, but I'll most likely be travelling to New York for auditions. How about you? What do you do?"

"I work as a middle school teacher. So that's why I have the summers off."

"Wow, that's pretty cool." She smiled in excitement to me. She seemed a nice person.

"Yeah. It's entertaining. Does Lisa work somewhere?"

"Right now, she works from home. She sells software. She can work from anywhere. She also performs. You do realise she's a musician, don't you?"

"To be honest, I don't know much about her anymore."

"What happened between you two in the first place? If you don't mind, I'm asking?"

"Has she ever told you anything about me?"

"It's just that you grew up together and are Mrs. H.'s granddaughter. To be honest, she never mentioned you until we got the letter from the attorney."

Even though it was predictable, it made me sad, still. I had no right to be sad because it was my choice to leave and to stay far away from her. But one thing is certain: it was done for a reason, an unacceptable reason, to be sure.

"It's not surprising." I sighed.

"Why do you say that?" Winter asked in concerned.

"It's kind of a long story." I shrugged, recalled back all those memories that caused us to drifted apart.

"Have you ever dated?"

I widen my eyes and shook my head vigorously then let out a small chuckled. "No nah, of course never. That was far from the case. We were just good friends, but after I moved away, we drifted apart."

"Ah, I see. Isn't everything a little strange? I mean, how did you end up with a house like this out of nowhere?" She pointed to the house and I just grinned awkwardly, whilst nodding my head to her.

"Well, my grandmother was a very generous person, and she loved Lisa. My mother is her only child, and grandma loved Lisa as if she were a granddaughter, so..."

"Did your grandmother leave the house to you instead of your mother?" Winter cut me off.

"Mom and Grandma had a squabble a few years ago. Fortunately, they reconciled before she died, but things were never the same again."

"I'm really sorry to hear that."

"It's totally fine." I smiled to reassured her and she smiled back to me.

Winter extended her arms and drew me into a warm embrace. "Well, I sincerely hope we can become friends. It'll be nice to have a girl to shop with and explore the island with."

"Yeah. That would be nice." I smiled to her.

"I'm hoping you'll join us for dinner tonight?" She asked softly, hoping that I'd agree with her, which I obviously won't do in the first place.

Because goddamn, I wasn't prepared to confront Lisa. I needed to make up a story and get out of here as soon as possible. Meeting Lisa at this time will undoubtedly be detrimental. I simply cannot do it. This is far too much for me. I have to neglect her no matter what. I'll have to make an excuse for it.

I'm not ready, and I've never been ready.

"Actually, I doubt it tonight. I'd better get going—"

"Isn't that what you're good at?" From behind me, came a throaty voice that I didn't recognise. A voice that completely foreign to me, making me gulped hard.

"Uhh what?" I asked, nervously swallowing and refusing to turn around to look at the person.

"Leaving," she said more louder but stern. "That's what you're good at." I heard a loud sighed at the end and I've never been this anxious.

My breathing was laboured, but it was when I turned around that I almost passed out.

Holy shit.

3. THE VIVID

Lisa stood in front of me, and it was as if the girl I'd left behind had been swallowed up by a beautiful, perfect figure. She just didn't look like the woman I remembered from nine years ago. Her rage was visible on her face, and it somehow made her even hotter. It would have been better if it hadn't been directed at me.

Her skin was a lovely milky colour that complemented the natural black streaks in her black hair. The smooth face I remembered had become even softer, and there were no scars or flaws.

I just took her in for an indefinite amount of time. My heart was screaming even though I was too stunned to say anything. I knew deep down that my reaction wasn't solely motivated by my physical attraction to her. It was because, despite all of the changes, one thing had remained constant.

Her eyes.

They reflected the same anguish that I remembered seeing her with the last time I saw her.

I finally got her name out of my head. "Lisa..."

"Rosie." Her voice reverberated through me.

"I wasn't sure if you were going to show up at all."

"Why wouldn't I have?" She sneered.

"Well, I supposed you were avoiding me."

"You've exaggerated your importance to me. Of course I was going to show up. This is about half of my house." She looked at me with annoyed. Her words pricked me.

"I never said it wasn't. It's just... I-I hadn't heard from you in a long time." Damn it, my heart almost dropped out of my body as I stuttered. It was strictly tense.

"It'll be interesting to see how that plays out."

Winter cleared her throat, clearly annoyed by our sparring. "I was just asking Rosie if she wanted to join us for dinner tonight. Perhaps you guys can catch up."

"She seems to to have plans." Lisa said out of no where.

I turned to face her, unbelievable. "How come you say that?"

"Oh, I'm not sure... maybe because you're carrying a bag smelling like dirty snatch?"

"It's freshly caught seafood."

"It doesn't smell very fresh to me."

"God. We haven't seen each other in nine years, and this is how you act?" I shifted my gaze to Winter. "Is she always this rude?"

"I guess you bring it out in me," she cracked before Winter could respond.

"Do you think Grandma would be pleased with your attitude right now? I guess she didn't leave us in this house just so we could fight."

"She left this house to both of us because we each meant something to her. But that doesn't mean we're meant to each other as well. And ah anyway, if you were so concerned with what Mrs. H. thought, perhaps you shouldn't have run away."

"That's a low blow" I said, almost whispering-endured with the pain.

"I guess the truth hurts."

"I tried to contact you, Lisa. I-"

"I'm not talking about it right now, Rosie," she said, her teeth clenched. "It's pretty outdated."

It was unsettling to hear her address me by my given name. She'd always called me Patch or Patchy since the first day we met. Hearing my name come out of her mouth felt like a slap in the face for some reason, as if she was emphasising how far apart we'd grown.

As she shut down, Lisa went from hot to cold, returning outside to retrieve her groceries from her car but not before slamming the door behind her.

I shuddered, looking over at Winter, whose eyes were darting from side to side in confusion.

"Well, that was a good start," I joked.

"I don't know what to say. To be honest, I've never seen her act that way toward anyone. I'm really sorry."

"It isn't your fault. Believe it or not, I pretty much deserve it."

The only thing worse than her rude reception was her blatant ignoring of me during dinner and the rest of the night. That hurt more than anything she'd ever said to me.

-

If I thought the evening was bad, a lack of sleep guaranteed that the next morning would be even worse. Lisa appears to have found a way to vent her rage by venting it on Winter.

Let's just say that playing the guitar wasn't the only skill she'd honed over the years. I was awakened in the middle of the night by Winter's moaning as Lisa pounded into her. The walls shook violently.

It was impossible to sleep again after that. I tossed and turned, my thoughts interchanging between rehashing Lisa's earlier words to me and imagining what the scene in the other room looked like. I knew I shouldn't have been thinking about the latter, but I couldn't stop myself.

It was 7 a.m., and the house was silent, so I assumed they were both catching up on slumber after their sexcapade. When I crept downstairs to make some coffee, I was surprised to find her standing alone in the kitchen, staring out the large window overlooking the water. The coffee was brewing. Her back was turned to me, so she hadn't noticed me yet.

I took advantage of the opportunity to admire her stature, and she was wearing a crop top that showed off the flawless skin of her defined waist. Her beautiful round ass was hugged by black gym pants. I had no idea how amazing her ass was.

Under the circumstances, my physical attraction to her irritated me, but that didn't stop me from checking her out. She tied her hair up.

Squinting, I tried in vain to figure out what it was. She caught me off guard when she turned around and met me with an incendiary stare.

"Do you always ogle people when you think they can't see you?"

The lump in my throat was swallowed. "How did you find out I was here?"

"I saw your reflection in the window, smarty."

Shit.

Literally embarrassed with myself.

"You didn't even make a flinch. I didn't think you noticed me." I explained, trying to cover up myself eventho it was useless already since it was too obvious.

"Clearly."

"Are you attempting to make me hate you or something? Because if it was true, you're doing a damn good job."

Lisa did not respond to my question. Instead, she simply turned back toward the window.

"How come you do that?" I questioned.

"Do what?" she asked undoubtedly.

"Say things to irritate me, then shut down?" I asked, holding back my rage.

"Would you rather I just continue to irritate you? I'm trying to keep my mood swings with you, Rosie. You should be glad I know when to shut up....unlike some people." She said, still facing the window.

"Will you at least look me in the eyes when you're speaking to me?"

She turned around and walked slowly toward me, leaning in. "Is this better? You'd rather have me in your face like this?" She asked. I could feel her words on my lips.

I could almost could taste her breath. As a result of the close contact, my entire body felt weak, so I backed away.

"I didn't think so," she said sarcastically.

I walked over to the refrigerator and opened it as if looking for something. It irritated me that my peaceful mornings were no longer a thing.

"Are you always up this early?" I inquired.

"I'm a morning person."

"I see what you mean...You're so bright and cheery," I opined sarcastically. "However, some of us need to sleep." I said again.

"I had a good night's sleep last night."

"Oh, I see... after you have traumatised me. After all that screwing, you must have passed out. Could you have been any more raucous last night?"

"Well, excuse me. Where do you expect me to fuck if I can't fuck in my own house?"

"I never said you couldn't do it. Just be more respectful."

"Define respect."

"Do it quietly."

"Sorry. I don't fuck quietly."

As much as I despised that response, I had a feeling those words would be playing over and over in my head later tonight.

"Ignore it. Clearly, you don't understand the concept of respect."

"So I need to respect you? Ah is that what you mean? Why Rosie? Is it because you're not getting laid? Why don't you meet some salty dude down at the dock? Maybe then you won't be as concerned about other people's problems."

"Hah? Salty what? Salty dude?"

"Yeah. You know, the guys who live on boats...the ones who sell you that nasty fish you ate last night."

I just shook my head and rolled my eyes, refusing to respond to that comment.

She caught me off guard when she abruptly lifted the carafe. "Would you like some coffee?" She asked, lifted her brows and looked straight into my eyes.

"Are you being nice now?"

"No? Why would I?" She laughed cynically, "I just assumed you were staying for some reason. It's got to be the coffee."

"This is my kitchen." I said with a small groan.

She gave a wink. "This is our kitchen. So how do you take your coffee?" she asked, taking two mugs from the cabinet.

"Cream and sugar."

"I'll handle it while you go put on a bra." She said without any expression, purely just to tease me, maybe?

I looked down at my boobs, which were protruding from beneath my white t-shirt. I hadn't expected to see her this early, so I hadn't thought to put one on. I went back to my room quickly and dressed, too embarrassed to acknowledge that she'd noticed.

When I returned, she was still drinking her coffee at the window.

"Is this better?" I inquired, referring to my outfit.

She turned around and inspected me.

"Define better. If better means I can't see your tits anymore, then yes. If better means you look better, that's debatable."

"What's the problem?" I frowned.

"It seems you sewed it yourself."

"It's actually from one of the shops on the island. This is handmade."

"From a potato sack?"

"I don't think so." I shook my head.

Maybe? Duh.

She smirked. "Your coffee is on the counter, Raggedy Ann."

My first instinct was to try to come up with a response, but I realised that was probably what she wanted. Instead of being angry, I needed to kill her with kindness.

"Thank you very much. It was thoughtful of you to make it for me."

Asshole.

I took a sip and then spit it out. "Fuck! What did you put in this? It's so strong!"

Instead of responding, she burst out laughing. Her laughter echoed throughout the kitchen, and as much as I despised the fact that it was at my expense, it was the first time she'd laughed.

For a brief moment, it transported me back in time and served as the only tangible reminder that the smoking hot asshole in front of me was once my best friend.

"You don't like it?"

"It's a little strong. Can you tell me?"

"It's actually coffee fusion."

"What does that even mean?"

Lisa strolled over to the cabinet and removed a can and a package. "This is my own recipe. Cuban coffee with this one." She indicated the black packaging with the white skull and crossbones on it.

"What in the universe is that?"

"It's coffee. I order it online. Nothing else is sufficiently caffeinated for me."

"Wasn't that why you wanted to serve it to me? You knew I truly hate this...concoction."

Instead of responding, she simply let out another raspy laugh, only this time she was laughing much harder than before Winter walked into the kitchen wearing a long black t-shirt that had to be the one she wasn't wearing.

"What's the big deal?"

Lisa's sly eyes peered out from behind her mug. She smirked. "We were just having coffee."

Winter shook her head in disbelief. "You didn't drink her mud, did you? I'm not sure how she likes that stuff."

I reminded myself of my plan to kill her gently. I nodded, taking another sip of coffee. "Actually, the first taste was quite strong, but I think I really like it."

It was fucking disgusting.

"You'd better be careful. That shit is lethal. Lisa is immune to it, but it kept me awake for four days the one and only time I drank it."

Lisa laughed. "Apparently, we kept Rosie awake last night."

Winter shifted her gaze to me. "Oh my gosh, shit. I'm sorry."

"It's no big deal," I shrugged. "After a while, I got used to it."

"Was that when you realised you wanted to join in?" Lisa burst out laughing.

Fuck her.

That was not going to get a response from me. I became more determined to beat the entire bloody mug of coffee to spite her as I looked over at her smug expression. "I'm really surprised at how much I like this," I lied.

Winter chose to disregard Lisa's earlier snarky comment. "How about we go to town after breakfast, Rosie? I'd appreciate it if you could take me on a tour of the island."

"Alright. That would be great."

Winter approached Lisa, wrapping her arm around her waist. "Would you like to accompany us, babe?"

"No. I've got some work to do," Lisa said as she finished the last of her coffee and tossed the cup in the sink.

"Okay. Then it's just the two of us, Rosie."

"No one cares," Lisa said, making me want to murder her right off the bat.

-

I'd become a spaz because of the coffee. Winter had to tell me to slow down as we walked around Newport that morning. Apparently, she couldn't keep up with me in her heels.

We came to a halt later in the afternoon to rest our legs. As the sun shone over the water, Winter and I sat on a wooden bench overlooking the dozens of docked sailboats.

"So, how did you and Lisa meet?" I asked.

"I was in the audience at a city club called Hades. That night, Lisa was performing. She was staring at me the entire time she was singing, and she came to find me after the show. I nearly died when she said she was thinking of me while singing the last song. Since then, we've been inseparable."

My face was red-hot. I refused to admit to myself that it was jealousy. For some reason, the thought of them attaching so intimately while she was performing made me uneasy. Perhaps it was because it reminded me of the songs she used to write for me. After having to put up with their fucking last night, you'd think nothing would bother me.

"What kind of music does she now play?"

"Well, she covers artists like John Mayer, but she also writes a lot of original material. She mostly performs in clubs, but her manager has been working hard to get her a record deal. Of course, the girls and boys are all smitten with her. For me, that part took some getting used to."

"I'm sure it's difficult."

"Yeah. Big time." She cocked her chin. "How about you? No girlfriend? Boyfriend?"

"I just got out of a relationship."

I spent the next half-hour telling her about Shawn's situation. Winter was a really easy person to talk to, and I could tell Shawn's cheating on me upset her a lot.

"Well, it's better to learn these things while you're still young than to waste a century with someone like that."

"Valid." I laughed.

"This summer, we'll have to find you someone. Today I've seen a lot of hot girls walking around here." She wiggled her brows with a silly smirked on her face.

"Really? Because the only ones I've seen holding hands were those who were holding each other's hands." I shook my head and swung my legs.

She burst out laughing. "No. Others existed."

"I don't want to get into another relationship."

"Bestie, nah. You need to find a girlfriend...Enjoy yourself duh, especially after what that asshole of an ex did to you. You deserve a hot summer fling, someone who blows your mind, someone you can't stop thinking about even when they're not there."

Ironically, it's your girlfriend who I can't get out of my head right now.

She meant well, so I just smiled and nodded, despite the fact that I had no plans to sleep with anyone this summer.

We passed Starlight's on the Beach on our way home, a restaurant known for live music at night and really good food. Temporary Summer Help Wanted was written on a sign outside. Because there was a university just over the bridge, many students returned home for the summer, leaving some local restaurants in need of temporary wait staff.

I came to a stop in front of the door. "Do you mind if I come in and ask about this? I want to have some fun!" I smiled in excitement.

"Sure. I'd like to look into it as well!" She screamed a bit and made a small dance and I just laughed at her.

Starlight's turned out to be in desperate need of summer help. Winter and I had both worked as waitresses, so we sat down and filled out applications. We each had a job by the time we walked out of there. We were basically told by the manager that we could work any night we wanted. The extra money and flexibility were too good to pass up.

Winter was especially relieved that she'd told her it wasn't a problem if she had to cancel a shift unexpectedly in the event she was called back to Manhattan for an audition. We were both going to start the next day.

That night, Winter suggested we celebrate our new jobs with dinner and drinks on the upper deck of the house. It hadn't occurred to me how peaceful the day had been without Lisa.

As soon as we walked in the door, butterflies began to swarm in my stomach again as I smelled her cologne. Winter ran over to Lisa and wrapped her arms around her neck while she was standing in the kitchen drinking tea. Lisa was tall-she stood over five feet-but Winter wasn't much shorter. I was basically not have that much different in comparison to both of them.

God, she cleaned up nice.

Lisa had changed out of her camouflage shorts and into a pair of cute night clothes that clung to her body. I couldn't figure out what she'd done to her hair. Perhaps, washed it? Whatever it was, it heightened the shades in her eyes, which were now staring into Winter's.

Winter kissed her after running her fingers through her neck. "I've been missing you, babe. Guess what? We both got jobs at this beachside restaurant named Starlight."

"Did you tell them you could be called up to New York at any time?" Lisa asked and playing with Winter's baby hair.

"He said it didn't make a difference. She stated that I could basically work whenever I wanted."

"Really. That sounds a little sketchy to me. But, hey, whatever. Are you sure she doesn't just want to get into your pants, babe?"

"She said the same thing to me," I cut in.

"Well, then, that can't be it."

It took a while for me to realise she'd just insulted me. Sometimes I just want to smack her ass down the floor, dip her head into the pool of water, and then bury her alive 8ft deep down into the earth.

Winter intercepted me before I could respond. "It's a nice day outside. Let's have dinner on the upstairs deck tonight. We could grill the steak I've been marinating in the fridge."

I didn't have the guts to tell her I don't like red meat, so I remained silent. She'd probably think I was looking for an excuse not to join them for dinner.

Kill her with compassion.

"I'm not a great cook, but I can make a big salad." I said nonchalantly.

Lisa slammed the counter. "Great. While Rosie tosses her large salad, I'll start the grill."

When I yelled after her, she began to walk outside.

"Do you know what Grandma would say to you right now? She'd tell you to go wash your dirty mouth with soap."

She raised her brow and turned around. "Soap isn't going to cut it."

I suppose I should have been relieved that she was speaking to me rather than pretending I wasn't there. I suppose we were making some progress?

I dressed the salad with homemade honey mustard vinaigrette after chopping lettuce, carrots, red onion, tomatoes, and cucumbers. Then, I carried it upstairs to the table where Lisa and Winter were already seated.

Winter had poured three glasses of Merlot, and Lisa was sipping one as she looked over at the choppy waves.

Lisa refused to look at me or engage in conversation once we began eating. I piled salad and bread on my plate, and it took a while for anyone to notice that I wasn't eating anything else.

"You didn't even touch the steak," Winter said, her mouth full.

Darn it, Winter.

"I'm not a big fan of meat." I shrugged and sipping on my water.

Lisa laughed. "Does that explain why you can't find a girlfriend?"

My fork fell to the ground. "You're an asshole. Seriously. I no longer recognise you. How did we ever get to be best friends?"

"That was a question I used to ask myself all the time before I stopped giving a shit." Lisa stared at me with stern.

I rose from my seat at the table and went downstairs. Leaning against the kitchen counter, I took slow, deep breaths in and out to calm myself.

Winter approached quietly behind me. "I'm not sure what's going on between you two or why she won't talk about it. Are you sure you never dated?"

"I told you, Win. It wasn't like that at all." I stared at her eyes, hoping she'd just believed in me.

"Would you mind telling me what happened?"

"I think she should be the one who explains it to you. To be honest, I don't want to irritate her any more than I already have by going too far. Besides, I can honestly say that if she's upset, it's because of how I left...my leaving. Everything that happened before that is now irrelevant. She's upset with me because of how I handled it." I explained, with a sigh.

"Let's just go back upstairs and try to eat something nice." Winter reassured me and we walked to the upstairs again.

Lisa was stone-faced on the upper deck, pouring more wine into her glass. A part of me wanted to slap her across the face, but another part of me felt guilty for inciting such rage in her. She claimed she didn't care, but I refused to believe she'd be acting this way if she didn't.

I stroked her arm. "Will you just talk to me?"

She snatched her arm away. "I'm done with it. I'm not talking anything."

"Would you do it for grandma?"

Her beautiful eyes darkened as her head tilted up. "Stop bringing her into this. Your grandmother was an amazing woman. She was the mother I didn't have. She, unlike almost everyone else in my life, never turned her back on me. This house symbolises Mrs. H., which is why I'm here. It's not because of you that I'm here. You want me to speak, but you don't seem to understand that I have nothing to say about anything that happened nearly a decade ago. I've taken down everything. It's too late now, Rosie. I don't mind if you and Winter become friends, okay? But don't bother trying to reach me because we're not going to be friends. You've put me in a shit mood, and I don't want to spend the rest of the summer in a shit mood. We live together. Nothing else. Stop acting as if there's something more to it. Stop acting like you like the goddamn coffee. Stop acting as if everything is great. Cut the bullshit and look at things for what they are. We don't mean anything to each other.. Never." She stood up and grabbed her plate. "I'm finished, Winter. I'll see you in the room."

Winter and I sat in silence, listening to nothing but the crashing waves beneath us.

"I'm truly sorry, Rosie"

"Please. Please don't, okay? She is right. You can't always fix things." A tear streamed down my cheek, despite the arrogant words I'd uttered.

-

Eleven Years Ago

Mom had left to go out once more. Lord knows where she went or who she was with. Jessica, my mom that I could never rely on her for anything. In my life, there were only two people on whom I could rely: Grandma and Lisa.

The one advantage of Mom leaving me alone most nights was that it gave me the freedom to sneak out of the house and go wherever I pleased. Grandma assumed my mother was at home half the time, so she couldn't intervene.

Lisa and I had agreed to meet in fifteen minutes. We were going to the mall to meet up with some of the other eighth-grade students from school. These kids belonged to the cool crowd that Lisa and I were attempting to break into. We weren't really affiliated with any clique because we mostly hung out with each other.

She was standing at the corner, hands in her pockets. I liked how she wore her baseball cap backwards and how her black hair peeked out from the sides. I've been noticing little things like that more and more lately. It was difficult not to.

She took a step toward me. "Are you ready to go?"

"Yeah."

Lisa began to run. "We need to get moving now, Rosie. The next bus will arrive in five minutes."

I couldn't figure out why the prospect of hanging out with these kids made me so nervous. Lisa didn't appear to be nervous at all. In general, she was more self-assured than I was.

The fluorescent lights inside the mall were a stark contrast to the dark winter outside. We were supposed to meet these kids at the food court, so we went to look at a map of the three-story structure.

As we approached the two boys and a girl who were standing outside of an Auntie Annie's pretzel stand, my heart was pounding. Lisa could tell I was nervous.

"Don't worry, Patch."

The first thing I remember Chandler saying was, "What the hell is that?"

"What?"

"Did you shit yourself, Roseanne?"

As I looked down at myself, my heart was now slamming out of my chest. Despite my nerves, I knew I hadn't lost control of my bowels. Who knows if that happens, right? No.

This was not poop; it was blood. It was the first time I'd ever gotten my period, so I wasn't prepared for it. At thirteen, I was pretty late than most of the other girls I knew. This was probably the worst possible timing.

Lisa looked down, then up, into my terrified eyes.

"It's blood," I said to her.

She gave me a quick nod, as if to say she had everything under control.

"It's blood," Lisa explained.

"Blood? Ew...gross!" Ethan, the other boy, stated.

"On the way here, Rosie stabbed herself with my knife."

I'd been looking down, but I jerked my head up and stared incredulously at my friend.

Chandler's pupils dilated. "Did she stab herself?"

"Yeah." Lisa smiled broadly. She took a pocket knife from her jacket, which surprised me. "See this? I keep it with me at all times. It's called a Swiss Army knife. Anyway, on the bus, I was showing it to Rosie. I challenged her to stab herself in the stomach. Being the crazy girl that she is, she did it. So, that's why, she now has blood on her pants."

"Are you joking?"

"Wish I was, dude."

The three of them exchanged glances before Chandler exclaimed, "Fuck! That's the coolest thing I've ever heard!"

My arm was smacked by Ethan. "Roseanne, I'm serious. That's some epic shit right there."

Lisa burst out laughing. "Yeah, so in any case...We figured we'd stop by and say hello since we were almost there. But, we should probably get her to the emergency room."

"That's cool, man. Let us know how it goes."

"Sure thing." Lisa nodded.

"What in the hell did you just do?" As we walked away, I murmured.

"Don't say anything. Just walk."

As we exited the mall's rotating doors, the cool night air hit us. We stood on the sidewalk for a moment, staring at each other, before bursting out laughing.

"I can't believe you made up that ridiculous story."

"Not that you should be ashamed of the truth, but I knew you were embarrassed. So I decided to take action. You were biting on your nails like mad."

"Was I? I didn't even notice." I said, embarrassed.

"Yeah. When you're really nervous, you do that." Lisa nodded to my hair.

"I had no idea you noticed that."

"I notice everything about you," she said, her eyes travelling down to my lips for a moment.

I changed the subject because I was suddenly flushed. "I had no idea you carried a knife."

"I always do. You know, just in case something bad happens while we're gone. I need to be able to protect you."

My heart, which had been pounding incessantly for those jerks only moments before, and was now pounding incessantly for an entirely different reason.

"I'd better get home."

"Right there is a drug store. Why don't you go get yourself something? Ask if they have a bathroom where you can use it."

I nodded and went inside then bought a box of maxi pads and some cheap granny underwear with the money I had set aside for video games at the mall arcade. Tampons would come later, when I had time to figure out how to use them.

When I came out, Lisa removed her jacket and handed it to me. "Take this and wrap it around your waist."

"I appreciate it."

"What are we doing now?" she asked.

"What do you mean? I need to get home! I-I have b-blood on my pants."

"With my jacket wrapped around you, no one can see it."

"But it was very uncomfy, Lili."

"I don't want to go back home tonight, Patch. I know where we can go...somewhere where we won't know anyone. It's a place I visit on my own from time to time. Come on."

Lisa escorted me down Providence's streets. We turned a corner after about ten minutes and approached a small red building. I raised my eyes to the illuminated sign.

"Does this look like a movie theatre?"

"Yup. They show movies that no one knows about or about which no one speaks. What's the best part? They don't give a damn about your age."

"Are they bad films?"

"No. Not like those naked movies, or the ones I told you my father watches. No. These are like foreign movies with subtitles and stuff." Lisa chuckled.

Lisa ordered two tickets and a bowl of popcorn for us to share. The theatre smelled musty and was nearly empty, which was ideal given that I didn't want to see anyone tonight. Despite the sticky seats, this was exactly what I needed.

The film, L'Amour Vrai, was a French film with subtitles. The cinematography was stunning, and the plot was more serious than most comedies we watch. But it was flawless. Perfect not only for what was on the big screen, but also for who was sitting next to me.

I rested my head on Lisa's shoulder, grateful to God for a friend who always knew just what I needed.

There was also a gnawing feeling running through me, something unidentifiable that would eventually identify itself and reach its climax shortly before I ran away from it all.

That wasn't the last independent film Lisa and I would watch together at the little red theatre. Then, over the next few years, that location became our secret hangout. Indie films became our priority.

Going there wasn't about being seen at the big screen or running into old friends. It was a place where we could both escape reality without being watched, a place where we could be together while also getting lost in a different world.

I listened from my window the next afternoon as Lisa sat on grandma's stoop, playing a new song I'd never heard her perform before. It sounded like the Divinyls' I Touch Myself, but she'd changed it to I Stab Myself.

She's funny and weirdly cute.

Gotta love that girl.

End of flashback.

4. THE MOMENT

After a couple of weeks, things between Lisa and me had not improved. Rather than taunt me, she'd resigned herself to totally ignoring me.

There were four bedrooms in the house. Lisa used the other one as an office during the day because I'd converted one of them into an exercise room. As she made work calls, her muffled voice could often be heard from behind the closed door.

Meanwhile, Winter and I were working almost every night and every afternoon at Starlight's. We were on break one day when we overheard the restaurant owner, Brayden, complaining that the band that played most nights had abruptly quit. Starlight's was probably the most popular live music venue on the entire island. Even more than the food, this was what it was known for. As a result, this did not bode well for business.

Winter's voice was hushed. "I'm wondering if Lisa would like to play here."

I'd already been feeling a little queasy this afternoon, but the mere mention of her name made my stomach churn even more. "Do you think she'd want to perform in a venue like this?"

"Well, she's used to larger venues, but she's not doing anything else after all at this moment. She took the summer off, but I have a feeling she regrets it. She's been in a grumpy mood since we arrived. I believe she is itching to play again. It might be beneficial for her to return to the game on a smaller scale. It's not like there's any pressure. Nobody knows who she is out here."

I got goosebumps just thinking about seeing Lisa perform. On the one hand, it would be incredible. On the other hand, I knew it would be emotionally draining for me to have to put up with her here at night. Her actually agreeing to it was unlikely, so I resolved not to make a fuss over it unless it became a reality.

"I'm going to talk to Brayden later," Winter stated.

I attempted to change the topic. "Do you think you and Lisa will tie the knot?" I'm not sure why I asked that. I'd been wondering how serious they were, and it just spilled out.

Winter paused. "I'm not sure. I truly love her. If we can work out our differences, I hope so."

"Differences? Such as what?" I was baffled.

She sipped her water and frowned. "Well, Lisa doesn't want kids."

"What? Did she told you that?" My eyes widen and almost couldn't believe my ears.

"Yeah. She believes it is irresponsible to bring children into the world unless you are completely confident in your abilities as a parent. She claims that her parents should never have had children, and she clearly does not believe it is for her."

"Uh really?"

"Don't misunderstand me. I don't plan on having children anytime soon. Right now, my career takes precedence, but I would like to have them someday. So, if she truly doesn't want kids, then that could be a problem."

"She'll probably change her mind as she gets older. She's still young."

She shook her head. "I'm not sure. It's very ugh, bad. Even though I'm on the pill and we're monogamous, she won't have sex with me without a condom. Because she is so afraid, she refuses to take even the smallest risk. She's extremely paranoid."

I simply said, "Wow," trying to block out the images of them having sex.

It saddened me that Lisa felt this way because of her parents. When we were kids, they were always working and never paid enough attention to her. Her mother was frequently away on business trips. That was one of the reasons why grandma was so important to her. My mother, to be honest, should not have had a child either. But her poor parenting did not deter me from wanting to have my own child someday.

Winter examined my face more closely. "Are you okay anyway?"

I believe the stress of my reunion with Lisa was finally getting to me. My nerves were shot, and everything was making me sick.

"I've actually been feeling sick all day. My stomach is upset, and I have a headache."

"Why don't you leave early? I'll cover your shift and notify Audrey of the situation."

"Are you sure?"

"Of course," she said, nodded.

"Then I'll owe you."

"Trust me, there will come a point that I get called back to New York, and you'll make due on that."

"Alright, thanks." I said as I stood up and untied the black smock tied around my back.

Despite my vow not to think about it the entire walk home, my thoughts returned to Lisa and the fact that Winter was going to try to get her the job at Starlight's. I hadn't heard her singing voice in years. I was curious how it sounded now that it was deeper and had been practised for years.

Outside the house, Lisa's black Range Rover was parked. She expected both Winter and I to be at work. I had to go through the kitchen to get to my room, and I hoped I wouldn't have to run into her without Winter there to protect me.

As I walked into the empty kitchen, a wave of relief washed over me. I snatched a water bottle and some Advil for my headache and crept up the stairs, hoping Lisa wouldn't notice me.

At the top of the stairwell, I was stopped in my tracks by the sound of heavy breathing coming from her bedroom. Sheets were rustling in the wind. My heart rate increased. She didn't expect to see anyone at home.

Oh god...

She must have a girl in there.

Shit.

How could she do such a thing to Winter?

I had to pass through her room anyway to get to mine. Thank goodness Grandma had carpeted this hallway. I crept slowly toward her door, which was cracked open, my hand obscuring my chest. I briefly closed my eyes to prepare myself for what I might see when I peeked inside.

Nothing could have prepared me for what was waiting for me behind that door.

There was no girl.

Lisa's eyes were tightly shut as she reclined on the bed by herself. Her jeans had come undone about halfway down her legs. Her left hand was tightly wrapped around her massive cock, while her other hand pressed down on her balls.

Holy Mary, Mother of...

Swallowing the saliva that was forming in my mouth, I watched her hand as she stroked herself hard in a twisting motion. She'd worked herself up to the point where you could hear the slick sound of the wetness as she pumped into her palm.

I knew I was doing the wrong thing by staring at her. In fact, this was probably the most heinous thing I'd ever done. But there was no way I was going to look away. There is no way. If this was to be the reason I went to hell, so be it. I'd never seen anything so intense, or imagined she could get so much pleasure from herself.

I was curious to find out how this would end.

I had to know how it ended.

Lisa's mouth was agape, the tip of her tongue slowly sliding back and forth across her bottom lip, as if looking for a taste of something or some-one.

I wanted to be the one.

My own body was trembling, and my clit was throbbing. The desire to be with her, to be with her, was intense. I was so engrossed in every move she made that I didn't care if I was watching her correctly or incorrectly.

Hypnotized.

She was fucking her palm faster and fisting the sheets with one hand. My muscles clenched tighter with each movement. I was drenched and perplexed by my mind's complete surrender to my body.

The low and deep groans of pleasure that came from her mouth were exacerbating the situation. I knew without a doubt that this-watching her enjoy herself-was the single biggest turn on I'd ever had.

Normally, getting off was a chore for me. I needed my vibrator and porn, and even then, it was sometimes difficult to relax enough to truly make myself come. I had to cross my legs right now to keep the need from building between them.

My tongue tingled as she licked her bottom lip again, imagining what her wet mouth would feel like against my own lips. I imagined myself wrapped around her cock as she pumped into her hand. I imagined myself wrapped around her cock. I had never wanted anyone as badly as I wanted her in that moment.

As the back of her head pressed against the headboard, her dark black hair was matted and unkempt. The clank of her belt buckle grew louder as she thrust her hips forward, her fist working harder to keep up. I was simply blown away by the intensity of her self-satisfaction.

As her eyes rolled back, her breathing became even more ragged. I swallowed hard and watched, enthralled, as streams of cum shot out like a fountain from her large crown. The sexiest sounds I'd ever heard come out of a woman's mouth were the grunts of pleasure escaping her as she orgasmed.

My heart felt like it was pounding against the inside of my chest. I'd completely lost my vision of the world while watching this whole thing unfold. I felt like I'd been there with her, experiencing every movement and feeling, except I wasn't allowed to come. It was as if I'd gone insane during the process.

That was the only explanation for my body's decision to betray me, letting out a spontaneous sigh....moan?

Shit.

I wasn't sure and couldn't even tell you what it was, other than to say that whatever sound I made caused Lisa to jump back. Her head jerked toward me, and her stunned eyes locked with mine for a split second before I dashed back down the stairs.

Humiliated.Mortified.

My heart felt as if it were inside my mouth. I ran aimlessly on the sand after escaping through the front door and down to the water. I had to stop about a mile down the beach to catch my breath, despite the fact that I wanted to keep running.

I'd become so engrossed in Lisa that I'd forgotten how sick I was this afternoon. It all hit me again as I staggered over to the beach and vomited into the sea.

I collapsed into the sand and sat there for at least an hour. The sun was beginning to set, and the tide was coming in. Everything seemed to be closing in on me. I knew I couldn't put off going home indefinitely.

What if she exposed what I'd done to Winter? That I was spying on her. Oh my God.

She was going to crucify me because of this.

What explanation could I possibly give her for why I was hiding behind her door, watching her ejaculate like it was a Fourth of July fireworks show?

I made the decision that I needed to get home before Winter did. Maybe I can persuade her not to say anything. I brushed the sand off my thighs and made my way up to the house.

My heart almost stopped when I found Lisa standing in the kitchen, drinking from a half-gallon of orange juice. I stood silently behind her, watching as she replaced the container. Lisa finally turned around and noticed me standing there.

Her hair was wet, so it appeared brown rather than black. She had to have taken a shower to wash away the awkwardness of our meeting. She just stared me down, looking painfully beautiful in a brown distressed t-shirt that fit her chest like a glove.

Here we go buddy.

I braced myself for her scathing comments. My heart was pounding in my chest as she stared at me blankly without saying anything. She walked slowly toward me, and every muscle in my body tightened. She was going to get in my face and do it.

Shit.

Lisa was only a few feet away from me. She smelled heavenly, like soap and cologne. I could feel the heat from her body, and my knees began to weaken. She locked her eyes on mine. It wasn't an angry glare, but it wasn't a happy or amused expression either.

She took a deep breath in and said, "You smell like vomit," after a few seconds of silence.

She turned around and walked back toward the stairs before disappearing just as I opened my mouth to respond.

Was that it? I smelled like vomit?

Was she really going to let it all go? Or was she just putting it off until Winter got home? I'd have to wait with anxiously to find out.

—

Starlight's had suffered greatly since the loss of their headlining band, The Ruckus. Brayden had filled the spot with mediocre local talent each night, but people were noticing the difference. The restaurant would close much earlier than usual, and we weren't getting as many customers in general.

I knew Winter had discussed taking on a few nights with Lisa, but the last I heard, she wasn't interested. So imagine my surprise when she showed up at Starlight's early one Friday evening with her guitar strap wrapped around her.

I didn't realise it was her until she turned around and looked at me. When I noticed her standing near the door, looking as if she didn't know where to go, butterflies swarmed in my stomach.

She was dressed in a navy hoodie and a beanie because it was unusually cool outside. She looked so hot in that hat. It always seemed to bring out her eyes. She looked sexy in anything, but she was particularly hot today.

My physical attraction to her never ceased to amaze me, given how she'd treated me. I suppose it was easier to concentrate on the physical.

Lisa's exterior, which was so different from what I remembered, served as a distraction from what I knew was going on inside.

The truth was, no matter how much I wanted her physically, it couldn't compare to the longing I still had for my old friend. I knew she was still there, somewhere beneath the brawn and beauty, and it irritated me.

Lisa, as far as I knew, never told Winter about the jerk-off encounter, nor did she torture me about it. I'm not sure why she decided to let me off the hook on that, but I'll be forever thankful.

While Winter was called away from town for an audition this morning. So I'd assumed she'd accompany her back home.

I walked over to her after finishing wiping down the table I'd been cleaning. "What are you doing here?"

She removed her guitar from her neck. "What does it look like I'm doing?"

"I thought you were with Winter in New York."

"She isn't going to be gone for long. And I've already agreed to this...gig." She said it almost mockingly.

"I thought you were against playing here. I overheard you telling Winter that you'd rather perform in a prison than a down-to-earth beach hut."

"Yeah. So, I guess she showed your boss some recordings of me and made me an offer I couldn't refuse."

"How long will you be playing here?"

"I'm not sure. A few weeks. Until we depart." Her arm was crossed across her chest.

"You're not staying for the entire summer?"

"No. That was never the idea." She said it calmly.

Disappointment began to set in. I should have been relieved that she was leaving soon, but hearing that news did the opposite.

"Wow. Okay. So...do you want me to show you around?"

"No, I'm good," she said as she walked away from me, toward the back of the restaurant.

Lisa gone for at least an hour. She was scheduled to perform at eight o'clock, so she only had about twenty minutes before the show.

As I went in search of her, my curiosity got the best of me. I could see her downing a bottle of beer and looking stressed through the door to one of the back rooms. I was curious if she ever got nervous before a performance.

Even though she thought performing here was a pun, she was still going to put herself out there.

Her stare switched to the side, where she noticed me standing. We just stood there staring at each other. It was ironic, but the only times I could feel the echoes of our old connection were in brief moments of silent eye contact. Sometimes silence speaks the loudest.

I abandoned her once more, returning down the hall and into the restaurant to attend to the customers I'd been ignoring. Things began to pick up steam. We were short-staffed tonight because Winter was not working, and I was struggling to keep up with the orders. Starlight's offered both indoor and outdoor seating. Normally, I would only work one section at a time, but tonight I was switching between the two.

Because the weather was nice, I knew Lisa would be performing outside. I kept checking the small stage to see if she was there. It was past eight o'clock and she still hadn't shown up.

I was in the middle of serving a large party of ten when I first heard it: the chilling sound of a soulful voice that was not at all familiar to me.

She made no introductions. No warning. She had only begun to sing the first few words, followed by a strum of her guitar. Lisa had chosen a cover of Ain't No Sunshine by Bill Withers as her first song.

The entire room quickly died down a bit, and all eyes were fixed on the stunning black hair female specimen who was under the spotlight. I couldn't move despite the fact that I was carrying a large round tray of dirty dishes. Her thick, smoky singing voice had completely paralysed me, penetrating both my body and soul.

Except for the lone teardrop that fell the night she lost it on me during steak dinner, I hadn't cried in a long time-until now. It was all a bit much. Hearing how different her voice sounded, how she'd honed it over the years, was a stark reminder of how much I'd been missing.

All of the hours of practise that must have gone into perfecting that lovely voice, and I wasn't there to witness any of it. The guilt, the emotions, the reality of a decade gone...it all hit me at once. Not to mention the song, which is about a girl who is leaving. It probably had nothing to do with me, but it sure felt that way in my head.

To perform solo acoustically, you had to be a true artist. Everything was focused on you and nothing else. There were no distractions to distract from a cracked voice or other gaffes. Lisa performed the song flawlessly. Her voice vibrated through my entire being like a deep massage. My heart was brimming with pride.

I was so proud of her, whether she liked it or not.

At the same time, I felt a rush of antsy excitement, similar to when I was a teenager and saw a girl band perform live. Adrenaline was coursing through my veins. A part of me wanted to yell, "This is my Lili! I knew her a long time ago!" Another part of me wanted to dash onto the stage and wrap my arms around her.

Her fingers effortlessly worked the guitar, almost rivalling the sexiness of her voice. Women and men began to leave their tables, tossing money at her feet.

Oh wow.

Did they expect her to start undressing if they gave her enough? I'd never seen anyone throw money around this place before. They certainly never threw money at The Ruckus. That was probably Lisa's effect on both men and women.

I needed a break by the third song. I went to the bathroom, splashed some water on my face, and returned to the tables just in time to hear her finally speak into the microphone in a low and sultry voice.

"My name is Lalisa Manoban, and I'm from New York City. I'll be here for a few weeks. Thank you for showing up tonight."

There was applause and a few whistles. My attention had been drawn to Lisa, and I had neglected my customers as a result. A few of them waved me down, eager for refills, so I took their orders and walked over to the bar.

Lisa sipped her beer before speaking into the microphone once more. "The next song is an original that I wrote recently. I hope you enjoy it. It's called She Likes to Watch," she said after strummed the guitar once.

My body froze when I heard the title, and it took a few seconds for it to sink in.

"This song is dedicated to all the sneaky little voyeurs out there. You know who you are." She said and I felt like she was smiling mockingly with pride.

The retaliation I'd assumed she'd waived was, in fact, simply postponed and about to be unleashed in full. I refused to look up at the stage. The drinks were placed in front of me by the bartender, and I forced my wobbly legs to move long enough to deliver them to their rightful owners before the song began.

She pretends to be a good girl,Quiet and refined.But Daddy always said,Those are the worst kind.Turns out he was right.As I found out the other night...

She likes to watch.Mmm hmm...she likes to watch.You think you are alone,Until you hear that little moan.She likes to watch.Mmm hmm...she likes to watch.

She'll catch you naked and exposed,When you think the door is closed. She's a princess and a voyeur,Curiosity will destroy her.Maybe therapy will heal ya,It's not too late for you, Rosie,She likes to watch.Mmm hmm...she likes to watch.And my kinky little friend,Insists on staying till the end.She likes to watch.Mmm hmm...she likes to watch.

When the song finally ended, the audience erupted. They appeared to be enamoured with the concept. Was it really necessary for her to include my name? A part of me was mortified, but I had to admit that another part of me was...relieved. Her songwriting was a small reminder of how things used to be.

When I finally got up the courage to look at her, she gave me a mischievous smile before moving on to the next song. She could tell by the look on my face that she'd succeeded in embarrassing me.

Well played.

—

Back at the house that night, Lisa went to her room without saying anything to me. It felt strange to be alone for the first time since Winter had left. However, the sensation was fleeting.

I was still in bed at eleven in the next morning when I heard the front door open. As she joined her in their bedroom, I could hear the muffled sounds of Lisa and Winter's voices. She had to leave the city very early in the morning to come back here.

Even though I adored Winter, her reappearance was unsettling. There was an underlying jealousy that I couldn't help but feel. When the bed began to creak, nausea set in.

Damn.

She was only home for three minutes before she pounced on her. I couldn't say I blamed her in the least, but I didn't want to hear it. I buried my face in my pillow, closed my eyes, and reminded myself that they'd both be gone in a few weeks.

Three weeks.

I changed into a terry cloth sundress around noon before joining Lisa and Winter downstairs. The sunlight streaming into the kitchen was blinding.

Lisa grinned as she lifted the carafe. "Coffee?"

I gave an exaggerated grin. "You know what? Sure, I'd like some."

I refused to back down, determined to maintain my facade of enjoying Lisa's coffee. Unfortunately, my body had grown accustomed to the abnormally high level of caffeine. The regular coffee hadn't done the trick the one morning I'd skipped it. I was becoming addicted to Lisa's coffee fusion, which was terrible.

Very terrible.

"How did Starlight's last night go? Did my baby rock the house?"

"She was amazing. Everyone loved her." Lisa's gaze met mine for a matter of seconds. I wanted her to know how much I meant it.

She brushed it aside. "It was good. It'll give me something to do while I'm here."

"What did you play?" Winter questioned.

"I tried out a new song." Lisa smiled smugly.

I took a big gulp.

"The one you played for me the other night?" She asked.

"No. Another one." Lisa smirked and I damn well knew what was that smirked for.

It occurred to me that Lisa probably chose to perform She Likes To Watch last night in particular because Winter was not prevalent. It still flummoxed me that she kept the entire incident to herself when she could have told her and embarrassed the shit out of me.

She gave me a friendly smile. "Would you like a refill, Rosie?"

I broadened my grin. "Don't mind if I do. This is really starting to grow on me. That was quite a surprise."

"Well, I know you like surprises."

I gave her a sidelong glance. Fortunately, Winter had no idea what she was talking about.

Her serving me coffee remained a running gag. She assumed I was drinking the mud to irritate her. The joke was on her. She had no idea I was becoming addicted to it and actually desired it. In any case, the morning coffee exchange was the only real chance for normal communication with her, so I took what I could get.

Winter ran her fingers through Lisa's unkempt hair in the morning. "Last night, I noticed Niki commented on your Instagram post." Winter pouted.

She yanked Jade's hand away from her, her face flushed.

"Baby...don't."

I had to ask. I just had to... "Who is Niki?"

"Lisa's ex-girlfriend. She works in the music industry and is extremely irritable. She makes comments on everything she does, despite the fact that she knew that Lisa has a girlfriend. It's so disrespectful."

"I can't help it that she comments on my shit," Lisa grumbled.

I was sure there were a lot of ex-girlfriends.

Niki.Huh.

Was I seriously jealous of someone else now, too, when I had no right to be? That was fairly pathetic. When it came to her, my jealousy was nothing new.

My inability to deal with these emotions played a significant role in my decision to leave, which ultimately altered the course of our lives.

Flashback 10 years ago.

"I don't like it when they start playing these games."

"We don't have to stay here if you don't want to, Patch," Lisa said quietly in my ear. Her hot breath sent shivers down my spine.

"It's fine," I said.

"Are you sure?"

"Yeah."

A group of students from Aaron Bosley's school were hanging out in his basement. Aaron would occasionally suggest that we all start playing Truth or Spin. It was a cross between Truth or Dare and Spin the Bottle. Aaron would choose the "victims," as he referred to them. He'd ask a question, and if the respondent pleaded the fifth, refusing to answer, Aaron'd spin the green Heineken bottle. The victim would then have to kiss whoever was pointed at by the bottle.

It was entertaining to watch as long as neither of us were called upon. Playing along with Aaron's games was part of the deal in getting invited back. Lisa and I had never been chosen to participate the previous two times we came here.

"Lisa!"

When I heard Lisa's name, my heart sank.

"Yeah?" Lisa frowned.

"You're up."

Lisa muttered under her breath, "Shit."

Before Aaron asked the question, she gave me a worried look.

"Question. Do you, or do you not secretly want to bone Roseanne?"

My best friend's face flushed. I don't recall ever seeing it in that colour before. My heart was racing. I couldn't believe Aaron had asked her that, and I was terrified of the outcome.

She shook her head. "Pass."

Aaron seemed flabbergasted by Lisa's refusal. "P-Pass? A-Are you sure?"

"Pass."

"Okay, then." Aaron didn't waste any time in bending down to spin the bottle. Before coming to a halt, the glass spun around, scraping across the laminate basement floor.

"Oh! Sophie is your oh-so-unlucky victim!"

Lisa gave me a look. The worry in her eyes was palpable, but she knew she had to do it.

"One minute," Aaron said.

Sophie slithered toward her from where she was sitting on the ground. I watched, heartbroken, as Lisa pressed her lips against hers. She opened her mouth wide and wrapped her hands around Lisa's head, pulling her closer to her and almost eating her face. I always knew she liked her.

My heart felt like it was tearing with each passing second. That was the longest minute of my life. It was the first time the jealousy beast had reared its obnoxious head to such an extent. It was also the first time I realised how strong my feelings for her were.

Lisa returned to me after the minute was up, wiping her lips with the back of her hand. I'm not even going to look at her. I knew I shouldn't have been angry, but my emotions were beyond my control.

"Are you alright?" she inquired.

I kept looking down at my shoes. "Let's just get going."

She was following me. "Patch... it's just a game."

"I don't want to talk about it."

We began our quiet and awkward walk home. I came to a sudden halt in the middle of the sidewalk and turned to face her. "Why didn't you just answer the question?"

"I didn't know what to say," she admitted after staring at me for a long time.

"What do you mean?"

"Your feelings would have been hurt if I had said no. And things would be strange between us if I said yes. That's something I don't want. Ever."

"Did she give you your first kiss?"

She paused, looking up at the dark sky, before whispering, "No."

I shook my head and began to walk in front of her.

I felt as if I didn't know her anymore.

"Come on, Rosie. Don't do it.

Tears began to fall. I was crying for reasons I couldn't even fathom. That's when I realised I'd fallen in love with her for the first time. I loved Lisa. More than just a friend, more than anything else. I was extremely upset at myself.

My greatest concern was losing her. It dawned on me that it would happen someday.

Perhaps it was already happening.

End of flashback.

5. THE reason

Lisa had practically become a local celebrity in Newport overnight a week later. The crowd at Starlight's had nearly doubled since she became the nightly entertainment. Of course, the newest customers were mostly girls who had heard about the hot new headlining guitarist.

Winter and I were about to leave for work one late afternoon when her phone rang.

"Shit. Hold on. It's my agent," Winter explained.

I stood in the doorway, waiting for her to answer the phone. Her hands began to tremble after a few seconds. "You're joking, aren't you? Are you serious?" She covered her mouth while jumping up and down. "Oh my God! Yes! Of course, I can."

Finally, she let out a delighted yelp. "Thank you very much, Marcus. Thank you for informing me! Oh my goodness. So, what's next? Oh okay! I'll call you later tonight," she said before hanging up the phone.

"What's going on?" I wanted to know.

Winter screamed with delight and drew me into a hug, her boney frame pressing against my ample chest.

"I was cast as an understudy for a major role in The Phenomenals...on Broadway! It was one of two auditions I had the previous week. I had dismissed it as a long shot. My agent was not even going to send me at first!" Lisa came downstairs when she let out another loud squeal.

"What the hell is going on down here?" Lisa asked, lifted her brow, then Winter dashed up to her and threw herself into Lisa's arms.

"Baby! I was cast as Veronica's understudy in The Phenomenals!"

"Are you serious? Holy shit. That's fucking amazing!" She spun her around and lifted her up in the air.

"Congratulations, Win!" I cleared my throat, feeling awkward and like a third wheel. "I'm extremely happy for you!"

Lisa finally put her down. "When does this all go down?"

"They want me to be in New York in a few days."

She appeared frazzled. "Aw, shucks. Alright...um... I wish I hadn't agreed to work at Starlight's. I would have just gone back with you."

"It's fine. Isn't it just a couple of weeks that you promised him? It'll go by quickly."

"Yeah."

Winter grinned. "Be nice to Rosie."

Lisa made an extra effort to stay in her room during the day after Winter left, and she also ignored me at the restaurant. She never performed She Likes To Watch again.

There was no other interaction besides my purposefully joining her in the kitchen when I knew she was having her coffee. Winter's departure seemed to be increasing the distance between us. That went on for a few days until one afternoon when everything changed.

I'd just gotten home from an afternoon shift at Starlight's when I noticed what sounded like wretched hurling coming from upstairs. I dashed up the stairs, not thinking twice, to find Lisa keeled over with her face inside the toilet.

"Oh my God, are you vomiting?"

"Nah. I'm flushing cunilingus down the toilet...What the fuck do you think?"

"Did you eat something bad?"

She shook her head as another puke volcano erupted within her. I avoided my eyes and closed my eyes until she was finished.

"Can I get you some-"

"Just go, Rosie." She flushed the toilet.

Something about someone being sick and helpless made you see the child in them. Despite her efforts to look tough, Lisa appeared helpless in that moment.

"Are you sure I can't get you-"

"Leave!" My whole body shook as she screamed. As another bout of vomiting began, I reluctantly returned downstairs.

I could hear her returning to her bedroom after a few minutes. I spent about an hour downstairs. It was unusually quiet. She'd be moving around in her room on a normal day, so I knew she'd either fallen asleep or was lying down.

Being the paranoid person that I was, I began to suspect she'd passed out from dehydration. She hadn't come down to get some water. Given all that she'd thrown up, that was dangerous.

I took a deep breath and marched up the stairs. I didn't bother knocking lightly on her door and didn't wait for her to respond before entering.

"Li-Lisa?"

She was lying on her side, her head resting on the pillow, her eyes open. She just stared at me blankly, but her eyes were glassy.

"Are you okay?"

"No."

I approached her and placed my hand on her brow without asking permission. It was hot to the touch. "You're on heat. We need to take your temperature."

Before returning to Lisa, I hurried to the bathroom and rifled through the medicine cabinet for a thermometer.

"Put this in your mouth."

She chuckled. "That's usually my line."

"Just do it," I said, rolling my eyes. I was relieved that she was just joking with me.

Surprisingly, she did not object to me taking her temperature. The thermometer beeped, and it showed that she had a significant fever.

"It's a hundred and twenty-five. Did you know you were supposed to play tonight?"

She hummed, "Mmm hmm."

"I'm calling Brayden to let him know you won't be able to make it."

"Don't. I'll wait an hour and see how I feel."

"There's no way you'll be able to perform like this."

"I'll call him in an hour," she said emphatically.

Lisa's phone rang, and she reached over to check it before resetting it on the nightstand.

"Was that winter?"

"Yeah."

"Does she know you're sick?"

"Yes."

"Does she have rehearsals tonight?"

"No."

"Is she on her way?"

"No. Why would she come all the way here just to see if I had a fever?"

I couldn't think of anything to say. I just knew if my girlfriend was this ill, I'd want to be with her. Maybe she'd played it down.

"Can I get you something?"

"Nothing. Privacy. That's all you can get for me."

"I'm going to get you something to drink. Whatever you say, I don't care. You'll become dehydrated."

"If you're going to keep playing nurse, make it a stiff one," she yelled after me.

I went downstairs and returned with a small towel and a bottle of water. I handed her the bottle and two Tylenol pills. "Here. Drink up."

Lisa swallowed the pills and sipped her drink before glancing at the wet cloth.

"What in the planet are you going to do with that?"

"It's a dripping wet cloth." I put it on her forehead. "It will bring the fever down."

She took my hand away from her. "I can look after myself, Rosie."

I ignored her comment and simply stated, "I'll call Brayden. Get some rest."

Lisa went to bed after yet another bout of vomiting. Despite the fact that I'd left some extra water for her, I was concerned that she wasn't drinking anything. So, before I went to bed, I decided to check in on her one more time.

She was awake and sitting up in bed, looking very pale.

"How do you feel?"

"Like shit."

"We should take your temperature once more."

When I pulled the thermometer out of her mouth this time, my heart almost stopped. "Oh my goodness. It reads one hundred and four point five. That's dangerous, Lisa. We need to get you to the hospital right away."

"I'm not going to the hospital," She groaned.

"This is not debatable." I grabbed my phone and began searching the Internet for information on adult fevers. "It says here that a fever of 105 degrees Fahrenheit can be fatal. You could suffer from brain damage."

"That's a little extreme. Don't you think?"

"I don't care if it's extreme. You must do check up." I stated sternly.

"I'm not leaving."

"If you saif so, then I guess I'll stay here all night until you agree to leave."

"Emergency rooms freak me out."

"Would you rather die?"

"Hmm. It's either that or being stuck in this room with you yelling in my ear."

"Wow, that's really nice."

"Why are you getting involved in this, Roseanne?"

"I don't care what you think of me, okay? I am worried about you. I've always done so and will continue to do so, and I don't want anything to happen to you."

She closed her eyes and took a deep breath after a long pause. "Alright. I'll fucking go. Hope you satisfied."

"Thank you, very satisfied indeed."

During the dark ride to Newport Hospital, Lisa shivered. I texted Winter before we left and promised to keep her updated throughout the night.

We were lucky that the emergency room was relatively quiet when we arrived. They ushered Lisa into one of the small, curtained-off treatment rooms in the back. No one, not even Lisa, objected to my accompanying her back there.

She was hooked up to an IV and given Motrin. They also done a battery of blood tests over the course of an hour.

A new doctor who had just started work entered the room.

"How are you feeling, Ms. Manoban?"

"Like crap." Lisa squinted her eyes to get a better look at the doctor's hospital identification. "Is your name really Dr. Danger?"

The doctor sighed and rolled his eyes. "It's actually pronounced hanger. Dan-ger."

"Do they know what's going on with her, Doc?"

He extended his hand for a handshake. "Call me Will, please."

And I accepted it. "Roseanne…"

He gave me a flirtatious look with his smile. "Well, we think it's a combination of things going on here. An unidentified bacterial infection that resulted in a high fever, vomiting, and dehydration. We've ruled out any more serious problems."

He turned to face Lisa. "You're very lucky that your girlfriend brought you in. Fevers of that magnitude can be extremely dangerous in adults."

Lisa gave me a quick glance before returning her attention to Dr. Danger. "How long am I going to be sick?"

"It'll probably last a few days, but because of the severity of your fever, we'd like to keep you overnight for observation and to get some more fluids and vitamins into you."

"Do I have to sleep here?"

"Yes. We'll put you to a more comfortable room."

Lisa scowled. "May I object?"

"I'm afraid not. I'm sure your girlfriend will keep you company."

"Oh, I'm not her girlfriend," I clarified. "Her girlfriend is currently in New York."

"Sister?" He asked again and I shook my head.

"Uh…No. We're just…" I was unsure. What were we? "We used to be friends. We now share a home that we both inherited."

Dr. Danger was puzzled and asked, "You're not dating each other then?"

"No," Lisa replied quickly.

"No," I said again.

"Do you live in the area, Roseanne?"

"Yes. I'm only about ten minutes away."

"I've just moved here from Pennsylvania. Would you mind showing me around the island someday?"

He'd caught me completely off guard. Dr. Danger-Will-was definitely appealing in a clean-cut semi-older way. He was attractive enough with his dark hair and large brown eyes. I couldn't say my body reacted to him in the same way that it did to Lisa. Accepting his offer, on the other hand, might be a good idea.

"Sure. That would be great."

"Great." He rummaged through the pockets of his white jacket for his phone. "Can you give me your phone number? I'll programme it right here."

Lisa frowned as I recited my digits.

"The nurse will be back in soon to check on him. I'll contact you." He gave a wink.

"Okay." I gave a small wave and smiled.

Lisa huffed as Will left the room and looked over at me from her bed. "What a fucking loser."

"Loser? Why? Because only a loser would be drawn to me?"

"What kind of doctor picks up a patient's friend on the job like that?"

"Oh, we're now friends?" I smirked.

"Seriously, that was lame," she said, ignoring my question. "He's a cheeseball."

"I like cheeseballs, especially if they come in the form of attractive doctors. Cheeseballs are better than downright mean people."

"Whatever." She rolled her eyes.

Then a nurse came in to let us know that the other room was ready. She led us to an elevator that took us to the second floor, where Lisa was assigned to an overnight suite. She finally fell asleep while still hooked up to the IV. I quickly followed suit, dozing off on the cot next to her bed.

It was early in the morning about an hour later. I awoke before she did, marvelling at how, despite her illness, she was still as attractive as ever with her matted hair and, especially, her overgrown stubble. Lisa then abruptly opened her eyes. She looked surprised when she saw me lying on the makeshift bed next to her.

"I thought you'd left the hospital."

"No. I couldn't leave you."

"You didn't have to stay."

"It was fine. I'd have been worried."

She didn't say anything, but her expression softened.

The nurse entered and took her vitals and temperature.

"Your fever is still high...one-hundred two point five...but at least it's responding to the medicine and going in the right direction. I'll check with the doctor on call about your discharge."

"Thank God," Lisa grumbled.

-

Lisa climbed back into her bed when we returned to the beach house. Thankfully, the vomiting portion of the illness seemed to have subsided, despite the fact that the fever had not. Winter would text from time to time, and I would keep her updated.

I boiled some chicken broth for her and brought it upstairs because the nurse had said it was important for her to eat something and stay hydrated. She was sleeping, and I didn't want to wake her up, so I took it back downstairs until she awoke. She must have heard the mug moving against the saucer because her voice stopped me as I was about to walk back out the door.

"What are you doing?"

"I made some broth for you. The nurse told you to eat."

When I returned to her bedside, she scooted up against the headboard and began to sip it. When I turned around to go back out the door, I felt her hand grab my arm.

"You don't have to leave."

"I'll just return for the mug." I muttered.

Her voice stopped me again as I was about to walk out the door.

"Patch."

My entire body froze.

Her referring to me by my old nickname had taken me completely by surprise. I never expected to hear it again.

"Turn around," she instructed.

When I did, her face lit up with a sincerity I hadn't seen in years. "Thank you...for everything," she said as she placed the mug and saucer on the table. "Thank you for taking care of me."

I was so caught off guard and overcome with emotion that I just nodded once and walked out the door, unable to stop thinking about her words for the rest of the night.

-

Lisa's fever had finally broken two days later, but she still wasn't feeling up to performing. I was watching tv downstairs when she sat down next to me on the couch. She crossed her arms and put her legs up on the ottoman. It was the first time she had chosen to hang out in the living room while I was relaxing.

She'd just gotten out of the shower and smelled lovely. Even though we weren't touching, my body reacted immediately to the proximity of her legs to mine.

I wished she were mine.

Where did that thought come from?

"What is this bullshit you're watching?"

"Some sort of reality show. If you want, I can change it."

"No. I invaded your space."

"I'm just glad you're feeling better." I said, focusing on the screen.

"Me too though."

"Seriously, take the remote," I said, hurling the controller at her.

She passed it back to me. "Nah. I owe you. When I was sick and whiny, you put up with my shit. The very least I can do is sit here and listen to these whiny butches."

"Well, there is something else you can do to thank me for nursing you back to health." I offered.

She arched her brow, baffled. "Alright..."

I just realised how ridiculous that sounded.

"You can talk to me."

"T-talk?" She stuttered and looked at me in disbelief, sith a frowned on her face.

"Yes." I nodded slowly and bit my lower lip.

She exhaled a deep sigh. "I don't want to open an old can of worms. We're both aware of what happened. It's not going to make a difference."

I looked into her eyes, not wanting to beg but, "Please?"

She sat up abruptly.

"Where are you going?" I wondered.

"I need a drink for this," she said as she walked toward the kitchen.

"Can you get one for me as well?" I chased after her. In preparation, my heartbeat began to quicken. Was this really going on? Was she going to ask me questions about what had happened or just listen to me ramble?

She returned with a bottle of beer and a glass of white wine for herself. It surprised me that she knew exactly what I wanted despite the fact that I hadn't specified it. It proved she'd been paying attention even when she pretended to ignore me.

She took a long sip before setting his beer on the coffee table. "But we have to set some rules."

"Alright."

"Rule number one, when I say we're done talking, we're done talking."

"Okay." I nodded in agreement with her. I felt better, well at least better than nothing.

We finally gonna have a real talk after years and I seemed cam't hide my nervousness.

"Rule number two...we don't talk about shit that happened in the past after tonight. That's it. Only for one night."

"Okay. That's something I can handle." I agreed with a nod again.

She grabbed the bottle again and drank half of it before slamming it down on the table. "Alright. Go."

Where do I even begin? I just needed to get it all out there.

"Honestly, there's no reason for me to leave the way I did. I was young, stupid, and terrified. My greatest fear had always been being hurt by you, because you were the only person on whom I could rely aside from grandma. When I found out you were aware of what was going on behind my back... It felt like a betrayal to me. I didn't realise you were just trying to protect me at the time."

Flashback 9 years earlier

Mom was out, as usual, so I'd sneak out with Lisa to the little red theatre. This week, they were showing an Italian film called Si Vive Una Volta Sola, which I had been looking forward to seeing.

Lisa greeted me at the corner, as she always did. "We'd better get moving," she advised. "We don't want to miss the show at nine o'clock."

"We're on time. Relax."

When I realised I didn't have my bus pass, we started walking to the bus stop. It was inside a hoodie that I knew I'd left inside Lisa's house the other day while we were doing homework.

"Shoot. We need to get into your home. I left my bus pass in the pocket of my jacket in your dining room."

She shook her head dismissively. "I'll just pay for you."

"No, Lili. That's a bad idea. We've still got plenty of time."

I began to walk back toward her house. She snatched my arm. "Stop. I've got it covered. I'm going inside."

Her face was flushed with an uncharacteristically panicked expression. "No, we can't."

"Why?"

Tiffany, her mother, was on a business trip out of town, as she did every other week. I couldn't understand why she was so adamant that we not enter her home. She appeared to be struggling to come up with an excuse. My instinct told me something was wrong when her eyes moved from side to side.

"What are you hiding from me?"

"Nothing. We just can't go in there right now."

"I don't get it. The car of your father is parked outside. He has returned home. How come I can't just run in and get my jacket?" I furrowed.

"My father would be furious if he found out I was seeing you. I told him I was meeting up with Rob."

"I don't think so. Your father knows we hang out. He's fine with it."

"Not at night."

"You're lying."

"Will you just trust me, Patch?"

I hurried to the front door and knocked frantically. Marco finally answered the door after almost a full minute of silence.

"Hi. Lisa and I had planned to go to the movies, but I need my bus pass. I left it in my jacket in your dining room. I just need to come in and get it." Lisa's father gave her a worried look.

Meanwhile, Lisa's face was almost completely white.

I pushed my way past Marco when he hesitated to let me in. "All I need is my jacket." I noticed my sweatshirt hanging on the chair as soon as I walked into the dining room.

But something else drew my attention,

...My mother's faux fur coat.

What was she doing here?

It didn't take long for me to figure it out. As I stormed upstairs, I knew exactly where I'd find her. I stormed into Lisa's parents' bedroom, where I found my mother desperately trying to put on her clothes.

I shook my head in disbelief, covering my mouth with my hand, before running back down the stairs and out the front door.

Lira chased after me. "Patch, please wait. Please!"

"You knew about this?" I snarled as I turned around. "You KNEW my mother was here messing with your father, didn't you? How long has this gone on?"

"I-I didn't know how to tell you." She said, stuttered.

"I can't believe it!"

"I'm sorry, Patch. I'm so sorry."

I crushed back into my house and slammed the door, unsure which hurt more : my mother's actions or Lisa's cover-up of everything from me.

End of flashback.

6. THE DISCLOSURE

Her pain was noticeable in her eyes. As I struggled to find the right words, Lisa leaned back against the couch.

"It was wrong of me to throw my rage on you. My mother was essentially an irresponsible child, a selfish person. She'd had a slew of boyfriends and affairs with married men. That she would stoop to that level with your father never surprised me. But at the time, I felt betrayed by everyone, including you. However, I was misleading in punishing you in any way for their actions."

She rubbed her eyes suspiciously and turned to face me. "What is it that you want to know, Rosie?"

"How did it all begin? How long have you known about them?"

She shifted her weight to my side and wrapped her arm around the back of the couch. "I'm pretty sure it was my father who pursued her. Before they got together, he was always asking me questions about Jessica."

"Really?" My eyes widen and she just nodded.

"What I didn't realise at the time was that my parents had an open marriage. If you know what I mean, my mother went on far too many business trips. But I hadn't figured it all out at the time. When I arrived home from school unexpectedly early one day, I found your mother with him. I happened to walk in on them having sex."

I shivered. "Oh my god."

Lisa took a long swig from her beer. "Later that night, my father sat me down and told me that he believed my mother, too, had been having an affair, and that he and Jess had only recently begun seeing each other. Your mother made me swear I wouldn't tell you anything. She said you wouldn't be able to handle it, that your relationship with her was already overstretched, and that you were dealing with a lot of stress that I wasn't aware of. She convinced me that telling you would ruin your life. She told me that if I truly loved you, I wouldn't tell you. I trusted what she said."

"I never kept anything from you, Lisa. I didn't have anything going on. She was using you to keep her antics buried deep from me."

"I wanted to tell you, but the longer I waited, the more difficult it became to admit that I'd been keeping something from you for so long. So, as a consequence, I chose not to say anything. I was only trying to keep you safe."

"Lisa, I-"

"Let me finish it first" she said, lifting up her index finger on the air.

"Okay." is all I could say.

"We both came from broken homes, but ever since I met you, my world has seemed a little less broken. I've always felt like it was my job to protect you in some way. And the fact that I kept what they were doing from you was just an extension of that. It was not intended to be deceptive."

I get it now

I was embarrassed to admit so much about my feelings all those years ago, but I couldn't stop myself. She was giving me one last chance to explain myself and I'll use this opportunity wisely to explain thing. I took a long swig of my wine and prepared to lay it all on the line.

"I ran away because I couldn't control my emotions. It wasn't just that you kept that secret from me. It meant to me that there would be other things in the future that you would keep from me as well." I took a breather.

Just say it motherfucker Rosé. Damn it, it is what it is. Go for it.

"I was having really strong feelings for you that went beyond our friendship, and I found myself unable to deal with them. I didn't know what to say to you. I didn't want to scare you away. It just felt like I was destined to be hurt, so I chose to leave before it happened. It was my way of keeping it under control. It was reckless and stupid." That was the first time I admitted to having feelings for her other than friendship.

She just looked at me for a moment before saying, "Why didn't you tell me how you felt before everything happened with our parents?"

"I didn't think you felt the same way about me, and I didn't want to scare you. I didn't want to lose you."

"So you ran away and lost me anyway. Did that make any sense to you then?"

"It felt as if if I left before the worst happened, it wouldn't hurt as much. But the bottom line is that I was a stupid, hormonal fifteen-year-old girl. It was the wrong choice. Running away to live with my father was a bad way to deal with it. You never gave me the time of day to say sorry when I came to my senses the following year. So I'm going to say it now. I am so sorry if my leaving like that hurt you in any way."

"Hurt me?" She let out a slight angry laugh, and then she said something that shocked me.

"It changed my life, Roseanne. I loved you. I was in love with you." Lisa was frustrated and ran her fingers through her hair. "How the fuck did you not know that?"

Her words felt like they slashed through my heart, leaving me speechless. I never expected her to say that in a million years. I knew she cared about me, but I had no idea she loved me the way I loved her.

She had loved me?

"I would have died for you back then," she continued. "When you left, it felt like the end of the world. Aside from your grandmother, you were the only person I could rely on. You were always there...until you weren't. Losing you taught me to rely entirely on myself. It shaped who I am today...which isn't always a good thing."

Hearing her say that hurt me so much.

"I'm sorry."

"You don't have to apologise again...you've already done so."

"If you don't forgive me, I'll have to keep doing it."

She exhaled a long, deep breath. "I've moved on from it, as I've told you before."

I didn't want her to move on. I wished I could go back in time and hug her. Never let go of her. I dug my nails into the back of the couch, still reeling from her admission, and said, "I don't want us to be virtual strangers. You are still very special to me. The fact that you're mad with me isn't going to change that."

"What do you hope from me?" She asked, looked at me with no expression and that scared the shit out of me. I need to be honest for that, though. I missed the old us.

"I'd like for us to try to be friends again. I'd like for us to be able to sit in the same room and talk to each other, maybe even laugh a little. We'll always own this house together. We'll be bringing children here someday. We need to get along."

"I am not going to have children," she stated unequivocally. The fact that Winter had told me about Lisa's aversion to having children had slipped my mind.

"Winter told me."

"Did she, didn't she? What else did you discuss? My dick size? Did you tell her you had a good look at it?"

I chose not to entertain the quip and instead focused on the topic at hand. "How come you don't want children, Lisa?"

"You, of all people, should understand that it's insane to bring a child into this world if you're not completely confident in your abilities. My parents are prime examples of people who should never have had children."

"You're not your parents."

"No, but I'm a fucked-up product of their mistakes, and I'm not gonna repeat the past."

It saddened me greatly that she felt this way. I knew Lisa would make an excellent parent because of how protective she was of me. She definitely couldn't see it. Knowing that I had promised we wouldn't recall the past beyond tonight, an urgent need to get more off my chest overtook me.

"I beg to differ. I believe you are a much stronger person because you had to mature much faster than children who were coddled and given everything they wanted. You've given to others what your parents didn't give to you. I'll never forget how you could always make me laugh when it seemed impossible, how you always knew exactly what I needed, and how you always protected me. Those are the characteristics that would make a person a good parent. And, whether you have children or not, you are a wonderful person. Not only that, but your musical talent completely astounds me. It saddens me to think of all that I missed because of my stupidity and fear. I know we've both changed a little, but I still see the best in you, even when you're trying so hard to hide behind a mask." My eyes began to water, and a teardrop fell from my cheek.

"I miss you, Lisa."

Everything seemed to pour out of me before I could consider the consequences of being so open about my feelings.

She surprised me by reaching over and wiping a teardrop from my cheek with her thumb, prompting me to close my eyes. Her touch was so soothing.

"I think we've had enough talking for tonight," she said.

"Okay..." I said, nodding then she got up from the couch and turned off the television. "Come on. Let's get some fresh air."

I walked out the front door and down to the beach, following her lead. We walked for what seemed like an eternity in silence. Except for the sound of the waves crashing, the night was silent. The ocean breeze was soothing, and the silence between us seemed to be some kind of therapeutic exercise. It felt like a huge weight had been lifted because I'd finally gotten to say what I wanted to say. Even though there wasn't a clear resolution to our conflict, it was the closest I'd ever come to with her.

The ringing of Lisa's phone broke the silence of our walk. She took it up. "Hey there, babe... Everything is fine. That's great... Wow. It's really happening...Ah I'm just going for a walk."

It was interesting to me that she didn't mention she was with me.

"Me too. I can't wait... I love you too. Alright. Bye." I looked at her after she hung up the phone. "How's Winter?"

"She's fine. Since the lead actor's grandfather died, she will be able to perform tomorrow night."

"Wow. That's amazing. But well, of course not that the grandfather died..."

"Yeah no worries. I've got it."

We didn't say anything else until we got close to the house. Lisa indicated something off in the distance. "Do you see that?"

"Where?"

I felt weightless the next thing I knew. Lisa had lifted me off my feet and was running toward the shore. There was nothing to point out, judging by her laughter; she'd just been trying to distract me long enough to snare me.

Jerk.

She threw my fully clothed body into the water. Salty water ran up and down my throat and nose. Lisa immediately ran back to the sand, leaving me to wade through the water after her. She was still laughing as she sat on the sand. She'd taken off her shirt which had gotten wet, leaving her with sport bra, and her pants were soaked.

"Are you feeling better now?" I sighed.

"A little." She laughed. "Actually...a lot."

"Well...good. I'm happy for you," I said as I wrung out my dress.

She rose to her feet. "Let me."

Lisa surprised me by standing behind me and twisting my long hair to help drain the water. Her hands lingered for a few seconds, tingling my nipples. When I turned around to distract myself, I was met with her black eyes staring into mine. They glowed in the reflection of the light from our house. She was heartbreakingly beautiful.

"Um...thank you," I said, stumbling a little. "But not really thank you because you caused it."

"It had been a long time coming. I've wanted to throw you in the water since the day I arrived."

"Oh, really..."

"Yeah. Really." She gave a mischievous grin.

"By the way, how come you're still here?"

She squinted. "What do you mean?"

"You could easily have returned to New York with Winter. You know this..."

"Are you implying at something?"

"I'm not implying anything. I just know you've been blaming it on the Starlight gig, which I find hard to believe."

"What do you want to hear, Roseannea? That I'm here because of... you?"

"No...I just...I didn't mean that way. I-"

"I'm not sure why I'm here. Alright? That is the truth. It just didn't feel like the right time to go."

"That's cool."

"Are you done questioning me for one night, pain-in-my-ass?"

"Yes." I cracked a grin. She loved to call me that way during old good days whenever she teased me. It felt good to hear that again from Lisa.

"Good."

"For the record, I'm really glad you stayed."

"Trying to hate you is exhausting," she said, shaking her head and rubbing her eyes.

"Quit it, then." I smiled and it was getting cold outside, so my teeth began to chatter.

"We should go inside," she advised.

I couldn't help but think that the cold air outside had nothing on the warm feeling inside of me from reconnecting with her tonight as I followed her to the house.

"Are you hungry?" she inquired.

"Starving...actually."

"Go change. I'll prepare dinner."

"Really?"

"Well, don't we have to eat?"

"Yeah. I suppose we do. I'll be right back." I laughed all the way to my room, giddy at the thought of her cooking for me.

When I returned with a dry outfit, I saw Lisa standing at the stove, and my heart felt a thing. She was frying vegetables in a pan while wearing a sport bra and a grey beanie.

I cleared my throat. "It smells nice. What are you making?"

"Just a teriyaki stir fry with rice...seems like you have a limited palate. When the hell did you stop eating red meat in the first place? You were once a carnivore."

She must have remembered how much we used to enjoy Burger Barn together.

"I just woke up one day and thought about how crazy it was to be eating a cow. It didn't make sense. And I just quit cold turkey."

"Seriously? That's a little ridiculous."

"Yes."

"Roseanne, you've always been a little odd. That does not surprise me."

I gave a wink. "That's why you love me."

I'd intended it to be a joke, but given her previous admission, I immediately regretted using the word "love."

When she didn't respond, I panicked and developed diarrhoea of the mouth. "I did not mean to say that you still love me. I was only joking. I-"

She held out her palm. "Stop while you're ahead. I knew exactly what you meant."

I pursed my lips, trying to come up with a quick change of topic. "Do you think you'll play at Starlight's again tomorrow night?"

"Probably."

"Good. I'm really excited to hear you perform again."

She grabbed two plates, poured the contents of the pan onto each, and slid mine across the counter. "Here."

"Thank you very much. This smells luscious."

The dish she'd prepared was actually quite tasty. She'd thrown in some sesame seeds and water chestnuts. "How did you learn to cook so well?"

"Self-taught. I've been cooking for myself for a great many years." She said, then take a sipped of her water while her eyes set on me.

"What happened to your parents?"

"I thought we'd done talking about it." She put down her glass and take a napkin to wipe her hand.

"Sorry. You are right."

Despite her words, she looked up from her plate and answered my question. "When I was in college, my mother moved back to Cincinnati. They sold the house. My father now lives in a Providence condo."

"How long did things last between my mother and him after I left?" I asked, scrunched up my brows.

"It's been about a year. My mother discovered what they were doing under our roof and evicted him. He lived with Jessica for a while before things between them soured."

"Did he live with her?"

"Yeah."

I couldn't catch my breath.

"My mother withheld that information from me at the time. That explains why Grandma stopped speaking to her at that point. She was disgusted by their behaviour."

"Before I moved away, I spent a lot of time over there with your grand mother... She was the only one who could keep me sane." Lisa said, toning down her tone. She's looking everywhere but me.

"Did you ever tell her about me?"

"She tried to convince me, but I refused."

"Lisa...do you think she left us both in this house because she knew we'd have to face each other?"

"I honestly don't know, Roseanne."

"I believe she did."

"I had no plans to come here and try to make amends with you."

"No...really? I didn't get it. Do you still feel the same?" I asked, as she cracked a slight smile.

"Things don't change in an instant. We talked about it. That isn't going to undo years of shit. We won't be able to magically become best friends again."

"I didn't expect that." I thought long and hard before speaking again, while playing with the remains of my food. "I'll just say one more thing. And then I promise I won't bring it up again."

"I wouldn't bet on that." When her mouth curved into another smile, it gave me the courage to spill my guts one more time.

"I'm going to spend the rest of my life wondering what would have happened if I hadn't run away, if I'd just put my fear aside and told you everything I was feeling. You told me tonight that you used to be in love with me. I honestly didn't know, Lisa, but I wish I had. I had no idea you felt that way. I need you to know that I loved you as well. I just had a really shady way of showing it. And to think you've spent your entire life hating me. All I want is for you to be happy. If being around me makes you angry or stressed, I don't want to force anything, and it might be best if we keep our distance. But if there's a chance that we can truly be friends again, I'd give anything to have it. And I'm not an idiot. Of course, I'm aware that it won't happen overnight. That's all. I'm not going to say anything else about it." I said, honestly, from the bottom of my heart. I felt very light, as if all of my burdens had been lifted. I finally told the truth, which made me feel a lot better.

Lisa was deafeningly quiet and said nothing. She just stared at her plate, as if she was thinking about something. I gather all of my cutlery and plate without waiting for her response.

I rose from my seat and placed my plate in the dishwasher. "Thank you for dinner and for taking the time to talk to me. I'm gonna turn in early."

I made my way upstairs after finished washing my plate. Her voice stopped me as I was about to take the first step up the stairs.

"I've never hated you. I couldn't possibly hate you if I tried. Believe me... I tried."

Turning around and smiling, I said, "Good to know."

"Good night, pain in my ass."

"Great night, Lisa."

I happily smiled.

7. THE HECK

[re-publish bcs someone literally unpublish this one hahaha dang it]

Two days later, I was having my morning coffee when my phone lit up with a text notification. It was sent by Dr. Will Danger.

Will D. : What about tomorrow night's dinner?

I deliberated on my response. It would probably be beneficial for me to take advantage of Lisa's distraction. Things had improved between us since our conversation the other night. At the very least, she was no longer avoiding me. We actually drove home from Starlight's together after she performed last night. It wasn't a thrilling ride, but it was a step in the right direction. So everything was as good as it could have been.

It was my fault. I still couldn't control my feelings for her and didn't know where to draw the line. Every second of the day, I thought about her. We'd be splitting up soon, not to mention the not-insignificant matter of her committed relationship with Winter. I would never do anything on purpose to jeopardise that. But I still couldn't keep my emotions in check.

My fingers squeaked out a response to Will.

Rosé : Tomorrow night sounds fantastic! Just let me know what time you'd like.

Lisa's deep morning voice caught me off guard. "I see you created a coffee fusion."

I jumped, quickly putting the phone down.

She smirked. "Oh. Did I interfere things? You texting a guy, huh?"

"No, shit. Why would I?" I rolled my eyes to her and she snickered and just shook her head.

She gave me a suspicious look. "Liar."

I let out a nervous laugh. "Would you like some coffee?"

"Are you trying to change the subject?"

"Maybe."

"So, who was it?"

"Will."

"Doctor Danger?"

"Yes."

"Have you ever heard of stranger danger?"

"Yes."

"They coined that phrase to describe him."

"Oh, really?"

"I'm genuinely sure. Really." She poured himself another cup of coffee and returned her attention to me. "But seriously? Dr. Cheeseball? Are you going to go out with him?"

"Tomorrow night," I said, nodding. "What is your beef with him?"

"He's disrespectful."

"How so?"

"He was eye fucking you before confirming we weren't together." Lisa sighed loudly.

"Perhaps he's just perceptive."

"How?"

"He sensed your contempt for me. It was quite clear." I smiled and she just shook her head, drank all of her coffee in one way down.

"Where is he taking you to?" she asked in a hushed tone.

"I'm not sure yet." I said slowly.

"You should look into it."

"What difference does it make?" I furrowed, scanning her face with many question in my head.

She smirked and licked her lips.

"If you go missing, I'll know where to direct the police to begin their search."

-

Evening came and went, and I had no idea what to wear. Will informed me that he was taking me to a restaurant on the water in nearby Tiverton. Because it was going to be a humid night, I chose a lightweight floral tube dress that I'd purchased earlier this summer while out shopping with Winter.

From down the hall, I could hear Lisa panting.

Not again...

After what happened the last time I found myself witness to that jerk-off jamboree, I didn't dare to go over there to assess the situation. After a few minutes, there was what sounded like punching added to the mix. I broke my plan to stay out of it and marched out of my room to investigate.

Lisa was discovered to be in the gym, beating the crap out of an Everlast punching bag.

Sweat was dripping down her sculpted back. Sweat mixed with her cologne filled the room. Her hair was drenched. She was wearing ear-buds, and I could hear music blasting through them. She gritted her teeth and pounded the black rubber contraption harder and harder. With each punch, my heart rate increased.

"Get out of the way," she growled as I approached cautiously. As her arm swung dangerously close to me, I flinched.

I took a step back, but remained in the corner of the room, watching her. I'd seen her exercise before, but never like this. She was ferocious and virile, like a beast.

I guess that was maybe because of Winter had been gone for so long, she must have been sexually frustrated. Maybe that's why she was hitting the punching bag. Whatever the reason, I was transfixed by the energy she was expending and couldn't take my eyes away from her.

She came to a standstill, removed her earbuds, and moved over to the doorway, where she'd set up a metal bar for pull ups. My gaze followed her body as she lifted her own weight, her rock hard abs tightening and curling with each lift.

She jumped down from the bar and wiped her brow with the back of her hand. "What could be more entertaining than watching me work out? Shouldn't you be getting ready for a date?"

"I'm all dressed up." I pointed to my body up and down.

"Isn't that Winter's dress?" She furrowed and scrutinised me properly.

"No. It's the same one she has, but this one is mine. We both bought these on clearance from the same store on the same day." I explained to her and she clenched her jaw.

"It looks normal on her but it looks ridiculous on you."

My stomach churned. "Are you saying I'm fat?"

"No, but your body isn't like hers. That dress looks obscene on you."

Looking down at myself, I suddenly felt naked. "What are you on about?"

"Do you want me to spell it out?"

"Yes." I widen my eyes to her and she smiled.

She came up behind me, grabbed my shoulders, and pushed me in front of the wall-mounted full-length mirror. The feel of her rough hands on me sent shivers down my spine.

"Look. Your tits are bursting through. Your nipples are poking out of the middle of those daisy flowers."

My mind was fogged by the fact that all I could see was myself in the mirror, with Lisa's hot, sweaty body behind me. Then she flipped me around quickly, her gaze burning into mine. She was too close for comfort, and the surge of sexual awareness made my legs feel like they were going to collapse beneath me.

"Look in the mirror at your ass. The material can barely just about wrap around it. Do you think Dr. Doolittle will be able to look you in the eyes in that outfit?" She sternly stated to me.

"Do you really think this looks that bad?"

She spontaneously walked away from me and back to the pull-up bar. My genital nipples were tingling. All I wanted was to feel her hands on me again.

"I think it makes you look like a whore," she said before doing a few more silent reps. She hopped down, her weight causing a loud thump against the wood floor. "Are you really that oblivious, don't you?"

"What do you mean?" I was curious.

"You had no idea what kind of impact you have on people."

"Please be specific."

"When we were younger, you'd sit on my lap, put your hands on my shoulders, run your fingers through my hair, and hug me all the time with your massive tits pressed against me. I spent half of my teenage years walking around with a fucking hard on that I couldn't get off. And you obviously had no idea the entire time."

"No, I didn't."

"I know that now. And you've got no idea how many times I've had to defend you behind your back. Guys talking about your body and saying sexual things about you right in front of my fucking face. Do you know how many fights I got into because of you?"

"You never told me."

"No. No, I didn't. Because I was trying to safeguard your feelings. I tried so hard to fucking protect you from shit, and it was the one thing that bit me in the ass in the end."

"I'm sorry."

She raised her hands. "You know what? Never mind. It was my fault. Let's not do it again. I told you we'd had enough of talking. And we are."

"Okay."

"If you don't mind, I'd like to continue my workout in peace."

"Alright." I lifted my hands up to her and walked away.

Back in my room, I could hear her returning to the punching bag with vigour. I couldn't help but wonder if she was right, as I was still reeling from her words. Maybe I was just a bumbling idiot. But she also never expressed her feelings to me at the time. Was she thought that I supposed to be able to read people's minds?

I felt compelled to make that point. It was bothering me. I went back down the hall and spoke to her through her violent grip on the bag.

"You asked me the other night why I never told you how I felt. But well, clearly you didn't even have the balls to tell me how you felt, either."

Lisa's punching stopped, but she kept her arms on the bag and leaned against it. She paused for a few moments to catch her breath. "I assumed it was understood. How much clearer could I have been? All the fucking songs I've written for you? Have you ever seen me with any other girls?"

"No. But you did admit to kissing someone the night before at Aaron's."

"I had kissed one girl prior to that night. Want to know why? Because I didn't want to be in the dark about what the fuck I was doing when I finally worked up the courage to kiss you. I never considered it a real kiss. I wanted to spend my first real one with you. I wanted to share everything with you. But I was worried you were too young, so I waited. I didn't want to rush things and mess them up. But you're right. A part of me also didn't have the balls to tell you how I felt."

"I wish you had. You were being careful, and I was just clueless. Together, we were...careless." I sighed.

"Careful plus clueless equals careless? Did you make that up just now?" She bit on her lower lip and look at me with full attention.

"Yeah...I guess."

"That's pretty fucking cheesy."

"Yeah thanks." I grinned.

"You should prepare for your date with Trapper Con M.D." She made an annoyed face to me and followed by a playful smiled afterwards.

I laughed, relieved that he was now happy about things. "Will you help me?"

"Help you? What the fuck do you need help with?"

"Help me pick out what to wear. Because I think you're right. This is a little skimpy on the small side."

"A little skimpy? If I sent them a picture, Hustler would call you the next day."

"Alright. A lot skimpy."

"You can't figure out this nonsense on your own? It's quite simple. You keep your tits and ass covered. Done." Lisa's eyes checking me out, up and down and then set her eyes on me.

"Yeah. But damn, I still want to look good. You know that I have a penchant for selecting unusual items. Potato sack couture included. I feel like I'm going from one extreme to the other, and I'm not sure how to dress in between."

"Fine." Lisa took a deep breath and followed me to my room.

I began to take dresses from my closet and place them one by one on the bed. "How about this?" I asked.

"Slutty."

"This one?"

"Sluttier."

"Okay. This?"

"Did you get some Birkenstocks to go with it?"

"Alright...How about this one?"

"At least that's one way to get rid of him."

I shielded my face. "Aishh shit! This is so stressing. You're not helping at all, Lisa poop!"

"I've got a solution."

"What?"

"Don't go on the date."

"Just because I can't decide what to wear?"

"Yeah. I think you should stay at home."

"You just don't like him."

"You're dead on."

"Again...why?"

"All he wants is to get into your pants, Roseanne."

"Well, he's not going to get in my pants."

"Are you sure about that?"

"I don't sleep with guys on the first date."

She raised her brow in scepticism. "You've never slept with a guy on the first date?"

"Well..."

"Exactly."

"Even if I wanted to sleep with him-which I don't-it wouldn't be tonight."

"How come?"

"I stabbed myself again."

When she realised I was talking about my period, she shook her head and laughed. "Ah, I see."

"What makes you think he's only interested in me for my body?"

"It was his eyes," she explained. "I don't believe them. The look in someone's eyes can reveal a lot about them. I got a bad vibe from him," she continued.

"Well, I've got more going for me than just my tits and ass. So, hopefully, you're mistaken."

"You're right. When you smile, you have nice deep-set dimples as well with that perfect moles on your face."

My face flushed as a result of the unexpected compliment. I didn't know what to say, so I just said, "Shut up."

"Just be careful," she said solemnly as she reached into her back pocket.

"Speaking of which...take this with you." It was her old red Swiss Army knife from our childhood.

"You still have this?" I asked, perplexed with it. How I missed seeing this thing and finally got to see it again after a long time.

"I'll never be able to live without this." She grinned sweetly. Typical Lisa.

"Are you sure you want me to take this with me?" I asked again, to make sure about it.

"Yes." She nodded her head slowly.

"Alright," I said, taking it from her.

"Are we done here?"

"We still haven't decided what I'm going to wear." I laughed and she did the same thing too.

Lisa approached my closet and ran her hand slowly down the row of outfits, finally stopping at a simple black sleeveless dress that was far from revealing. It seemed to be something you'd wear to a funeral. Actually, it was the dress I had purchased to wear to Grandma's funeral before realising she had specifically stated that she did not want one. She wanted to be cremated and her ashes scattered in the ocean with no ceremony.

"This one? Really?"

She was holding the dress in her hand. "Don't ask for my help if you're not going to listen."

"Okay. This one it is." I took it from her and stood there watching as she walked out the door. My gaze was drawn to the rectangular tattoo on her back. Even though I've always thought it was sexy as hell, I've never been able to get a good enough look at it until now.

"Lisa."

She swung around. "Yes, Rosie?"

"What is that tattoo on your back?"

Her body tensed. "It's a bar code," she said nonchalantly.

"That's exactly what I thought. I was always curious. Does it have any meaning?"

"Get dressed," she said, refusing to answer my question. "You definitely don't want to be late for Dr. Dick."

Will was supposed to come get me in about twenty minutes. To freshen up, I sat at the kitchen counter, sipping a glass of white wine. Lisa's choice of a black dress was actually quite nice. There was no extra skin showing, which is probably how it should have been. I ended up twisting my long, blonde hair up in a bun.

A whiff of her cologne drew my attention to the side. When I saw Lisa standing in the doorway, my heart clenched. I hadn't realised she was there until I smelled her. She seemed to be watching me without my knowledge.

She'd just showered after her workout and looked stunning in a simple black shirt that clung to her figure. Her jeans were the ones that always showed off her ass in the best way. Despite the fact that I had the night off, Lisa was scheduled to perform at Starlight's. Tonight, the women were going to go apeshit over her.

She came over and sat down next to me on a stool. My nipples pricked up at the closeness of her body.

"You don't look too excited," she said after examining my face.

"To be honest, I'm not sure how I feel."

"Are you nervous about going out with that jackass?"

"A little."

"Why? He's not worth your nerve."

"This is the first date I've had since Shawn."

She almost angrily sucked in her jaw. "That's the jerk who cheated on you..."

"Yeah. How did you find out?" I asked, almost can't believed my ears. That confession literally shocked the shit out of me.

"Winter told me."

It surprised me that they'd been discussing me. I wasn't sure how I felt about Lisa knowing about Shawn.

"Oh."

"Don't let what happened with that asshole convince you that you have to settle for the first Tom, Dick, or Harry who comes along."

"Have you ever cheated on anyone?"

She paused before responding, "Yes. I'm not proud of myself. But I was younger back then. It's not something I'd do nowadays. If you want to cheat on someone, you should just break up with them. Cheating is a trait of cowards."

"I concur. Shawn should have just broken up with me."

"I'm glad you're no longer with him."

"Me, too."

"He was attempting to get the best of both worlds. He'll do it to the other girl as well. Watch."

"Winter is lucky to have you, to be with someone who is faithful."

"Temptation is natural," she said, her expression darkening. "That doesn't mean you should do anything about it." She appeared to be pondering her own words in an attempt to persuade herself of this fact.

"Right. Without a doubt."

Lisa quickly changed the topic. "Do you have your pocket knife?"

"Yes. I'm not going to need it, but it's in my purse, just in case."

"Good. Do you have my phone number?"

"Yes." I nodded.

"You should drive your own car."

"Well, I've already agreed for him to pick me up."

"Call me if he does anything odd. I'll come and get you."

"But you'll be in the middle of a performance."

"Doesn't matter. If you need a ride, give me a call."

"Okay. I will."

Her protectiveness reminded me of my childhood. It felt great to know that someone was looking out for me. In fact, I hadn't felt anything like it since I ran away from home all those years ago. I drank another sip of my drink.

Before I could set it down on the counter, I felt Lisa's hand on mine, snatching the glass from my grasp and gulping down the rest of the wine.

My voice was barely above a whisper. "I had no idea you liked white wine."

"I guess I'm in a different kind of mood tonight." She walked over to the small bar area and refilled the glass before returning to her seat and placing it in front of me.

We drank quietly from the same goblet, passing it back and forth, making silent eye contact. It was completely arousing whenever she licked the Chardonnay off her lips. I felt terrible for feeling that way, but it was out of my hands.

Temptation, as she said, was natural, right? But knowing that I couldn't and wouldn't act on it made the feelings all the more potent. It was all-consuming because she was unattainable.

If I'm being completely honest, I had no willingness to go out with Will tonight. Every piece of me, on the other hand, wanted to go see Lisa perform, especially since it was the last few days before she had to return to New York.

The knock on the door was confident and loud. Lisa massaged the back of her neck to relieve tension. If I didn't know any better, I'd think she was the one who was nervous about the date.

"Wait," she said as I hopped down from the stool to answer the door.

"Yeah?"

"You look really nice. I think you made the right choice with the dress." Lisa said, more like whispering but her eyes are not on me, but down the floor whilst she rubbed her neck.

My heart was fluttering. "T-thank you, Lisa."

My heels clicked on the tile as I walked over to the front door.

Will was holding a small flower bouquet. Hi eyed me up and down and I noticed Lisa was giving a hard look at him. "Good evening, Roseanne... .And, oh my dear, you look stunning."

"Hi, Will. Thank you. Come in." I said and made a way for him.

Lisa had her arms crossed. Her demeanour was more akin to an armed guard at a bank than a person standing casually in her own kitchen.

"You remember Lisa, my housemate?" I pointed to Lisa and Will just grinning and nodding his head.

"Of course I do. How are you feeling, Lisa?"

"Feeling very energised right now, Dr. Danger." Lisa said and seemed to annoyed Will.

Will seemed annoyed by Lisa's mispronunciation. "Dan-ger," Will clarified and Will just gave out a thin smiled to her.

"Sorry, didn't mean to anger Dr. Dan-ger." Lisa smiled and scrutinised Will as if she wanted to had an competition with him. I wonder what's going on with Lisa.

Will was irritated, it was just too obvious. Painted all over his face but he just played it cool in front of me. "No problem."

"Where are you kids going tonight?" Lisa asked again but this time her eyes were on me and her face relaxed and seemed a bit worried.

"The Boathouse," he says. "Have you been there?"

"Right on the water. Smooth. We're pulling out all the stops."

"Well, we should get going," I said, taking my purse.

Lisa extended her hand. "I'll take care of the flowers."

I wondered if they'd end up in the trash as soon as the door shut behind us.

"Thanks."

"There's no problem."

Will looked at me when we got outside. "Your roommate likes to butcher my name. She's a bit of a sage."

"Yes. She can be."

Will opened the door to his Mercedes and invited me to take a seat on the passenger side. On the way to Tiverton, the conversation flowed easily. He asked about my teaching experience, and we discussed his time at the University of North Carolina Medical School in Chapel Hill.

My phone then vibrated.

Lisa: Those were supermarket flowers.

Rosé: How do you know?

Lisa: He didn't take off the orange sticker. What a tool.

Rosé: It's the thought that counts.

Lisa: Look in the backseat. I'm sure you'll see milk and eggs.

Rosé: Don't you have to be at Starlight's?

Lisa: I'm about to leave.

Rosé: Break a leg tonight.

Lisa: Stay away from Danger. Better yet, keep Danger away from you.

Rosé: You're a goof.

Lisa: Order the lobster. At the very least, you will get something out of tonight.

Rosé: Duh, adios Lisa!

"What's so funny about it?"

"Oh, it's nothing. Sorry."

He turned to face me. "So, what were we talking about? Oh, you were about to tell me when you're going back to Providence..."

"It's the last week of August. I need to get my classroom ready for the start of the school year in September."

"I bet your students really love you."

"Why do you say that?"

"I wish I had had a teacher like you when I was in middle school." Will winked, and I just awkwardly smiled.

"Well, I like to think they appreciate me for other reasons."

"Oh. I'm sure they do."

Because it was already dark when we arrived at the restaurant, the waterfront view was not as spectacular as it would have been during the day. We chose a window seat inside but overlooking the water because it was starting to get cold. Some of the sailboats' lights illuminated the dark ocean. The white Christmas bulbs hanging inside the restaurant created a cosy atmosphere. The air was filled with the aroma of fresh seafood.

I laughed to myself, picturing Lisa saying the place smelled like dirty snatch.

Will ordered Chicken Marsala while I ordered swordfish with mango salsa. While we waited for our food, we had a fairly mundane conversation. We talked briefly about the upcoming presidential election. Will was a Democrat, while I was a Republican. I also told him how I ended up inheriting Grandma's house.

My phone vibrated once more.

Lisa: How's it going?

I didn't want to be rude and respond to him. So I ignored the text until Will excused himself to use the restroom.

Rosé: Aren't you supposed to be singing?

Lisa: It's my ten-minute break.

Rosé: Everything is fine.

Lisa: I'm just checking to see if you're still alive.

Rosé: No, I haven't had to use the knife.

Lisa: Did you order the lobster as I told?

Rosé: No. Swordfish.

She didn't respond, so I assumed she was done texting me, which was good because Will was about to return to the table.

When our food arrived, the waitress brought me another glass of wine. We were eating quietly when I noticed my phone buzzing on my lap. I was curious to look down, assuming it was Lisa, but don't want to seem rude. I decided to excuse myself halfway through my meal to use the restroom so I could check my phone.

I leaned against the sink in the restroom as I took out my phone.

Lisa: You were right.

What does this imply?

Rosé: What is it that you're right about?

I decided to return to the table after five minutes of waiting.

"Is everything okay?"

"Yes. Everything is fine."

"I was thinking we could drive back to Newport and take an evening stroll down Main Street, stopping for coffee or ice cream, whichever you prefer."

To be honest, all I wanted to do was go home, take off my heels, and soak in a nice hot bath.

"That sounds fun," I lied.

My phone vibrated once more. I looked down on my lap this time, hoping to catch a glimpse of Lisa's response.

Lisa: I didn't stay because of the gig at Starlight's.

Lisa: I could have returned to New York.

Lisa: I wanted to stay.

Those words guaranteed that I would be a goner for the rest of our time at The Boathouse. I didn't respond to the text message because I didn't know what to say. She might not have expected a response. My heart just felt strangely heavy.

We'd just returned to Newport in the car when Will said he needed to stop at a convenience store for a minute. My nose started running out of nowhere. I desperately needed a tissue, so I opened the centre console, hoping to find something to wipe my nose with. While I didn't find a tissue, my hand did come across something: a men's gold wedding band.

What the fuck is this? My heart began to pound incessantly. You've got to be kidding me right now.

The asshole was probably buying condoms for a tryst with me. I got out of the car and slammed the door without thinking. I wasn't in the mood for a fight and honestly didn't care enough to call him out.

All I cared about was seeing Lisa. Looking down at my phone, I realised she would still be playing the last set at Sandy's, which was about a half-mile walk from my current location. Running in my heels, I panted my way through downtown Newport.

Before entering the restaurant, I paused to catch my breath. Lisa was performing on the inside stage tonight because it was cooler. I crept inside and hid in a corner where she couldn't see me but I could still keep an eye on her. This had to be near the end.

Her voice abruptly vibrated through the microphone. "This last song is dedicated to anyone who has ever had a friend who drives you crazy-that kind who gets under your skin and stays there even when they're not physically present. The kind with dimples you've wished for since you were a child. You know, the kind with woods brown eyes that you get lost in. The kind that's as confusing as hell. That sort. This song is for you if you can relate."

Oh my God.

Lisa started playing a cover of a song I knew. It was Colbie Caillat's Realize. When I tried to listen to the words, I couldn't because I was too focused on the way she sang them.

The lyrics were mostly about realising one's true feelings and how they can be one-sided at times. Her eyes were closed for the majority of the song, despite the fact that she was playing the guitar. She had no idea I was there, and I was pretty sure she was thinking of me. I wasn't sure if I should leave. I felt like I was invading some of her privacy. It was unlikely that she would have chosen to sing this song in front of me.

When Lisa finished the song, she thanked the audience and stood up right away. She walked to the back of the restaurant, ignoring the bunch of women trying to approach her for an autographed CD. I needed to decide whether or not to make my presence known.

My phone vibrated while I was still in the corner of the room.

Lisa: I'm done for the evening. Heading home. Is everything kosher?

Rosé: Not quite.

Lisa: ???

I chose to pretend I hadn't heard the song or what had come before it. Nothing of it was intended for my ears. I typed as I walked back outside.

Rosé: Everything is fine. I just got to Starlight's. I'm now outside.

Within ten seconds, the door opened, and Lisa was outside carrying her guitar.

Her face was red-faced with anger. "What the fuck?"

"Hi to you, too."

"What happened?"

"Your suspicions about his character were correct."

"Did he try to touch you?"

"No. He didn't touch me."

"So, what did he do?"

"He didn't mention that he's married."

"What? How did you figure that out?"

"I found a men's wedding ring in the centre console of his car."

"Fucker." Lisa said in a throaty voice.

"Thank you for looking out for me."

"I guess old habits die hard." She looked up at the night sky. "Anyway, I'm sorry for wasting your night."

"The only regret I have is that I was unable to attend your performance. I dropped him off at the Cumberland Farms convenience store and dashed here as quickly as I could, but I didn't make it in time."

"You didn't leave much out."

"How come?"

"I felt a little off tonight."

"I'm sure that's just your perception."

"No. I was distracted."

A group of girls approached her and lingered outside. One of them approached her and handed her a CD. "Would you mind signing this, Lisa?"

"Not at all." She was incredibly gracious about it.

The girl squealed and dashed away with her friends.

I laughed. "Do you think I could snag a ride from a local celebrity?"

"I'm not sure. Your house may be too far out of the way for me." She nudges her head. "Come on. I'm in the parking lot across the street." She smiled generously.

I enjoyed riding in Lisa's Range Rover because her intoxicating scent was amplified tenfold inside. I closed my eyes as I leaned against the seat, overjoyed to be with her. It dawned on me that she'd only be gone for a few days before returning to New York. I'd be closing down the house and wouldn't see her every day.When I opened my eyes, I saw that we were about to cross the Mount Hope Bridge. She was driving away from the island.

"Where are we going?"

"We're going to take a detour. Is that all right with you?"

I was filled with excitement. "Yeah."

We arrived in Providence, where I lived and where we grew up, forty minutes later.

"I haven't been back in ages," she admitted.

"You're not missing out on much."

"I'm trying not to think about what I'm missing."

We drove through our old neighbourhood and eventually made our way down the city's East Side's congested streets. It finally dawned on me where she was taking me when she turned onto a particular side street. There was an open parking spot directly in front of the little red theatre, as if it had been reserved for us. Lisa parallel parked and turned off her car.

She sat there for a few seconds before turning to face me. "It looks open. Do you think they still have a midnight show?"

"I haven't been here in a long time. We could take a look." I had not anticipated this trip down memory lane.

Lisa approached the unkempt old man behind the counter. "Are you still showing indie films?"

"Whatever you want to call them."

"When's the next movie?" Lisa asked.

"Ten minutes."

"We'll take two tickets." Lisa said, giving out some money note to him.

"Number one to your left."

"Thank you," Lisa said as she led me into the dimly lit theatre.

"I'm so glad you thought of this," I said, looking around.

"Do you remember this exact room?" she inquired.

"Yes, I do." I pointed to the centre. "We used to sit right there. It smells even worse than I recall."

"It does smell a little raunchy." Lisa laughed.

The only other person in the theatre was a man who sat diagonally across from us. The lights went down, and the feature presentation began.

Within a few seconds, it was clear that, while the little red theatre appeared to be the same, everything else had changed.

A musical montage of women sucking various men off was featured in the opening sequence. Our little red movie house seemed to have lost its innocence in the years since we'd abandoned it.

It was now a porno theatre.

Lisa was laughing so hard she was practically crying when I looked over at her.

"Swear to me you didn't know," I said quietly.

She wiped her brow. "I swear to God, Roseanne, I swear to God. I had no idea. Did you see any signs...anything?"

"No. But there were never any signs indicating what was going on, so I just assumed..."

"You know what they say about assuming..."

"Do you make a fool of you and me?"

"Close. When you make assumptions, you can end up in an adult movie theatre watching anal."

She pointed to the screen, which showed nothing but a massive ass getting screwed. "Our little red theatre has been corrupted, Patch."

To make matters worse, the only other customer appeared to be jerking her hand up and down under a blanket. We both looked over at the guy and burst out laughing.

"Do you think that's our cue to leave?" I inquired.

"It's possible." Lisa giggled.

A new scene appeared on the screen out of nowhere. It wasn't as hard-core as the other, and it felt more cinematic, like an actual film rather than a cheap triple X video. The music had become softer. The snippet showed two guys slowly and sensually going to town on a girl. She was having oral sex with one of them while the other was going down on her.

We were supposed to be leaving, but I was stuck in my seat, unable to take my eyes away from it. Lisa was quiet, so I knew she was watching it as well.

The whole thing took about ten minutes. When it was finished, I turned to face Lisa, who was just staring at me. Was she watching the film, or was she watching me watch the film? Did she know it aroused me? In any case, she didn't say anything snide, and she wasn't laughing at me.

When she did finally speak up, her voice was strained as she whispered in my ear, "Do you want to stay?"

"No. We should go."

"Okay."

She put her hand on my arm to stop me from getting up. "I need a minute."

"Why?"

She just stared at me as if I should have guessed why.

I finally figured it out. "Oh."

I couldn't decide whether watching that scene or knowing Lisa was hard from it turned me on more. It was all a little much for me. She closed her eyes for about a minute before looking at me. "It's not going down."

"Staying in here will not help."

"I doubt it."

"Let's just get going." I didn't mean to laugh, but it was quite amusing.

We both stood up and left the theatre. I tried really hard not to look down, but my gaze was drawn to the bulge straining through her jeans. My mind was filled with dirty thoughts. I wished things were different because there were a million ways I could help her in taking care of it.

The drive back to Newport was quiet. The sexual tension in the room was palpable. My nipples had turned to steel, and my panties were soaked because I knew she was still hard. It occurred to me that certain situations, where you wanted something badly but couldn't have it, could be even more arousing than sex itself. My body was in an unfathomable state of arousal.

We arrived at the house. When she turned off the ignition, she leaned back against the seat and turned to face me, as if she wanted to say something but couldn't think of what to say.

"Thank you for attempting to make my night better," I said to break the ice.

"Attempt is the operative word. It was an epic fail."

"No, it wasn't," I said.

"Wasn't it? I took you to see a porno by accident and got a boner in the process. What the fuck...am I fifteen?"

"I was turned on too. It's just not as obvious."

"I know. I could tell. That's what..." She paused and shook her head. "Never mind."

"Well, anyway. It was still better than the date with Dr. Danger."

"I can't believe that asshole. I should go to the hospital tomorrow and beat the fuck out of him."

"He's not worth it." I cast a glance out the window. "Anyway, let's go inside."

"Yeah." she agreed.

We lingered in the kitchen when we returned home. Even though it was well after 1 in the morning, I wasn't ready to sleep. We didn't move an inch.

"Jesus, it's so late," I said, "but I'm not tired at all." I continued.

"Would you like some coffee fusion if I make some?"

"Yeah. I'd like some." I cracked a grin.

As she brewed the coffee, I kept a close eye on her every move.

I love you.

God, the thought had just popped into my head out of nowhere. When I was with her, those three words would play in my head from time to time. I did love her, just as much as I always had. But I had to keep these emotions under control or I'd set myself up for major disappointment.

"Win will be back in a few days," she said with her back to me.

My heart skipped a beat. "Really? Are you going back to New York with her?"

"No. I'll stay an extra few days after she leaves to keep my promise to Brayden."

"Oh, I see."

She sat me down with a steaming hot mug in front of me. "Here you go."

"Thank you."

Something seemed to have shifted between us in the last 48 hours. Perhaps her change in attitude was caused by the impending end of summer.

"I don't think either of us will be going to sleep anytime soon after this," I said as I sipped my coffee.

"Might as well just stay up."

Lisa and I just talked for the next two hours, opening up about the things we'd missed in each other's lives. I found that before moving to New York, she had completed a semester at Boston's Berklee College of Music but couldn't afford to continue. Her parents had refused to pay for her education if she decided to major in music. Instead, she moved to New York and worked odd jobs and gigs until she was able to return to school, where she majored in business with a minor in music.

She told me she met Jisoo, her ex-girlfriend, a few years after she moved there. They lived together for a few years and remained friends even after she ended her relationship with her. Before Winter, she'd been her only serious girlfriend.

Winter believes the ex wants to rekindle their relationship, despite the fact that Jisoo is now with someone else. She'd slept with a lot of women in the time between those two relationships. I appreciated her candour, but it still hurt to hear that.

I told her about my time at UNH and how I chose education as a major because it seemed like a safe bet rather than because it was something I was passionate about. Even though I enjoyed teaching, I admitted that there was something missing, something else I was supposed to be doing with my life that I hadn't figured out yet.

We had literally talked our way through the night, fueled by coffee. I was still dressed in the black dress I wore on my date. I went upstairs to use the restroom at one point. When I returned to the kitchen, she was sitting on a stool by the window, playing her guitar.

The sun was beginning to rise over the sea. Her back was turned to me as she began playing the Beatles' Here Comes the Sun. Listening to her soothing voice, I leaned against the doorway.

Stop falling in love with her, Roseanne.

How was I supposed to change my feelings? I couldn't do it. All I had to do was accept that Lisa was with Winter. She was happy. I needed to figure out how to be her friend again without hurting her feelings.

When the song ended, she turned around to see that I had been watching her.

I walked over to where she was sitting and looked out the window. "Isn't the sunrise beautiful today?"

"Really beautiful," she agreed, except she wasn't looking at the sun.

8. THE HELL

Winter was arriving tomorrow, and that was making me feel very much on edge.

I needed to talk to someone, so I coerced my friend and co-worker, Jennie, to come for a visit to the island. She met me for lunch at the town's Brick Alley Pub. Jennie hadn't seen me since the end of the school year. She hadn't been able to get away from her kids' busy summer schedules until now.

The first half of our lunch date was spent over nachos, recalling my history with Lisa and rehashing what had happened at the beach house up to this point.

"I wouldn't want to be in your shoes," she admitted. "What is your plans?"

"Is there anything I can do?"

"You could express your feelings for her."

"She's with Winter, and Win is a good person. If that's what you mean, I can't make a move for her right under her nose. I'm not going to do that."

"But she clearly wants you."

"That's not something I'd say."

"Come on...the song she wrote for you? Sure, she had no idea you heard it, but she clearly has lingering feelings."

"It's one thing to have lingering feelings...Acting on them is entirely different. She's not going to abandon her gorgeous, talented, Broadway star girlfriend, who'd been there for her when I wasn't, just because some old feelings resurfaced. Win is an amazing young lady."

"But Win is not you. She's always wanted you. You're the one who got away."

"I'm the one who ran away. That's something she'll never forget. She may learn to forgive me, but I doubt she will ever fully trust me. It's not fair of me to expect that of her."

"You're being overly critical of yourself. You were a kid." Jennie took a bite of her corn chip and asked, "You said you're not selling the house, right?"

"No. We decided to keep it. That's exactly what grandma would want."

"Then, whether she stays with Winter or not, this house will forever bind the two of you. Do you really want to spend the rest of your life watching the woman you love move on with other women every summer?"

My heart felt like it was splitting in half. On fast forwards, images of many summers turning into winters flashed through my mind. That appeared to be a daunting prospect. I didn't want to endure year after year of unrequited love for someone I couldn't have.

"You're not helping my dilemma. I was hoping you'd talk sense into me, make me realise that I needed to accept things as they were and move on."

"But isn't that not what you really want?"

No. No, it does not.

—

It was my night off tonight. I couldn't decide whether I was disappointed or relieved that I wouldn't be able to see Lisa play. Since the all-nighter, we'd kept our distance. It was probably for the best, because things were bordering on inappropriate that night, at least in my head.

Jennie chose to stay and spend the night at the beach house. With Lisa out of the house, she had the brilliant idea of buying some liquor and having a girls' night in.

We arrived at the house carrying a paper bag containing tequila, limes, and coarse salt. When I saw Lisa's car in the driveway, my stomach dropped.

She was supposed to be at work. What did she do at home?

"Shit. Lisa's home."

"I thought she was working," she stated.

"Me, too though."

When we walked in, Lisa was nowhere to be found. I set the bag down on the kitchen counter and went upstairs to show Jennie the upper deck.

Lisa was sitting there, drinking coffee with her legs up on the balcony, looking out over the water. Her hair was wet, as if she'd just gotten out of the ocean. She was only wearing her sports bra. The top of her boxer briefs poking up from her jeans. She looked like a freaking Calvin Klein ad. Jennie's jaw dropped to the floor when she caught sight of her.

"What are you doing here? I supposed you were performing at the restaurant." I asked.

She thrown a glance at me. "I was supposed to be there. But the place almost burned down."

"Hah what?"

"This afternoon, there was a kitchen fire. When I arrived, they informed me that they needed to close in order to air out the entire restaurant. They won't reopen for at least another week. It doesn't seem that I'll be able to play there again before I leave."

"Woah hold on! Has anyone been hurt?"

"No, but Brayden was a fuck up." She glanced over at Jennie. "Who is this?"

"This is Jennie, a good friend from Providence who also happens to be a teacher at my school. She came down for the day to spend it with me. She'll be staying with us tonight."

Lisa stood up and wore her baseball cap backwards over her head. "Nice to meet you," she said as she extended her hand.

"Likewise," she said as she accepted it.

I shook my head in disbelief, not only about the fire, but also about Lisa possibly leaving with Winter sooner than I expected.

"Wow. I can't believe that about the fire."

"I wasn't in the mood to perform tonight, but I'd never wish that shit on Sal. Also, I'm not sure if I'll be working there again before the end of the summer." She flipped her hair and tied a small knot in it. There was something so sexy about that.

"What are you ladies up to tonight?"

"We were planning on having some drinks and having a girls night in."

"That sounds like a hot mess."

Jennie burst out laughing. "I don't get away from my kids every night. So, for me, a girls' night in is about as wild as it gets."

Lisa made a wink. "Well, then, I'll stay out of your way."

"You don't have to," Jennie pointed out. "You should come with us for a drink."

"That's alright. I'll pass."

When we got back downstairs, Jennie went to the restroom. Lisa came down and noticed the massive bottle of tequila on the counter as I was cutting up limes.

"Jesus Christ," he said in a shocked tone. "Enough tequila?"

"It was her idea. I've never had a tequila shot before."

Her eyes squinted. "You've never had a tequila shot?"

"Nope."

"Damn, Patch. What did they not know how to do in New Hampshire?"

"Until about a year ago, I had never really drank at all. In fact, I've never drank so much as I have this summer."

She gave a mocking grin. "Do you want me to take responsibility for that?"

"Maybe." I burst out laughing.

As Jennie returned down the stairs, our attention was drawn to her.

"I'm so sorry, Roseanne, but Jackson just called to say Bella is sick and vomiting. He desperately needs me to return to Warwick."

"Are you serious? I'm so sorry to hear that."

"I guess you'll have to enjoy the tequila without me. I'm just glad Jackson called before I got drunk and couldn't drive home." Jennie smiled but still couldn't hide the sadness on her face.

"Do you need anything for the ride?" I questioned. "A bottle of water or something?"

"No. I'm good. I'll see you back at school in a few weeks anyway," Jennie said as she drew me into a hug.

"I appreciate you coming down, Jen. I had a great time."

"It was a nice to meet you, Lisa."

Lisa gave a silent wave to Jen as I led her to the door.

With Jennie gone, the atmosphere changed from light to intensely tense. Lisa was leaning against the kitchen counter, arms crossed, when I turned around.

This was exactly what I had hoped to avoid. I'd encouraged Jennie to stay the night partly to avoid being alone with her. Tonight was probably the last time we'd be alone before she left for New York.

I moved slowly towards where she was standing.

Lisa grinned. "What are we going to do with all this tequila?"

"I don't know," I said, shrugging my shoulders.

"I think we should drink it."

"I'm not sure how to do tequila shots." Jennie was going to show to me."

"Simple. Suck, slam, lick."

"Excuse me?"

"There are three steps to it. You wet your hand, lick the salt off, slam the drink down, and then suck the lime. Suck, lick, slam. I'll show how to do it."

Hearing her say words like lick, slam, and suck made my skin prickle.

My phone vibrated against the counter at that precise moment. It was right besides Lisa. Her face darkened as she looked down at the screen.

Before handing me the phone, she lifted it and muttered, "Really fucking nice."

When I read Jennie's text, all of the blood in my body seemed to rush to my head.

Jenjen: Lisa totally wants you. You should fuck her hard tonight.

When I looked up, her gaze was piercing. I let out a fake laugh as I wracked my brain for a response. "She's a jokester. She likes to bust balls. I'm sorry."

She didn't say anything and just stared at me with an unpleasant intensity.

Shit. Thank you so much, Jennie!

My heart was racing wildly.

Lisa remained silent for a long time before finally saying, "I really need that fucking drink."

"Me, too," I said, exhaling a sigh of relief.

She looked over the bottle. "Did you pick this tequila?"

Good. She was letting go of it.

"Yes."

"This brand sucks. It's cheap."

"I told you. I know nothing about tequila."

"Actually, it's not the worst thing in the world because we'll chug it down so quickly that you won't even notice. That would be a waste if it was the expensive stuff."

Lisa took a small container of salt from the cabinet, grabbed two shot glasses from the cabinet, and set them on the granite before sliding one of them over to me.

Lifting her hand, she spread her thumb and her index finger open and pointed to the space between them. "Put your hand here and do what I do." She licked the space between her fingers after that. That single swiping of her tongue was so erotic. She made it clear what that mouth was capable of doing in other ways.

Winter was surely a lucky woman.

Lisa was watching my every move of my tongue as I did the same. She then rubbed some salt between her and my fingers. "You're going to lick the salt off quickly before downing the tequila in one shot. Don't stop. Take it all in. Then take a lime and suck it." Hearing the commanding tone of her words lick and suck come out of her mouth...it was nearly too much.

"Ready? We'll do it together. On the third count. One...Two...Three."

I licked my hand and slammed the tequila down, the tequila burning my throat.

I'd forgotten to bring a lime with me. Lisa snatched one and shoved it into my mouth. "Quick. Suck on it. The flavour will be diffused." I sucked the juice out, savouring the sour taste. My lips were brushing up against her fingers as she held it. She was staring at me as I sucked on it. I wished I could have swallowed her entire set of fingers.

I licked my lips when she took the lime away from me. "Oh my God, that was very strong. What should we do now? Another?"

"It's simple, drunksé. We should wait a little longer. You're a light-weight."

We timed our shots so that each one was more powerful than the last. "Alright," Lisa said when I lost my balance a little. "That's all. I'm going to cut you off."

I stood there as she fired two more shots. Her eyes were beginning to glaze over after a few minutes. We were both quite drunk.

As I walked over to the couch and closed my eyes, the room swayed. I felt a heavy weight as Lisa plopped down on the cushion next to me. She leant back and closed her eyes as well. She'd removed her hat, and her hair was rumpled. The recessed lighting in the living room was shining on her head, highlighting blond streaks.

After a while of staring at her, the desire to run my fingers through her silky hair became unbearable. I reached over and began to rake my fingers slowly through it. I knew it was wrong, but I'd convinced myself it was a harmless gesture between friends.

Just like we used to. I knew I was delusory deep down. The alcohol had lowered my inhibitions and given me the confidence to do something I'd wanted to do for a long time.

She took a long, shaky breath but kept her eyes closed as my fingers massaged through her hair. I didn't stop because she looked like she was in ecstasy at first. Her breathing became heavier after about a minute, and she began to fidget.

She startled me when she opened her eyes and turned to face me. "What the fuck are you doing, Roseanne?"

I pulled away my hand. As I tried to think of an excuse, my heart began to race. "I'm sorry. I...I got carried away."

"Ah, I see. Blame it on the alcohol?" She scoffed.

She stood up and paced to the other side of the room, pulling on her hair in frustration. Then she did the strangest thing. She knelt on the floor and began doing pushups in quick succession.

I watched as she continued the exercises for several minutes, trying to fight the tears of humiliation that were stinging my eyes. By the time she collapsed onto her back, she was panting and exhausted. She finally sat up, bowed her head to the floor, as she sat deep in thought. Sweat was dripping down her back.

I got up and started to go upstairs, deciding that I'd done enough damage for one night.

Her voice shut down me. "Don't go."

"I think I really need to just go to sleep," I said as I turned around at the bottom of the stairs.

"Come on," she said quietly.

Her voice became more demanding when I returned to my seat on the couch. "I said come...here." She indicated the floor next to her. I sat besides Lisa on the ground, still too shamed to look her in the eyes, as she sat with her arms wrapped around her shins.

She shifted her gaze away from me. "You questioned about the meaning of the tattoo on my back. Look at the numbers in three sets of four under the barcode."

They seemed to be random numerals in no particular order. Three sets of four. What did they mean?

The first set finally came to me: 0237. "It's your birthday in March, the twenty-seventh."

She gave a nod. "Yeah."

The following set was 0507. "What's that one?"

"May 7th, 2001," she stated.

"What significance does that date have?"

"Do you have no idea?"

"No."

"That's when we met."

"How did you remember the exact date?"

"I just never forgot."

I examined the next set of digits: 0726.

That was one date I'd never forget.

"July 26th, 2006 was the date I left Providence. The barcode represents your birth as well as the beginning and end of our relationship," I said after a brief pause.

"Yeah. Life-defining moments."

"How long have you had this tattoo?"

"I was in Boston finishing my first and final semester at Berklee College of Music the night I got it. I knew I couldn't go back because I couldn't afford it. That night, I was depressed and sad, and I missed you like hell. But I'd refused to speak to you the year before when you tried to contact me, and I wasn't about to change my mind now. I was young and obstinate. I wanted to make you pay for leaving. The only way I knew how to accomplish this was for you to do to me what you did to me—disappear. I went to a tattoo parlour near my school and had this inked on me. It represented finally letting you go."

"Did it do the trick?"

"You know...after that day, I really kept my promise to move on. And it did get easier to forget everything with each passing year, especially after I moved to New York. I'd go days and weeks without thinking about you. I thought I'd put you in the past, where you belonged."

"Until you couldn't get away from me any longer."

She gave a nod. "I had no idea what to expect when I came here. When I first saw you in the kitchen that first day, I realised that none of my feelings had really gone away. I'd just been ignoring them. Seeing you again as a grown woman...it was jarring. I didn't know how to handle it."

"Aside from being mean."

"At first, I was still angry at you. I wanted you to be a bitch to me so that my rage would be justified. You, on the other hand, were sweet and full of regret. My rage has gradually shifted from you to myself...for wasting all those years in bitterness. So, do you know what this tattoo means to me now?" She took a breather. "Fucking idiocy."

"I was the idiot for ever leaving you. I—"

"Let me finish. I need to get this done tonight."

"Alright."

The next thing she said was completely out of character for her.

"Roseanne, we need to talk about our attraction to each other."

I took a swallow. "Okay."

"That text message from your friend...she was right. I want to fuck you so badly right now that I'm practically shaking. My conscience is the only thing keeping me from doing so. It's completely wrong and messed up."

My body was in a state of flux as a result of her admission, unsure whether I should be turned on or sick to my stomach.

"Ever since that day I caught you watching me in my room...," she continued. "I can't seem to get you out of my head."

"I probably shouldn't have done that."

"No, you shouldn't have done that. But here's the thing... I couldn't even be mad at you because you watching me jerk off was the hottest fucking thing I'd ever experienced in my life."

Wow. I didn't believe she felt that way.

"I figured you thought I was perverted."

"I would have done the same thing if I happened to walk by your room and saw you touching yourself."

"You have a beautiful body, Lisa. It was hard to look away."

"What were you thinking?"

"What do you mean?"

"When you were looking at me. What were you thinking?"

I decided to tell her the whole truth because she was being so forthright with me. "I was imagining myself with you."

Her breath caught in her throat, and she averted her gaze for a moment before making eye contact. "Have you always been attracted to me in the same way you are now?"

"Yes. But now it's even more so. I know it's wrong, Lisa."

"Right or wrong, we can't help who we're attracted to. I don't want you to be like this. It's hard for me just to sit next to you right now. But wanting someone and acting on it are two different things. That's why I had to stop you from touching my hair."

"I wasn't trying to sleep with you at all. I just missed touching your hair. That's it. It was selfish." I said, slowly.

"Believe me, I get it. I'm not blameless in any of this. I've looked for excuses to touch you, too. But I have a girlfriend. In New York, we have a good life. There are no excuses. I'm beginning to feel like my father, completely out of control and with no regard for anyone else."

"You're not your father." I convinced.

"My mother was just as bad."

"Well, you're not your parents."

"I don't want to hurt you, Patch. I'm so fucking confused. The fact that we share a house makes things very awkward. Maybe we should work out an arrangement next year," she said after closing her eyes for a long moment.

"Arrangement?"

"Yeah, maybe we switch months so we don't have to be here at the same time."

It was as if she had punched me in the gut.

What I was hearing was unbelievable. "Let me clarify something. You can't trust yourself around me, so you don't want to see me physically again?"

"No, that isn't it."

"Then why wouldn't you want to be around me?"

She raised her voice, her tone veering towards rage. "Do you enjoy hearing me and Winter fucking?"

"No. But—"

"Well, I don't want to hear you fucking anyone either. I'm doing my best to protect both of us here."

My heart was pounding. "So you'd prefer not to see me at all?"

"I didn't say anything like that. But making a schedule is something we should at least think about. I think that would be a smart option."

The words flew out of my mouth. "As difficult as this has been for me, I've never considered that. That is the difference between us. I would put up with whatever inconvenience it took to have you in my life. I would never choose an option that required me to pretend you didn't exist. I'd rather have a piece of you than nothing at all. Obviously, you don't feel the same way about me. So, you know what? Now that I know... I'm perfectly fine with a schedule." My cheeks were flushed as hot tears streamed down my cheeks.

"Fuck, Patch. Don't cry."

As I stood up, I extended my hand. "Please. Don't ever call me that name again."

"Fuck!" she yelled into her hands as she buried her face in her hands.

I stormed into the kitchen and poured myself another shot of tequila from the bottle. I skipped the salt and lime and instead drank it straight.

Lisa snatched the bottle from me before I could pour another. "You're going to sicken yourself."

"That's none of your business."

At that precise moment, the door clicked open. We both turned our heads towards it at the same time.

Her face turned almost pale before she said, "Winter!" with the most phoney smile.

She dashed towards Lisa, wrapping her arms around her. "I just couldn't wait until tomorrow. I've been missing you terribly."

Her body stiffened as she planted her lips on her. After what happened tonight, you could tell she was hesitant to kiss her in front of me. She pulled away from her. "You have a strong tequila smell."

"Yeah. Her friend was here and brought it."

"I'm glad to see you two are still talking to each other." She looked over at me then approached to give me a hug and said, "I missed you, too, Rosie." With each second that her skinny frame pressed into me, guilt grew within me.

"I'm so glad you're back," I said, lying.

She looked at my face. "Your eyes look red. Are you okay?"

"Yes. I just drank too much. It's not something I'm used to."

"Tequila is rough." She laughed as she looked over at the bottle. "Especially when it's cheap crap like that."

Winter spent the next few minutes filling me in on all of the Broadway theatre gossip while Lisa and I exchanged awkward glances. I decided I needed to excuse myself after she finished rambling.

"Well, I'm exhausted. I'm going upstairs."

"I'm hoping we don't bother you too much tonight." She winked and turned to face Lisa. "It's been a while." Lisa obviously looked stoic and extremely uncomfortable.

"Don't worry about me. Go to town," I said, biting my lower lip.

To muffle the sound of her bed shaking, I covered my ears with my pillow upstairs in my room. Listening to them have sex was excruciatingly painful, but it paled in comparison to the emptiness I felt after Lisa and I talked.

My stomach was grumbling. I became violently ill all of a sudden. I swore to myself as I dashed to the bathroom that I would never drink tequila again for the rest of my life, not only because it made me sick to my stomach, but also because it would always remind me of that miserable night.

9. THE UNEXPECTED

Two days later, and I was still sick. Is it possible that hangovers can last this long? I had barely come out of my room. Lisa and Winter were getting ready to leave the summer house and return to the city for good. I could hear them slowly packing their belongings. It was still unclear when they would take off.

I had no desire to face her or even say goodbye because I was still mad at her suggestion that we schedule our stays at the house for next summer. She hadn't even bothered to come check on me. When Winter came in, I'd thank her but tell her to stay away from me so she didn't get sick before her return to Broadway.

I preferred not having to talk to them again before they left, but I was beginning to realise that I needed to leave my room long enough to see the doctor.

Today had to be my lucky day because they'd left the house together just long enough for me to wash up and sneak out without having to confront them.

When I arrived at the clinic, I had to wait for about a half-hour before being seen. I couldn't go to Newport Hospital's emergency room because the last thing I needed was to be seen by Will Danger. So I took a detour to find this small walk-in clinic.

A nurse eventually called me. "Miss Park?"

I followed her down the winding corridors into a cold, small examination room, where she made me wait for another fifteen minutes or so. When the doctor arrived, I explained all of my symptoms such as nausea, vomiting, and fatigue.

I told her I'd been feeling sick on and off all summer and admitted to drinking heavily the day before, but they ruled out alcohol poisoning. I also listed Lisa's illness in case it had anything to do with it.

When I admitted that I hadn't seen a doctor in over two years, she insisted on running some tests to make sure everything was fine with me. She directed me to the lab, where a phlebotomist took blood from my arm. I also peed in a cup. This was becoming far too complicated.

The blood test results would be back in a few days. I was about to leave the office when the doctor noticed me in the waiting room. "Miss Park?"

"Yes?"

"Could you please come back into my office for a moment?"

My heart was pounding. Something about this scenario didn't seem right. They stated that they would contact me. I'm curious why she needed to see me so suddenly.

"As you know, the lab downstairs took your blood, and the results won't be available for a few days, but testing the urine sample is a much faster process. You stated that you were not sexually active, but it turns out that you are pregnant."

Pregnant...

I'm pregnant?

What the actual fuck!?

Oh jesus. how is that even possible. There's no fucking way!

"That's impossible," I exhale heavily, I rubbed my chest and looked at the doctor, hoping she'd say she was joking about it.

Oh dear god, pease tell me this is all a joke.

"I'm afraid it is."

"I've even gotten my period."

"It could have been spotting or some irregular bleeding that wasn't menstruation. You mentioned recently that you'd been drinking a lot. Is it possible that you had sexual relations that you were unaware of?"

"Absolutely not."

Wracking my brain, I recalled the last time I had sex. I recalled the last time I had sex. It was with Shawn a few months ago—the night we broke up. It seemed impossible because we'd always used condoms.

"Are you sure?"

"Yes, these tests are quite accurate."

"Can you run it again?"

"I'll tell you what. There's an OB GYN office in this building. If they can fit you in, I'll see if they won't mind doing a quick sonogram. I can't promise they'll be available, but I'll call them anyway. Why don't you wait in the lobby?"

They seemed to have made me wait an eternity. I was convinced that everything had been a mistake and thus a huge waste of time.

"Miss Park?" the doctor asked, peering into the waiting room. "Good news. They'll take you right away. Just return to the first floor via the elevator and look for Reid Obstetrics. Ask for Bella. She works as an ultrasound technician. Our office has already forwarded all of your insurance information."

"Thank you." When I arrived at the office downstairs, a young lady in scrubs with Mickey Mouse heads all over her shirt greeted me with a smile. "Roseanne?"

"Yes, me."

"Hi. Come on over here." Bella led me into a dimly lit room. The temperature was much higher than in the cold examination room upstairs, and soft music was playing on the radio.

"First off, Congratulations." She spoke with a slight Spanish accent.

"Oh, I'm not pregnant. I'm infected with a virus. This is simply to confirm that they erred with the urine test."

She appeared amused. "Those tests are extremely accurate."

"Normally, they are, but not in this case," I stated matter-of-factly.

She ignored my comment and pointed to my shirt. "Would you mind lifting this for me? I'm just going to apply some warm gel to your stomach."

When she squeezed the clear gel onto my stomach, the tube made a strange squirting sound. She pressed the nozzle against my abdomen a little. A fuzzy white image appeared on the screen, and I recognised it within seconds.

It wasn't just a blob; it had a huge head and arms. It was moving and appeared to be enormous.

"Roseanne, I present you...your virus. As you can see, it has a beating heart right here, and all of the parts appear to be in place. You are definitely carrying a child."

It felt like the room was spinning. My heart stops. They're frozen to their place. Stomach twists. Can't breathe. Hands fly to chests. Goosebumps maybe.

"How can this be?"

"I'm sure if you think hard enough, you'll figure it out."

You also seem to be about twelve weeks along, which would put your due date somewhere near the end of March."

It was three months ago. Almost exactly the same as the last time I was with Shawn. Shawn was the one who cheated on me. Shawn, who was living with Dina in Boston. Shawn, whom I loathed.

That Shawn.

I was carrying Shawn's baby.

Hell.

"Unfortunately, it's a little too early to tell the sex," she continued the technician, "but we can make you another appointment for your eighteen-week visit, and we should be able to determine the gender then. But you'll see the doctor the next time."

"I'll probably see a doctor out in Providence, where I live most of the year, but thank you."

I was dazed and confused as she printed out three pictures of my baby and handed them to me. I looked down at the images of the alien creature, then down at my stomach, which didn't appear to be any different. I just looked a little bloated, which I attributed to stress and drinking.

Oh my goodness. Drinking!

I'd been drinking a coffee-and-alcohol concoction. Was the baby even okay? Damnit.

I exited the medical building, feeling numb, and sat in my car for several minutes before summoning the energy to drive home. The outside appeared to be different. Grayer. Scarier.

The future appeared to be completely unpredictable. For the first time in months, something other than Lisa had taken over my thoughts.

—

Back at home, Lisa and Winter were preparing dinner in the kitchen, while I sat in bed, clutching my stomach in disbelief. I'd gotten back into my room before they returned to the house with their groceries, so I still hadn't spoken to them.

Under the circumstances, the sound of Winter's laughter from down-stairs was driving me insane. I was still stunned. I felt as if I were in the middle of a nightmare. It was difficult to believe that I was pregnant.

How could I possibly raise a child? I was barely able to care for myself. My salary was insufficient to cover the cost of daycare. There were a lot of things up in the air. My frantic thought process was interrupted by the sound of the front door slamming. I heard footsteps coming up the stairs and approaching my room before I could wonder if they'd left.

A knock came on the door. "Who is it?"

"It's me."

I shivered at the unexpected sound of her low voice.

"What do you need?" I asked, a bit loud.

"May I come in?"

I stood up and opened the door. "What?"

She seemed tired, as if she'd been pushed to the limit.

"You look exhausted. Too much sex?" I scoffed.

"Win is making guacamole," she said, ignoring the question. "We were out of limes, so she hurried back to the store. It's the first time I've had the opportunity to speak with you alone. We don't have a lot of time." she continued and I wanna push her out of this room so bad. She was only here because Winter wasn't around.

"Do you have anything to say?"

"Why haven't you come out of your room?"

"Isn't that what you wanted? For me to disappear?" I said, without looking at her face. I sat back at the corner of my bed while she was just stay at the front door.

Lisa shook her head slowly and whispered, "No," her face filled with regret as I looked at her way.

"No?" I snorted, shaking my head

"No. The schedule idea was ridiculous. I'm sorry I ever suggested it."

"Well, guess what?" I smiled, in pain.

Pain is all I felt.

"What?"

"It's no longer going to be very hard for you to resist me. There will be no dilemma. Because after I tell you what I found out today, you will never have an inappropriate thought about me again. You're not going to want anything to do with me. Your worst nightmare has just become my reality, Lisa."

Her eyelids were fluttering as she tried to decipher what I was saying. "Wait, what the fuck are you talking about?"

I buried my face in my hands as I burst into tears and knelt on my knees. I became acutely aware of my pregnancy hormones. Lisa, who had never seen me cry so hard, sat next to me and drew me into her arms. That only made me sob even more.

"Rosie...talk to me. Please."

"I went to the doctor. It was supposed to be just a routine check-up. I'd been sick...just like you..."

"Did someone hurt you over there?"

I cried, wiping my nose with my sleeve. "No. That is not the case."

"So, what then?"

"The doctor ran some tests. A pregnancy test was one of them." I drew back, embarrassed, to look at her face.

"You..." She stuttered. She came closer a bit to me and looked at me in the eyes with full curiosity and deadly concerned face.

"You're...pregnant?" She let it out with a wrinkled on her brows.

My voice was nearly inaudible. "Yes."

"How is that possible?"

"I'm three months pregnant. It's Shawn's."

"Did that asshole not use a condom with you?"

"That's the thing. We did use one. I'm not sure how this happened. Clearly, they are not impenetrable."

"Is it too late to terminate it?"

"Didn't you hear me say I was three months pregnant? Yes, it's too late! Even so, I could never have an abortion."

Lisa got out of bed and began pacing. "Alright...alright, I'm sorry. I was just thinking out loud, making sure you know what your options are."

"I'm scared shitless."

"Lisa?" yelled Winter from downstairs. "I'm back!"

She came to a dead stop in her pacing. "Shit."

"Please don't tell Winter no matter what happens" I begged. "I don't want anyone to find out just yet."

"Okay. Yeah, of course."

"I think you should leave."

She refused to move from her position. "Roseanne..."

"Go! Just go! Please...I don't want her to see me in crying."

Lisa quietly slipped out of the room, still stunned and dumbfounded without any words.

I spent the rest of that night researching what to expect in the next six months on the Internet. I needed to think about how I was going to tell Shawn. He didn't want anything to do with it, but he had to know.

—

Lisa and Winter were putting the car away. I'd already said my goodbyes to Win over breakfast, but I hadn't had time to speak with Lisa. They'd be on their way back to the city in no time. I couldn't believe the day had arrived. It was both a relief and a source of dread. Seeing her every day would have been even more difficult, knowing that there was no longer any hope of a future for us.

Lisa had no desire to have her own children, let alone raise someone else's. This pregnancy proved to be the final nail in the coffin. Maybe I'll take her up on her offer for next summer. Better yet, perhaps I should sell her my half of the house. As heartbreaking as that thought was, I had no idea what kind of financial situation I would be in after the baby was born.

I watched from my bedroom window as they loaded suitcases and boxes into the back of the Range Rover. Lisa happened to look up at me at one point. She held up her index finger as if to signal that I should wait for something. I soon noticed that she was whispering in Win's ear. She sped away in the car a few seconds later.

Her footsteps were soon heard. Then she showed up at my door.

"Hi," she said, her face solemn.

"Hi."

"How are you feeling?"

"Not very good." I sighed and just shrugged.

"I asked Winter to go get gas so I could say goodbye and see if there was anything else I needed before we left."

"No. I'm fine. You need to get back to your life."

"I feel bad leaving you like this."

"I'll be back in a couple of days anyway. The sooner I return to Providence and begin preparing for this new reality, the better."

"Patch..."

"Don't call me that anymore...please." My eyes welled up with tears. "Not because I'm mad at you... It just makes me sad." My lips trembled.

"Uh yeah, okay," she said softly.

"What were you going to say anyway?"

"Please call me if you need anything...anything at all. Just call me right away. Promise me you'll keep me up to date on what's going on."

"I'll do it."

"And oh, let me know when I'm free to tell Win."

"Okay. It's not like I'll be able to keep it hidden for much longer." Her gaze was drawn to the bed. I'd been looking at the ultrasound snapshots earlier and had left them out in the open.

She walked over and took them. She looked mesmerised as she stared at the images. "Is that something inside of you. You're hardly displaying."

"I know."

While looking over the photos, she shook his head. "Oh my God, this is bizarre. I believe I'm still in shock."

"You wouldn't be the first." I smiled, barely.

She re-arranged the pictures on the bed and stared into space, deep in thought. She reached into her pocket and pulled out a red pocketknife. "I'd like you to keep it. You need it more than I do. Keep it next to your bed at night. It'll make me feel better because I'm currently feeling fucking damn helpless right now."

I was not about to argue with her. I don't want to waste her time because she has to leave, after this. "Okay."

Her gaze was drawn to the window. We could both see Winter approaching.

I wiped away my tears. I had absolutely no idea I was in tears. It just too hurt that I barely could sensed it coming.

"You'd better get going." I spoke slowly, with a crackly tone in my voice.

She didn't move an inch.

We locked our gazes on each other until we heard Winter enter the house.

She then...slipped away.

When my soul can't find her, the world becomes unquestionably cold. The ground suddenly crumbled beneath my feet, because it was terrifying to stand on the edge of a cliff alone.

10. THE VISITS

E ight Months Later...

I felt like I was breaking into someone's home, despite the fact that it was half my own.

Everything appeared to be exactly as we had left it. The beach house was bitterly cold. It was necessary to turn on the heat. It was the middle of May, and the island was still relatively cool. I wasn't supposed to return until the end of June, but the house where I was renting an apartment was sold, so I had to leave.

That left me with no choice but to leave for Newport as soon as possible; otherwise, we would have been homeless. It made sense because I was already on maternity leave until the end of the school year.

We couldn't find any temporary tenants in the off season, so the beach house sat empty. I was overcome by an unexpected sense of longing. This place used to make me think of grandma, but now it makes me think of Lisa. I could practically smell her cologne in the kitchen. It was my imagination, but it felt real.

I also imagined her standing near the coffeepot, smirking while stirring her coffee fusion...her muscled back as she looked out the window toward the ocean...the lick, slam, suck as she drank tequila. Gazing toward the living room, I remembered our awkward final night before Winter returned.

Closing my eyes for a moment, I imagined it was last summer when life was so simple. Then, the little cry coming from the baby carrier strapped to my chest snapped me back to reality.

Bea's head wiggled back and forth in search of my breast. "Wait...wait. I have to take you out of this thing first." Removing her from the Baby Bjorn, I mambled, "You were so good during the ride. You must be so hungry, huh cutie bear?"

Shit. Most of my stuff was still in the car. I carried my two-month-old daughter outside to retrieve the breastfeeding pillow from my backseat. Jennie had bought it for me, insisting it was the one item I'd need the most, and she was right. It was bright pink with white daisies and an absolute necessity in order to feed this constantly hungry baby without breaking my back. I stopped for a moment to admire the ocean before returning inside.

Bea was short for Bella. It sounds right like that. She was named after my grandmother. My baby girl was born in mid-March, one week before her due date. Shawn chose not to be there. He said he wanted proof that the baby was his, and until then, he wasn't going to acknowledge her as his daughter. Because we'd used condoms, he assumed that it was unlikely that he could be the father. He was the only person I'd slept with before getting pregnant, but there was simply no way to prove that to him if he didn't take my word for it.

I didn't want the stress of having to get Bea's blood drawn right now, and he was in no hurry to be there for us, so I chose to put off dealing with him. His bitch, Dina, was surely working this situation behind the scenes, and I was sure she was telling him that I was a liar. With much bigger fish to fry, I didn't need that shit right now. Life was too stressful as it was.

Bea fell asleep again after she finished feeding. I gently lifted her from my breast and slid her into the infant seat. I used the rare break to head back outside and retrieve the rest of our items. The majority of my belongings were in storage in Providence. But I did bring all of our clothes and Bea's bassinet. I'd have to buy a crib and figure out how to put it together.

A man with dark curls, probably in his early thirties, approached me. His big brown eyes twinkled. "Hello there, neighbour. I noticed your car. I was wondering when I'd get to meet the people who live in this beautiful house."

I pointed to the house directly to my right. "Do you live in that one over there?"

"Yes. I moved in last fall. Apparently, I'm one of the few year-round residents." He nodded his head and scratching his nape.

"So, you've met Naddy, haven't you? She's also available all year." I asked.

"Yeah, but I think that's all there is to it."

"You're probably right," I said, laughing.

He extended his hand. "Danny Holland," he says.

"It's a pleasure to meet you. I'm Roseanne Park."

"I see you have baby supplies in here. Do you have any kids?"

"Oh...just one. My daughter was born in March. She's sleeping inside."

"I have a daughter too! She is seven years old and lives in California with her mother."

"I'm sure you miss her."

"You've got no idea. I work for the Navy and have been stationed here for some time. My ex wanted to move back West to be closer to her family after her mother and I divorced."

"Ah, I see."

"Where is your husband?"

"Oh...I don't have a husband. It's a lengthy story. I'm not with my kid's father. It was an accidental pregnancy."

"I'm really sorry to hear that."

"Don't be. It's a blessing."

Danny took a peek inside my trunk. "Can I help you in carrying the rest of this stuff in?"

My fatigue overcame my apprehension about trusting this virtual stranger. Bea hadn't been letting me sleep, and I was grateful for any help I could get carrying all of this stuff inside.

"That would be great."

Danny unloaded everything from the car into the house, even bringing the bassinet upstairs and placing it next to my bed for me. He knelt down to look at Bea while she slept in her car seat on the living room floor after we walked back down the stairs together.

"She's precious," he said quietly.

"Thank you. She sleeps during the day and keeps me awake at night. I've been told to sleep when the baby sleeps, but I can't. I have too much work to do while she's sleeping."

He stood up and lingered for a moment before saying, "Well, if there's anything else you need, I'm right next door. Seriously... If something breaks or you need assistance lifting something, don't be afraid to ask."

"I appreciate it more than you know. Thank you very much."

A smile spread across my face as the door closed. Danny had no idea he'd be putting together a crib so soon.

I decided to go upstairs and put some of our clothes away while Bea was still sleeping. I couldn't help but stop in Lisa's room on my way to my room. I sat down and sniffed her side of the bed's pillow. It wasn't my imagination this time, it still smelled like her cologne.

There was that longing feeling again.

As I hugged the pillow, a tear streamed down my cheek. I'd done a good job of suppressing these emotions for nearly a year. This was the point at which everything began to fall apart.

I'm missing you, Lisa.

Lisa had called and texted me several times in the previous months. I'd tell her I was fine but insisted that I didn't need her help.

She wasn't very active on social media, other than posting a few pictures from gigs—mostly of her audiences—on Instagram here and there. I would stalk Winter's Facebook page for small glimpses into their city life, envious of their freedom. I missed her terribly, but I knew that keeping my distance was for the best.

I texted Lisa a picture of Bea shortly after she was born. She once again offered help, both financially and otherwise. I'd always said no. She and Winter ended up sending me a generous Babies R Us gift card, which I used to purchase Bea's bassinet and bouncy seat.

I hadn't told her I'd been evicted from my apartment. I was embarrassed and didn't want to accept the offer of charity again. So she had no idea I was living here yet. I was hoping against hope that they would stay away for as long as possible this summer. I doubted they'd appreciate being woken up several times in the middle of the night by Bea anyway. But, to be honest, the real reason I didn't want to see her was that it would be too painful.

—

There had been no sign of Lisa or Winter for nearly a month. I was finally getting back into the swing of things on the island.

Danny ended up putting the crib together for me. It was white, and I'd used the remainder of my gift card to purchase a bedding set online. Danny and I were getting to know each other. Knowing how difficult it was for me to leave the house, he'd bring me coffee or fresh seafood from the dock on occasion.

Even though I had a feeling he was interested in me, he wasn't making any moves, which was a good thing because I was in no position to date anyone.

Bea was going through a difficult time. She was colicky and still didn't get much sleep. She always wanted more food, no matter how much I fed her. When I was able to leave the house, I took her everywhere with me, to the market and to doctor's appointments.

I hadn't been out by myself since she was born. We were the only two of us. That was fine with me. The only times sadness would creep in were late at night, when I was exhausted from the day.

Rain was pelting my bedroom window one such evening. Bea was yelling and sobbing. She'd drained my breasts of milk but refused a bottle.

I was starting to see stars due to exhaustion, and I just wanted to sleep so badly. I burst into tears. This type of torture seemed appropriate for prison inmates.

How was I going to function if I didn't get any sleep? How could I possibly go back to work, and who could possibly care for her the way I did? As thunder rolled in the distance, I was overcome with a sense of helplessness. What if we were to lose power? In the dark, how would I change her diaper? I realised we didn't even have any candles.

A minor panic attack began to form within me. I decided to go downstairs and carefully descended the stairs while holding onto Bea.

My emotions had only gotten worse after a half-hour. My nipples were painfully sore and cracked. Bea was still squirming in my arms. The front door shook, and a full-fledged panic ensued.

As I frantically reached into my pocket for Lisa's pocketknife, I felt a rush of adrenaline. For that reason, I made sure to wear pyjamas with pockets.

Someone was trying to break into the house.

My cell phone was upstairs, it occurred to me. We couldn't even hide because Bea was screaming. The door was shaky once more.

"Damn key," she said as the door opened. When she saw me, her eyes popped out of her head. Bea was clinging to my boob.

My hair was rumpled, and I was pointing her own knife at her.

"Lisa."

Lisa is here. What the fuck!?

She averted her attentions from me. "What the fuck, Roseanne? Put the knife down and cover your tit."

Her unexpected arrival had taken me by surprise, and I hadn't even noticed that one of my breasts was protruding from my nursing bra. I wasn't wearing a shirt because I didn't usually sleep in one. It was easier to nurse Bea while only wearing bra.

I walked over to the kitchen, Bea in one arm, and grabbed my cardigan from one of the stools before covering myself up.

"What are you doing here?" I asked, fumbling with my sweater and speaking through Bea's agonising cries.

"Do you always walk around the house in just your bra these days? If that's the case, we're going to have a problem." Lisa shook her head.

"I didn't expect you to show up. It's earlier in the season than you were when you arrived last year. How come you didn't call me first?"

"For one thing, I didn't expect you to be here. I needed to get away from the city for a while. I was going to spend a couple of weeks opening up the house and getting it ready for you."

Bea's sobs had not subsided. In an attempt to calm her, I bounced her up and down.

"What's wrong with her?"

"She has colicky. I don't have enough milk to satisfy her, and she refuses to take formula."

She moved slowly closer to where I was standing, catching a glimpse of Bea's face. Lisa's lips curved into a small smile. "She looks like you. She's...beautiful."

"I know."

She took a good look at me now that she was close to me. "Jesus Christ, Roseanne."

"What?"

"You seemed like after been through a war."

"Is that another way of saying I look shit?"

"Your eyes are swollen with blood...The hair is tangled. Fuck. You're a mess."

"Do you think I'm not aware of that?" I lifted my brow.

"Have you gotten any sleep?"

"No. I don't get much sleep. She's going through a rough patch, she keeps me awake at night and sleeps only intermittently during the day."

"You've nailed the rough patch part."

"Very funny." I laughed sarcastically.

"You can't go on living like this."

"What exactly do you suggest I do?"

"You could begin by taking a shower." She pointed her index finger to me.

"I can't just leave her like this."

"Have you ever considered that maybe she's crying because you stink?" She laughed.

For a brief moment, I was speechless before burst out laughing at my own expense. Oh my God. She could be technically correct.

"You could be right."

"I'll hold her while you take a bath."

"Really? Would you do that?"

"I said I'd do it."

"Have you ever held a newborn?"

"No."

"Are you sure you want to do this?"

"I've got this."

This was an opportunity I couldn't pass up. Right now, the thought of a hot shower sounded absolutely divine.

"Watch her head," I warned as I handed her to Lisa with care. "Make sure that it is not bending too far back. Use your arm to support her neck."

"I've got it."

Bea seemed so small in her big arms. She seemed to enjoy her presence, and the little bugger stopped crying.

"You have to be kidding me."

"What?" she inquired.

"Didn't you notice she stopped crying?"

"I told you. Maybe you smell."

"Maybe." I burst out laughing. "Or it could just be that you're a chick magnet, and that title also applies to infants."

She waved me off as she rocked her body back and forth to calm Bella. "Shh. Rosie, go. Before she loses it once more."

"Okay." At the bottom of the stairs, I turned around. "Thank you...so much."

As the hot water poured down on me upstairs, I thanked God for Lisa's prompt arrival. I had reached the end of my sanity. Lisa came through exactly when I needed her, just like she always did when we were kids. She was my hero tonight, even if it wasn't on purpose.

I stepped out of the shower, feeling somewhat human again, and dressed as quickly as I could. It didn't escape my notice that it was quiet downstairs.

Still, I felt compelled to get dressed quickly in case Lisa lost patience—or, worse, if Bea had pooped.

When I got downstairs, the reality was very different from what I had imagined. As she lay stomach down on Lisa's chest, Bea's back rose and fell. She was out like a light. She was just sitting on the couch, and everything was as calm as could be. When she saw me coming up behind her, she put her index finger to her mouth to tell that I should be quiet.

Sitting next to her on the couch, I just stared in awe. She didn't even have to do anything but exist, and she managed to put her to sleep. Who knew Lisa-I'll-Never-Want-Children-Manoban was the Baby Whisperer?

She looked at me. "How about you go to bed?"

"What if she awakens?"

"I'll take care of it."

"She'll want to eat when she wakes up."

"If that happens, I'll bring her upstairs. For now, she's fine."

"Are you sure?"

"Rosie..."

"Yeah?"

"Does it seem that we'll be going anywhere anytime soon?" She pushed me away. "Go go!"

"Thank you," I said as I walked upstairs.

I only vaguely recall my head hitting the pillow. It was the longest stretch of uninterrupted sleep I'd had since the day before my daughter was born.

The sound of Bea crying woke me up six hours later. I could see Lisa standing in the doorway with her whilst rubbing my eyes.

"I tried to avoid coming up here for as long as I could..." She approached me and placed her in my arms. "I'm going to leave so you can feed her. I'm going to sleep for a while."

"Thank you so much Lisa. I was in desperate need of a good night's sleep."

"It was no problem."

After she left, I took out my breast, and Bea immediately latched on. She had Lisa's scent on her. I inhaled the masculine scent, and a long-suppressed sexual desire resurfaced in me.

It felt great not to be the only adult in the house, but I had to keep my emotions in check. I was not going to let myself become obsessed with Lisa again, no matter what it took. Because I was responsible for another person, I couldn't afford to be an emotional wreck.

11. THE SIGNIFICANCE

Lisa arrived downstairs in the mid-afternoon. As I cleaned the kitchen, Bea was strapped to my chest in the carrier.

"Good morning." I cracked a grin.

"Hey," she groggily said.

My body abruptly awoke with a strong desire. She embodied the term "scruffy." Her hair was rumpled, and in the light, it was clear that she'd been growing out her stubble.

Her muscles appeared to be painted on a grey fitted t-shirt. Don't even get me started on how hot her ass looked in those gym shorts.

"How is she doing?" She asked. My body reacted even more as she took a step closer to check on Bea.

"She's sound asleep."

"That makes sense. The sun is shining brightly. I should've known better this little princess loves to sleep at this hours." She smiled then she looked into my eyes. "How are you?"

"I'm feeling good. You were amazing last night."

"That's what they say all the time." She gave me a wink with a playful smile on her sweet face.

"Thank you again," I said, rolling my eyes.

"Please stop thanking me." Her expression became solemn and serious. "You know...every time I asked how you were doing, you said you were fine. Last night, you didn't look fucking okay to me. You lied."

"Lisa, I'm responsible for everything. What is anyone else going to do for me?"

"Has your mother ever paid you a visit?"

"She came to the hospital when Bea was born, but she didn't stay to help. She's apparently more concerned with things like going to Cancun with her boyfriend and selling those multi-colored leggings all over the Internet. Priorities, you know."

"Unfuckingbelievable." She sighed. "Grandma would have helped," she said after looking around the house.

"Of course she would have." I closed my eyes for a moment, thinking of my grandmother, before returning to my mother. "As for Jessica, I don't want her with me in the first place. Having to deal with her would be like having two babies. "

"Even if you refused, she should have had the decency to offer a helping hand."

"I concur."

She shook her head. "I forgot to bring my coffee. Do you have any lying around?"

"I actually stopped drinking coffee fusion when I found out I was pregnant. The withdrawal was excruciating. But I have some half-caf in the pantry."

"I guess that'll have to do for now." She bit her lower lips. She cast a glance over at Bea. "Do you think all that fusion did anything to her?"

"Do you mean why her sleeping patterns are erratic?"

"I feel bad for hooking you up on that shit. Neither of us had any idea what was going on."

"Don't even. It's not your fault. Look at her...she's fine."

She grinned as she rubbed her chin. "Yeah. She looks fine."

"I'm going to try to put her in the crib upstairs. Then I'll go downstairs and make some coffee."

"I've got it," Lisa declared.

"You sure?"

"Very much."

When I returned to the kitchen after putting Bea down, Lisa was preparing two mugs.

"Still want cream and sugar?" she inquired.

"Yeah. Thanks."

"How is she doing?"

"Sleeping like a baby."

"Good." She slid my mug closer to me.

I sipped my drink and asked the question I'd been dying to ask. "Why didn't you bring Win?"

"She has a regular role in The Alley Cats, a new musical. She can't leave the city."

"She's not going to come at all?"

"I'm actually not sure."

"How long will you be here?"

She shook her head and stirred her coffee. "I don't know."

I was filled with dread. Lisa had only been here one day, and I was already dreading the day when she'd leave me alone once more.

"Well, I'm glad you came."

We sipped our coffee in silence until I noticed Lisa looking down at my breasts.

"Did you spill coffee on yourself?" she asked, coughing.

When I looked down, I saw that breast milk was dripping from my nipples, forming two large wet spots. "Shit. N-no. I'm leaking milk. I'd go change, but it'll just happen again until she falls asleep."

"Jesus. I'm glad I'm a woman with dick and nothing like that happened."

God. I'm glad you're also that kind of woman.

"Welcome to my world." I joked as she continued to look down. "You don't have to look anymore. I've got my eyes up here."

"Your tits are massive. That is something you must be knowledgeable of."

"Oh, I'm well aware. It's a matter of supply and demand. The more she drinks—which she does constantly—the more I make. When she's awake, it's all she wants to do."

"I can't say I blame her."

My face was turning bright red, and I was aware of it. What was going on with me? I couldn't continue to be a walking zombie on no sleep while dealing with this infatuation. I hadn't felt sexy in a long time. Nonetheless, I found myself falling back into the pattern of lusting after this woman.

"Well, despite the fact that my breasts are larger, I've lost weight."

"Oh, I noticed. Have you been eating?"

"Not doing as well as I should. I force myself to eat cheese sticks and raw vegetables because I'm too tired to cook anything substantial."

"How long has it been since you had a home-cooked meal?"

"I can't even recall. The only time I've bothered to cook is when my neighbour brings me fresh seafood from the dock."

"Who is your neighbour?"

"Danny."

"Danny." Lisa said it again and I just nodded my head.

"Yes. Last summer, he moved into a vacant house. You know... the blue one?"

"Really..." She fixed her gaze on me. "Does he bring you anything else?"

"Occasionally, coffee."

"Give me a hunch. He's single."

"Yes, he's divorced, but he's only a friend. He's been extremely helpful. He actually put the crib together for me."

"Right. Of course, he did. No guy does that shit without a reason, Roseanne."

"Not all guys are the same."

"And not every fucking girl looks like you. Trust me, he's waiting in the wings. Just be aware of it and be cautious."

I cleared my throat, feeling hot from the compliment. "It wouldn't matter whether he had ulterior motives or not. Clearly, I'm not in the mood to be with a man. I can't even take a bath half of the time."

"You shouldn't be allowing strangers into your home so easily. You're in a vulnerable position right now. This guy is aware of it."

"Well, I was desperate for help, so..."

"You should have called me."

"You've arrived in New York. That would have been absurd. He's right next door."

"I'd come for the day if you needed me."

"I don't want to be a distraction to you, Lisa. I need to forge my own path." Even though a part of me was relieved she'd said that, another part of me was confused. "You were suggesting last summer that we avoid each other entirely." My tone was sour. "Forgive me if you weren't the first person who came to mind when I needed help."

Her face became gloomy. "Fuck, Rosie. Really? You're going to bring it up again? Do you think that's what I really wanted? That night, I was drunk as shit and said and did anything to keep my fucking dick in my pants. I thought I already told you that suggesting that to you was a mistake."

"Okay. I'm sorry." I extended my hands. "I don't want to get into a fight."

"Good." She took a deep breath and changed the subject. "So I told Brayden that if he wanted, I could play a few nights here and there. But I didn't make any long-term commitments."

"Because you don't know how long you'll be here?"

"Right."

"Well, he must be thrilled to have you back, even if it's only for a few nights."

"Yeah. He was."

"I wish I could come and see you play."

"Why you can't?"

"I can't take Bea to Starlight's. She'd break down in the middle of one of your songs. And it would be awkward if I had to feed her there."

"Who cares if she cries? People will simply have to deal with it. You could also feed her in the back room. You–You need to get the fuck out of here."

"I'll think about it."

She abruptly stood up and placed her mug in the sink. "I need to get some work done. And I'll make dinner tonight, so don't eat too many raw vegetables."

"That'll be great."

—

Bea slept for at least a few hours that afternoon, allowing me to catch up on laundry and other errands. Lisa spent a good chunk of the day working in her room.

She had just showered and was buttoning her black button-down shirt when she finally came downstairs. She looked too good to be staying home tonight.

"Are you going to be playing at Starlight's?" I investigated.

"No. Not tonight."

"I didn't believe so. It's just that you're dressed to the nines."

"Do you remember Hans from Starlight's?"

"Was it the old night manager?"

"Yeah. I told him I'd see him later at the Barking Crab for a drink. He's interested in picking my brain about music."

"Ah, I see."

"How about going upstairs and changing before dinner?"

"Are we just eating here?"

"Yes, but your shirt has boob milk stains on it. I was just thinking you might want to shower and change."

Bruh. She was right. I needed to be more self-assured about my appearance.

"I'd be delighted."

Lisa looked after Bea while I took a shower. I went all out and put on a tube dress. I brushed my hair and applied make-up to my eyes. It felt like I was getting ready for a date, and I needed to get that train of thought to stop.

When I returned downstairs, I expected to find Lisa cooking. I'd instructed her to sit in the bouncy seat. Instead, she was rocking back and forth with Bea, gazing out the window. She had no idea I was watching her.

"I'm back."

"Oh, hey. She refused to sit in the seat and began crying, so we've just been watching the sunset."

My heart clenched.

"Are you going to have to cook?"

"Yeah, but it won't be long."

When I reached out my arms, Bea began to cry in protest as I attempted to take her away from Lisa. "I don't think she wanted to leave you," I said, patting Bea on the back.

"No. It's just your imagination."

"Really? Would you like to try it?" I extended her hand once more towards her.

Lisa cradled Bea in her arms once more, and Bea stopped crying. She was staring at her. It appeared that the apple did not fall far from the tree.

"Was that my imagination?"

She looked down at Bea with a smile. "I'm not sure why she likes me. I don't do anything except hold her."

"That's everything to a baby."

She handed her back to me, suddenly looking a little uneasy. "You should take her."

Bea began to fuss again once she was back in my grasp, so I took her to the living room and fed her while Lisa prepared dinner.

A knock came on the door.

"Are you expecting someone?" From the kitchen, Lisa yelled.

"No. Do you mind getting it? She's still chowing down." For privacy, I repositioned the blanket over my shoulder.

From where I was sitting, I couldn't see the front door, but I could hear everything.

"Who are you?"

"I'm Danny. I live right next door. You are?"

Shit.

"Lisa. This is my house."

"Oh, that's right. She mentioned a seasonal housemate."

"Can I help you?"

"Is Roseanne here?"

"Yes, but she's feeding the baby."

"I was just at the dock. I went out and bought her some shellfish."

"Roseanne! Danny is here. He brought you some snatch," Lisa yelled, not in a nice way.

Great.

"Coming!" I yelled, covering myself as quickly as I could.

"Hey!" I said, trying to appear unconcerned.

"Hello, Roseanne. Sorry if I'm bothering you."

"No, no, not at all—"

"Actually, we were about to eat," Lisa said, interrupting.

Danny appeared irritated. "How long will you be here, Lisa?"

"As long as I want to."

"Roseanne told me your girlfriend is a Broadway star, right?"

"Yes."

"Wow, that's pretty gnarly."

"Gnarly? What are you? A surfer or something?" Lisa made a shaka sign with her hands.

"Woah!"

"Danny, don't mind Lisa. It was very thoughtful of you to bring the crabs. I really appreciate it."

Lisa scoffed, "Crabs...interesting choice."

"I guess I'd better let you guys eat."

"We'll talk later." I smiled.

"Take care, Roseanne. Nice to meet you, Lisa."

Lisa gave a small salute. "Roger that!"

I turned to face Lisa when she slammed the door behind Danny. "You're being a complete jerk."

"Come on. I was just teasing him."

"You may think it's funny, but he's my only friend here, and you're going to scare him away. I'm going to need someone to talk to after you leave for New York again. It's extremely lonely out here."

"You don't need that tool. Why would you need him? You live in Providence, after all."

"Actually...," I said, biting my lower lip. "I was going to talk with you about something." I continued, feeling a bit nervous.

"About what?"

"I'm thinking about taking a year off...from my teaching job. I got kicked out of my apartment because the owner sold the building. I no longer have a place to live in the city, and I'm not sure I'm ready to enrol Bea in daycare at the end of the summer. I was going to ask if I could stay in this house during the off season."

"This is your home. Of course it's fine. I would never tell you anything else. You shouldn't need to ask."

"Alright. Now that I've gotten that out of the way, I feel a lot better. Thank you."

"Dinner is ready. Just put her down so you can eat." Lisa had poured a glass of wine for each of us.

"Oh...I can't drink, Lisa."

"Shit. I wasn't even thinking."

"Well, they say I'm only allowed one drink, but I'm still hesitant."

"That's all right. It will not be squandered."

Lisa had prepared a rice casserole. We were about halfway through our meal when Bea began crying in her bouncy seat. Lisa stopped me when I got up to go get her.

"Finish your meal. I've got her."

She lifted her and dragged her to the table. Bea quieted in Lisa's arms as she stretched her neck to look up at Lisa's face, as she always did. She reached out her little hand this time and began to play with Lisa's lips.

"Hey cutie lil princess, are you trying to tell me that I need to kiss you, huh?" Lisa smiled and kissed Bella on her forehead.

I got goosebumps every time I saw Lisa with her. Those simple gestures literally made my heart bloom with happiness, excitement, and all kinds of emotions. Why was I still hoping Lisa would stay with us forever when I knew she wouldn't and had her own life in New York with Winter?

Roseanne, damn! Don't. Don't feel anything that out of your control.

Bea began to mumble. It occurred as if she was attempting to communicate with Lisa. Lisa pretended to understand her. "Oh, yes?" She didn't even flinch when she passed gas. "Well, excuse me!" she simply said. I couldn't stop laughing at the whole thing.

After I finished, I took her back from Lisa and fed her on the couch while Lisa cleaned up the kitchen. Bea dozed off again after her meal.

When Lisa joined us in the living room, I realised she'd made plans to go out.

"Aren't you supposed to go out for a drink with Hans?"

"Nah. I'm going to skip it. I'll be performing tomorrow night. Instead, I'll probably meet up with him after that."

When her phone rang, she answered, "Hey."

I wasn't sure who she was talking to until she turned to face me and said, "Winter says hello."

"Hey, Win." I smiled, despite the fact that I was starting to feel that old familiar jealousy creep back in. Maybe it was a good thing she called when she did, because a reality check was much needed. Then she exited the room to finish the call in the other room.

"I have to go back to New York this weekend," she said when she returned.

My heart felt like it had sunk to the bottom of my stomach. "Oh. Only for the weekend? Or what?

"Possibly a bit longer."

12. THE SURPRISED

Lisa had already left for her gig at Starlight's on Friday night. She was supposed to leave early the next morning for her return trip to New York. While I had initially told her that I would not be attending her performance, I was now seriously second-guessing my decision.

Who knew when or if she'd return? She'd come for some alone time, only to find Bea and I wrecking havoc on her life. If I were her, I'm not sure I'd want to go back.

I abruptly turned to face Bea. "Would you like to go see Aunt Lisa perform? Will you make a promise to be good, cutie bee?"

I hurriedly put her in the crib before ripping my clothes off, afraid that if I didn't hurry, I'd wuss out and decide to stay at home. I put on a red dress I hadn't worn since before I was pregnant and tucked breast pads into my bra to avoid wet spots. I put on makeup and styled my hair into loose curls. Bea and I were dressed and in the car within minutes.

I got the jitters when I returned to Starlight's. I hadn't been back since the summer of last year. I was also inexplicably nervous that Lisa would see me in the audience despite the fact that I'd already told her I wouldn't be there.

She was in the middle of a song I hadn't heard before. The crowd was transfixed on her as usual, with women creeping closer and closer to the front to be near her and get a better look at her beautiful face while she sang. Watching her perform was always an emotional experience for me. Thank goodness, Bea was behaving well in her carrier, allowing me to enjoy every moment of being here.

I made my way to the mahogany bar to say hello to John, the bartender, who offered me a free glass of seltzer. I closed my eyes and enjoyed the sound of Lisa singing as she began a cover of the Rolling Stones' Wild Horses. That melancholy song seemed tailor-made for her voice. I cursed myself when I noticed my eyes were getting watery.

Why did she always make me so emotional when she sang? Every word of every song seemed to have meaning and could be applied to my experiences with her.

Bea began to cry about halfway through the song. This was not the type of song that would effectively mask an infant's frantic cries. A lot of people were looking at me. There were whispers, probably from people wondering why I'd brought a baby to such a place in the first place.

My body was filled with hot flashes. Lisa's gaze drifted over to my corner of the room, despite the fact that she sang the song flawlessly. Our gazes were locked. I was mortified that I had interrupted such a beautiful song.

When it was finished, I began to make my way towards the back room. Lisa motioned with her hand for me to stay. I continued down the hall until her voice through the microphone stopped me dead in my tracks.

"So that crying baby is actually special to me. Her name is Bea. Her mum is Roseanne, who's also special to me—one of my oldest friends. Anyway, would you believe this is Roseanne's first night out since Bea was born three months ago? Roseanne refused to come here tonight. She was afraid that if the baby started crying, people would stare at her. I assured her that the people here were kinder and more understanding than that. She didn't believe me, but she took a chance and came anyway. Believe me when I say...she has not had an easy life. She's doing an awesome job raising that little baby on her own. Don't you think she deserves a night out?" Applause erupted, and Lisa motioned for me to approach her. Bea was still screaming.

"Give her to me...and the carrier," she said away from the microphone. Lisa slid Bea into the Baby Bjorn and secured her. My baby girl was finally calmed down because she was exactly where she wanted to be. Of course, she did.

Lisa repositioned her guitar to accommodate her and began singing a song that sounded like a lullaby at first. Then it hit me, Dream a Little Dream. As I watched Bea up there with her, I couldn't help but smile.

The women in the audience were gushing. If they thought they loved her before, now their ovaries were absolutely combusting. After she finished, the crowd's cheers was the loudest on record.

When Lisa took Bea out of the carrier, her butt was facing the microphone. A sound that sounded like an explosion rang out through the restaurant, magnified by the mic. All of these people were simply witnesses to my daughter's explosive diarrhoea, it occurred to me.

Lisa completely freaked out. She was laughing along with everyone else as she handed her back to me. "Bea just busted serious ass," she said quietly.

"I should go change her." I smiled.

She stopped me as I was walking away. "Uhm...Roseanne."

"Yes?"

"You look beautiful."

I shook my head. "I tried." Despite the fact that I brushed aside her compliment, I hadn't felt beautiful until that moment. My heart was now racing at a breakneck pace.

———

Lisa was gone when we woke up the next morning. On the kitchen counter, there was a note.

"It was the first night you both slept. I didn't have the heart to wake you before I left. Take good care of Bea. I'll see you soon."

There was no word from her for a week. I made an effort not to overreact. After all, we weren't her responsibility. The loneliness seemed so much worse now that I knew what it was like to be surrounded by people. Bea's insomnia was also worse than before. I truly believe she missed her. So did I.

In desperation, I called my mother and asked if she would mind staying with me for a week or so.

She'd only been at the beach house for three days, and I was already wanting to shoot myself in the head. She spent more time on the phone with her boyfriend or smoking her Benson and Hedges cigarettes on the upper deck than she did with Bea and me. It was reckless of me to think that her becoming a grandmother would make her less selfish.

While she was able to keep Bea entertained so that I could get a few hours of sleep each night, inviting her to stay with us proved to be a mistake. On the last night of her stay, rather than spend quality time with Bea, she chose instead to badger me about taking legal action against Shawn.

"Roseanne, when are you going to make that guy pay?"

I'd taken Bea to have her blood drawn shortly after Lisa had left. Shawn also visited a lab in Boston, where it was confirmed yesterday that he was her biological father.

"I don't want to put Bea through this right now. As far as I'm concerned, he must make the first move. I don't want him in her life because he's been so mean to her."

"Well, you won't be able to support yourself for much longer. You must find a man, even if it is not him."

"I'm not going to bring a man into Bea's life solely to provide financial support. I'll find a way to look after myself."

I am not you.

"Good luck doing that on a teacher's salary."

"At the very least, I have a respectable job to fall back on. I'm sure you think it'd be better if I just didn't work and mooched off strange men like you did. Luckily, my father was one of the good guys. But I can assure you that I will never subject Bea to the kind of upbringing I had, with men coming and going."

"You act as if you've been abused. Your upbringing wasn't all that bad."

"You'd have no idea. You were gone for the majority of it."

"Did you really invite me to fight here, Roseanne?" She hissed.

"I'm tired. I'm going to bed. You're leaving the next day. Let's put an end to the fighting. Would you mind staying up with Bea so I can get some sleep?"

"Sure. Go ahead."

I figured I'd take advantage of her last night here. She was unlikely to return after such a traumatic experience.

A few hours later, something disturbed my sleep. It was well past twelve o'clock in the morning. The faint sound of people downstairs chatting seemed to register. Who the hell was in my house when my mother was supposed to be watching Bea?

Panic set in, and I crept down the stairs, coming to a halt halfway down when I realised the other voice was Lisa's.

She'd came back?

As I hid in the stairwell listening to them, the conversation that ensued between her and my mother completely blew me away.

"What are you doing here?" My mom asked.

"This is my home," Lisa explained.

"Which, by the way, is a joke. This house should have been passed down to me." My mother's tongue clicking was very audible, and it annoyed me greatly. I'm not sure about Lisa, but I get the impression she's annoyed because of my mother as well.

"Did you come here on your own or was your daughter the one who invited you?"

"Roseanne asked me to come." She said nonchalantly. "God, you turned out to be fucking hot," my mother said after a pause.

"Excuse me?"

"You're like a better-looking young version of your father. I wish I could go back in time and be fifteen years younger. Unless you have a thing for older women..."

"Are you serious right now, Jessica? Haven't you already ruined our lives? Roseanne invited you here to help with the baby, and I find Bea alone in the living room while you smoke on the fucking deck. Now, you're trying to pick me up?"

"Calm down. I was only joking."

"I wish I could believe you were. Do you know what Roseanne has been through in the last few months? She's doing everything she can. She does not deserve this. You should have offered to assist her from the start, but she's better off without it."

I'd had enough of it. "Mom, I think it's best if you leave tonight," I said as I made my way down the stairs.

"Tonight? I was already planning to leave in the morning."

"Yes. But that was before I knew Lisa was going to come back. You're upsetting both of us because you're in her house. And why were you on the deck when you were supposed to be looking after the baby?"

"She was sleeping. It isn't a big deal."

"To you, nothing is ever a big deal!"

"Are you seriously asking me to leave in the middle of the night?"

"No. I'm telling you to get out. Please. You're my mum, and I love you, but you're fucked up and won't change."

"I can't believe it," my mother grumbled before quietly making her way upstairs to pack her belongings.

When she returned, she lifted Bea out of the carrier she was sleeping in, waking her up so she could kiss her. Bea began to cry as my mother handed her to me and walked out the door without saying anything else.

When the door closed, I closed my eyes, expecting to cry along with the baby. Lisa's arms then wrapped around me.

"I'm sorry," she said.

"I wasn't sure if you were going to be coming back." She snatched Bea from my grasp. She quickly calmed down, as expected. But something unexpected happened as well, something she'd never done before. As she looked up at her, her little mouth spread into a wide toothless smile.

"Oh my goodness, Lisa. She's smiling at you!"

"Has she never smiled before?" Lisa asked with excitement. She lifted the corner of her lips and looked stunning.

"There were times when I thought I was smiling, but I wasn't sure if it was just gas. But there is no doubt about this one. That is unmistakably a smile!"

She continued to grin at her, as if she was in awe. "Maybe she didn't think I'd come back."

She wouldn't be the only one.

"We're both happy you're back."

———

Lisa had already made coffee when I came downstairs carrying Bea the next morning. The aroma of freshly ground beans combined with her musky scent was a pleasant way to begin the day. There was also a new Keurig machine set up on the counter, which I noticed.

"Where did you get that?"

"I brought it back from my city apartment. That way, I can make coffee fusion for myself and half-caf for you in the coffee maker."

"That was very considerate."

Something occurred to me as she handed me my steaming mug. "What did you use in this? We had run out of cream. I haven't had the chance to go to the market."

"I used milk instead."

"We were out of milk either."

She pointed the refrigerator with her thumb. "In there was a glass bottle of milk."

I'm covering my mouth. "I didn't buy regular milk. That was my breast milk, Lisa! I pumped it and poured it into a glass bottle that was empty. My mother's only good deed for me while she was here was to buy me a breast pump. I've been putting it through its paces."

I pointed into the coffee, laughing. "You just dumped my breast milk in here!"

"On top of that...I've already drink two cups of your breast milk. This is my third!"

I put my hand over my mouth once more. "Oh my fucking god!"

She sipped some of her coffee. "It's fucking good, I swear to god..."

"Seriously bro?" I smacked my forehead and shook my head.

"Yeah...nice. I can see why Bea drinks it like crack."

"Are you serious?"

"No."

"You're nuts. I'm not going to drink this."

"How much of that shit can you produce in a day? We can sell it." She wiggled her brows.

"You've got to be kidding."

"As for selling it, yes. For drinking it? No, I'm not kidding. And I don't want to share it with anyone other than Bea."

"You're sick."

She gave a wink. "You just figuring this out?"

God, It felt great to have her back.

———

It was a typical weeknight evening at home a week later. Lisa was performing at Starlight's while Bea and I remained at home. She was being extremely quiet as she played with her phone on the floor, so I decided to surf the web while sitting on the couch with my laptop.

I'd been avoiding Winter's Facebook page because I didn't want to see pictures from Lisa's trip back to New York, which would only upset me. But I'd found myself on her profile anyway, scrolling through her recent posts. Much of it was the same as usual like a backstage scenes, theatre friends out on the town after performances, and photos with fans. However, there was one thing that was unexpected. Winter's relationship status had recently changed from "in a relationship" to "single."

They broken up?My heart was racing like crazy.When did this happen?

She'd also posted a cryptic status around the time Lisa returned to Newport, captioned "To New Beginnings."

They'd ended it while she was in New York! She'd been back for a week without telling me. Why would she keep it hidden? My thoughts were racing. Is she EVER going to tell me?

I remained in the same position in the living room, waiting for her to return home. When the doorknob turned, I sat up straighter. Lisa hung up her jacket and placed her guitar next to the door. "What's wrong? Why are you staring at me like that?"

"Why you didn't tell me you and Win broke up?"

She took a slow breath and sat down next to me on the couch. "How did you find out?"

"She changed her relationship status on Facebook."

"Things had been off for a while," she explained, taking another deep breath. "We'd been drifting apart for the past year. I arrived in Newport early in order to have some alone time to think. That's when I found you and Bea."

"I don't get it. I thought you were madly in love with her."

"No."

"No? Why were you always telling her you loved her back then? Isn't that misleading?"

"I used to think I loved her. So, yes, we confessed our feelings for one another. It becomes second nature to use that word once you start saying it. It is abused and thus loses its value. For a while, we had a good relationship, but it was never going to last."

"Why?"

"We're too different. She's currently engrossed in the world of theatre. There was no time for us to work on our issues."

"She also wanted kids," I added.

"That, too"

I took a swallow. Even though I knew how she felt about kids, a part of me hoped that being around Bea would show her that it wasn't so bad.

"You didn't sound like you had any issues. In fact, the opposite is true. I had to cover my ears whenever she came home."

"The sex was great. We never had any problems in that area. But it takes something more to last a lifetime with someone. I didn't want to take up any of her time. Time is precious."

"So you were the one who broke up with her?"

"Uh, yes. I was the one who were asked for it." She said in a lower tone.

I genuinely felt sorry for Winter. I knew what it was like to be in love with this woman, and she was a nice person. She didn't deserve to be dumped.

"Was that the reason for your visit to New York?"

"My emotions had been bothering me. I didn't want to spend the entire summer like that. She is now free to do whatever she wants."

"How about you?"

"The same," she said after a brief pause.

My body couldn't decide whether to feel relieved or nauseated. Is this a good or a bad thing? I honestly had no idea. Lisa's newfound freedom meant that she could potentially be out on the town, bringing girls home, and taking advantage of all of the lustful women gushing over her at Starlight's. That was too much for me.

But in a twisted way, knowing she was committed to Win gave her a bittersweet sense of relief because it meant there was only one woman to worry about. There could be a lot of them now.

At the same time, this could be an opportunity for me to finally be with her. I quickly shook that thought from my mind, knowing it was a long shot. She was absolutely convinced about not having children. I now had one, and there was no way in hell she was going to go for that kind of package deal.

Then it occurred to me that she might have purposefully kept the breakup from me in order to avoid any expectations on my part. That's it!

"Why did you keep this from me, Lisa?"

"I was planning on telling you."

"When?"

"I'm not sure."

"My knowledge doesn't change anything between us. I don't expect anything from you, especially now."

"What do you mean, especially now?"

"I mean…if I hadn't had Bea…" My head shook. "Never mind."

"Say what you were going to say."

"Things might have been different if I hadn't had a kid. We might have been able to see where things went."

She seemed to be unsure of what to say next. "You aren't any less attractive because you have a kid. Never…ever think that. But you are right in one point. Any man you end up with must be completely prepared for that responsibility." She looked over to Bea, who was kicking her legs around while playing on the rug. "It wouldn't be fair to her otherwise."

She was right.

I'd never felt more unsure about what lay ahead of me as my head hit the pillow that night.

13. THE HAVOC

Every evening when the door opened, I cringed, wondering if that was the night she finally brought a woman home with him. I continued to brace myself for it. Lisa was an extremely sexual person. Win was always referring to her insatiable appetite. That always made me want to throw up.

She wasn't going to be celibate indefinitely.It wasn't a matter of if she brought someone home; it was a matter of when. But each time she walked in alone, it was a bigger relief than the last. With each passing day, I wondered how much longer this peaceful camaraderie between us would last.

Bea was growing bigger by the day. She was finally dozing off. That meant being extremely cautious when changing her diaper because she could easily fall off the table. It was much easier for me to leave the house now that I was pumping milk. Lisa would watch Bea for short periods of time while I ran errands. Around her, I referred to her as Aunt Lisa.

She appeared to be happy with that. It was a safe title, and it was clear that I didn't expect her to play a larger role in Bea's life. She'd probably always be Aunt Lisa to her. I vowed to myself that I would learn to accept it.

The best part of my day remained mornings when Lisa and I sat in the kitchen with Bea and drank coffee together. However, the strangeo was still using my pumped milk as a cream replacement. At first, I assumed she was doing it for the sake of fun, but as time passed, it became clear that she truly enjoyed the taste.

"You think that's completely normal?" I asked as she poured some from a bottle into her coffee.

"I'd prefer to drink from you than from some random cow. Consider th is...you're the one who gave up eating meat after having a similar epiphany."

"Alright, but you do realise that the average person would find your drinking breast milk very strange."

"No. It would be strange if I stood in line while you fed her and asked to go next."

That made me laugh out loud. "That's true, but what happens when you start dating someone? You think she'll let you drink another woman's breast milk? Or even something you've had in the past?"

"I'll deal with it when I have to."

It felt like a good opportunity to pry. "So you're not seeing anyone?"

She looked at me from over her mug, her eyes amused. "I'm pretty sure you know the answer, Roseanne. If I'm not here, then I'm at Starlight's, and then I come home. When am I even have the time to see someone?"

"I understand. I guess I'm just confused."

She slammed the ceramic mug onto the granite counter. "Okay. Please explain why you're confused."

"You're obviously very attractive. On top of that, you're a musician. Women are literally throwing themselves at you. It's been a month since you ended your relationship with Winter. I'm expecting you to come in with someone. That's it."

"When I'm single, you think I'm a manwhore?"

"I've only known you with a girlfriend, so I'm not sure."

She leant in and placed her hands on the table. What she said next gave me goosebumps. "I enjoy fucking. LOVE it. Above and beyond anything." Those words went straight to my loins. She reclined her chair and crossed her arms. "However, the more I learn, the more I realise that you have to be cautious out there. I don't sleep around as much as I used to."

I decided to mess with her. "That's interesting because I was thinking that casual sex might be my only option."

She was on the verge of spitting out her coffee. "Are you sure?"

"Yeah. In fact, you aided in that realisation."

"Did I do it now? This is something I'd like to hear."

"Consider it. As you mentioned, any man who ends up with me has to be in it for the long haul. Isn't it true that it takes a long time to figure out that stuff? I can't stay celibate forever while I wait to see if Mr. Right wants to be my daughter's father. I, too, enjoy fucking."

Her pupils dilated. "Ah, I see."

"Although I haven't slept around in recent years, it may be better for me at this point in my life to have meaningless sex with a trusted person who's on the same page. Of course, he'd have to be clean and pass all the necessary tests."

"Are you serious right now?"

"I'm dead serious."

I was becoming more and more convinced of my own case. It made some sense.

"And where are you going to find this man who is just looking for casual fucking but also happens to be a clean, respectable person that you can bring around your daughter? Oh, and this guy doesn't seem to be sleeping with anyone else at the same time? Yeah. That makes perfect sense." She mocked.

"I wouldn't bring any man around Bea unless it was for a serious reason. So, he won't be getting to know my daughter."

"So, where are you going to meet said man?"

"Hotels."

"Who's going to keep an eye on Bea while you're fucking this guy in a motel?"

I laughed and snorted. "You?"

"Please tell me you're joking. Because I'm about to fucking lose it."

"Want the honest truth?"

"Yes."

"For the most part, I'm joking. But I do believe that at some point, I will need to find someone to satisfy my needs, someone I can trust but who understands that it will be nothing more than sex."

He clenched his teeth. "Someone like Danny next door, huh?"

"Maybe..."

Her face flushed with rage as she stood up and tossed her mug into the sink. "That's great, Roseanne. Just fucking great."

That was the last thing she said before stomping up the stairs to begin her day at work.

She didn't show up that afternoon.

Lisa was furious...and jealous as hell It wasn't even subtle.

I'd told her I was telling her the truth, but that wasn't the case. Because the truth was, there was only one person I'd ever fantasised about fucking in a hotel-and that was her.

Lisa appeared to be in a bad mood that night. She was flipping through the channels at breakneck speed, barely paying attention. She picked up my phone when it vibrated on the coffee table and looked down at the caller ID.

As she handed me the phone, she had a shocked expression on her face. "It's Shawn."

Shit.

I'd left Shawn a voice message the other day, asking if he'd be interested in meeting Bea in Newport. I didn't want to see him, but I felt I owed it to my daughter to at least try to establish a relationship between them.

Lisa watched me like a hawk as I responded. "Hello?"

Shawn's voice was a little muffled. "Hey."

"I'm guessing you received my voicemail."

He must have been driving because there was some static.

"Yeah. Dina has left. I'll be able to come down this weekend. When is a good time?"

Is he only able to come down because Dina is away? Very nice.

"I think it's best if we meet downtown. Perhaps in the park. I can text you the address. Would Saturday work?"

"Yeah. That should be fine."

"Okay. Why don't we plan to meet at three o'clock?"

"That'll work."

"I'll text you the details shortly."

"Alright. Bye."

"Bye."

He never even asked how she was doing.

Lisa was still staring at me after I hung up the phone. "Is he coming down here? When did he become interested in being a part of her life?"

"Because a blood test confirmed he's the father."

"You never told me you'd done that."

"It was merely a formality. It happened while you were away, and you didn't even think to mention it because there was never any doubt about it. In any case, the only person who cared about the test was Shawn, because he was accusing me of lying."

Lisa's demeanour was solemn. "I still don't want him anywhere near her."

"He's her father."

"He's a sperm donor," she gritted her teeth.

"What am I supposed to do then? Keep her away from him?"

"He doesn't deserve her." Lisa appeared to be deep in thought for a few moments before asking, "What exactly are his rights now?"

"I'm not entirely sure. I don't think he'll want any of the responsibility of caring for her, so I haven't even looked into it. By the same token, I'm not pressuring him in any way. And it'll be a brief meeting."

"I'm coming with you."

"No. You don't have to."

"I'm not going to let you go see that asshole by yourself."

"That isn't really necessary. We'll be there-"

"Roseanne, it's not a choice. I'm coming with you," she said again.

The look in her eyes told me I wasn't going to win this one.

-

The weather was ideal: dry and cool with low humidity. We'd meet at Colt State Park, which was just across the bridge and off the island. Lisa and I had been to this park when we were kids, so it felt a little nostalgic.

We packed a picnic lunch and spent the afternoon there, arriving an hour before Shawn was supposed to arrive. It's not a bad idea to have some fun after a stressful event.

I'd put Bea in her frilliest pink dress and one of those little thin ruffled headbands on her head. Her tiny feet were dressed in the most adorable white patent leather shoes.

Lisa stroked her hair with the back of her finger. "Bea looks adorable, but you know it kind of pisses me off you got her all dressed up for him."

"I wanted her to look her best and make him feel shit."

"No matter what you put on her, she always looks her best. He should feel like shit either way, whether she's wearing a dress or covered in poop. She's his fucking flesh and blood, and he hasn't seen her since she was five months old."

"You're right."

Our attention was drawn to a pair of teenagers flying a multi-colored kite. We sat quietly, taking in the scenery. Because it was a beautiful day to be out on the water, many sailboats could be seen in the distance, as the park bordered the ocean.

Lisa raised her eyes to the clear blue sky. "Do you remember when we were last here?"

"Yes," I answered quietly. "It was not long before I moved to New Hampshire. You were getting into photography."

During our previous visit, Lisa had taken her camera to Colt State Park and photographed me with the water as a backdrop. "Yeah. That was a short-lived hobby that gave way to music." She took out her wallet, which was quite old, with cracked and weathered brown leather. She slid it open. "Don't laugh if I show you something."

"Okay..."

She pulled out a small black-and-white photograph from the back pocket. The photo paper's edges were frayed. It was a never-before-seen snapshot of myself. "This is one of the photographs I took that day. It was the only one I'd created."

I took it away from her. "Wow. I never got to meet any of them."

"I liked this one because I took it when you weren't posing. When I took it, you were laughing at one of my jokes."

My gaze moved from the photograph to her beautiful brown eyes, which reflected the ocean behind me. "Have you been carrying this around with you your whole life?"

"Even when I was mad at you, I couldn't get rid of it. I'd hide it, so I didn't have to see you, but I couldn't throw you away."

"Throw it away or throw me away?"

"Both."

We locked gazes as I willed away the pangs of longing that were always present and had to be constantly suppressed.

I looked down at my watch and saw that it was ten minutes past three o'clock. "Shawn is late."

"What a jackass."

Lisa took Bea from me and leant back, holding her against her chest. She was blowing raspberries against her fingers while reaching out her little hand to Lisa's mouth.

"You want me to kiss you, huh little princess?" Lisa smiled and pampered lot of kisses on Bea's face, making Bea's smiled widely and cutely. Thr baby noise she made sounds very cute and it was enough to make me feel content.

Minutes passed and there was still no sign of Shawn. Lisa was getting irritated after an hour of waiting. "We have to leave."

"I can't believe he just didn't show up. Maybe he's stuck in traffic."

"Then why wouldn't he text you? That is fucking disrespectful. He doesn't deserve another second of our time. He'd be better off not showing up at this point, because he'll get punched in the face." Lisa barked out with her reddened face. She looked unsatisfied and I felt like, if she could punch Shawn in the face, she would.

I started packing, feeling terrible for Bea. It didn't matter to me whether Shawn was a part of our lives, but it would undoubtedly matter to her someday.

My phone suddenly vibrated. It was a text message from Shawn.

Shawn: I was on my way but decided to turn around. I m sorry. I just can't. This is impossible for me. I'll send you some money.

Lisa took the phone from me and began reading the text message. She shook her head in disbelief, then looked down at Bea, who was still sitting there in her lovely gown, as she looked up at her. Lisa was on her knees, and Bea rested her back against the incline of Lisa's legs. Her small hands were encased in her large ones. My daughter was as cool as a cucumber. She had no idea how that text would affect her life for the rest of her life. She had no idea her father had abandoned her.

I was pretty sure she thought she was looking into the eyes of her other parent right now.

"He doesn't know what he's missing," Lisa said quietly after a long silence. "He's a fool. Well, we don't need him," she said, moving her face towards hers. "Do we, Bea? Fuck him!"

Despite the fact that she probably shouldn't have sworn in front of the baby, the most amazing thing happened. As soon as Lisa said, "Fuck him," Bea burst out laughing, as if she understood. It wasn't a subtle belly laugh, but rather a contagious belly laugh.

When she has stopped, Lisa bowed her head back and bobbed it down quickly, repeating, "Fuck him!" She burst out laughing once more. Then she did it once more. "Fuck him!" There was even more laughter. Lisa and I were both laughing along with her.

Tears were streaming down my cheeks, and I couldn't tell if I was laughing or crying.

After we've arrived home, Lisa offered to put Bea up for the night that evening. Her soothing singing voice could be heard all the way downstairs. I closed my eyes and listened to her rocking her to sleep. The song she'd chosen was no accident: Stevie Wonder's "Isn't She Lovely."

14. THE POSITION

It was the middle of the day the following week, and Lisa was upstairs working. Bea was lying on her belly in the living room, playing, while I paid some bills. A knock came on the door. Danny was standing there with two medium lattes from Maggie's Coffeehouse when I opened it. It had been more than a month since he had last visited.

"It's been a while." I cracked a grin. "You didn't have to do that," I said as I took one of his drinks. "But it was time for my afternoon caffeine, so it was perfect timing." I waved my arm. "Please come in."

Then he knelt to greet Bea. "Oh my gosh, she's getting big."

"I know. She's going on six months. Can you believe it?"

"The clock is ticking."

"Yes...which is why I'm glad you came by. I was afraid Lisa would scare you away."

"Well, to be honest, I debated coming," he said quietly. "Your watchdog is a little intimidating."

"I'm sorry she was rude the last time you were here."

"I'm guessing she's still here?"

"Yes. Lisa is now at home. She works from home and is actually in her office upstairs."

"How long will she be on the island?"

It was getting close to the end of the summer, and Lisa had given me no indication of her plans. Every time I asked, she said she wasn't sure.

"To be honest, I'm not sure. We don't discuss it because she can stay as long as she wants because she owns half the house."

"Can I be a little nosey?"

"Sure. What's up?"

"Is there something more going on between you two?"

"No. Why do you ask?"

"Well, someone doesn't bark at another about a friend like that unless she wants her for herself."

"Lisa and I have a long history together, but we've never actually been together. In over a decade of knowing each other, we've never even kissed."

"Really..."

"She can be protective, but she doesn't want to be in a serious relationship with me-especially now. She loves Bea, but she isn't interested in having children. She doesn't want to be with me."

Something about saying those words aloud made me extremely sad-and angry. Why wasn't I enough? Why wasn't Bea enough? Lisa genuinely cared about us, but not nearly enough.

"It sounds like her loss."

"Some things are simply better left alone."

"Alright, now that you've cleared that up...May I ask you one more question?"

"Yes, sure."

"Are you available to go out this weekend? Downtown is hosting a jazz festival. I'd love to bring you...and Bea. We could go during the day."

"I've got to be honest because I'm not sure if you're asking me out on a date. I don't think I'm prepared for anything serious. However, I enjoy your company. So, if there are no expectations, I would love to."

"I understand. We won't call it a date then. There are no expectations... just each other's company. It can get lonely out here on the island, and I'm grateful to have met you, if only for companionship. I'd love to take you out even if it's just for that. Roseanne, you need to get out."

"You know what? You're right. Let's do it. Let's go out." I cracked a grin.

When he grinned, he got a few wrinkles around his eyes and asked, "Saturday then?"

"Sure. I'll see if Lisa will watch Bea. If not, I'll bring her along." Deep down, I knew Lisa was going to go ballistic. This, however, was necessary. If she didn't want me hanging out with other men, she had to explain why. If she wasn't going to give me affection, I needed to find it elsewhere.

"It's perfectly fine to bring Bea..." He gave a wink. "Especially since there isn't a date."

"We'll see."

Danny was able to leave the house without Lisa noticing.

My roommate's mood was unreadable when she finally emerged later that afternoon. "What do you feel like for dinner tonight?" she asked, lifting Bea off the floor and tickling her belly with her nose.

"Anything is fine."

She scratched the overgrown stubble on her chin as she carried Bea over to the cupboard. "I need to figure out what we've got."

She cast a glance over to the trash can, noticing the Maggie's Coffeehouse cup. "Did you get some coffee?"

"No. Danny brought it over this afternoon."

As she pondered that, her jaw tightened and her hand froze on the last item she was touching. "Was he here?"

"Yes." I exhaled a sigh. "We need to talk about it."

Lisa shut the cupboard door. "Alright."

Just say it.

"Danny asked if I wanted to accompany him to the jazz festival this weekend. I said yes."

She blinked a couple of times. "You're going on a date with him..."

"No."

"It's a fucking date, Roseanne."

"I told him that I wasn't ready to date."

"Oh, you're right. You're not looking for a relationship. You're just looking for a casual fuck."

"It's just a little outing."

She became more agitated. "This isn't just a fun outing. He's a man. I've seen the way he looks at you. He wants to fuck you."

Lisa was really starting to irritate me. My natural instinct was to scream at her, but I restrained myself. Instead, I just stared into her eyes-truly stared into them. "What are you doing?"

I hoped she could see my pain and frustration through my expression. Even though it was a simple question, I knew she couldn't give me a straight answer. It was complicated. I don't think she realised why she was acting the way she was. But it had to stop.

Then something changed in her eyes. It was as if she finally realised how unreasonable she was being. She didn't want anything more from me, but she also didn't want anyone else to have me. She couldn't have it both ways. It wasn't fair, and I believe that's when it hit me.

"I'm not sure," she murmured, staring blankly into space. "I'm not sure why it annoyed me so much. I'm confused. Fuck. I'm...I'm sorry." She still had Bea in her arms and handed her to me before walking over to the window to gaze out at the sea.

I responded to her. "I was going to ask you to watch Bea, but I think it's better if I bring her with me."

"No." Her hands were in her pockets as she turned around. "I'll keep tabs on her. You should go and have some fun."

"Are you sure?"

"Yes."

"Okay. Thank you."

We ate in silence that night.

-

I decided to go see Lisa at Starlight's on the Friday evening before my Saturday date.

She'd kept to herself aside from playing with Bea since our argument about Danny. I guess a part of me wondered if her mood had influenced her performance in any way.

When we arrived at the restaurant, Bea was sound asleep in her carrier. Lisa was performing on the outdoor stage tonight. She didn't notice my presence in the far corner.

It had been a breezy night. A few napkins flew off the tables, and Lisa's hair was blowing in the wind.

When she began singing a cover of John Mayer's Daughters, it pricked my heart because I wondered if she chose that song because of the situation with Bea and Shawn. I was also curious if she was thinking of her. The majority of the songs she'd chosen for tonight were slow and melancholy, and Bea slept right through them.

Her first intermission finally rolled around. She hadn't noticed us yet. In general, she didn't seem to be paying attention to the audience tonight, and she seemed to be lost in her own thoughts. She was usually much more engaged with the audience.

An attractive young redhead made her way over to the stage just as I was about to get up and announce that we were there. I stood there for several minutes, watching as she shamelessly flirted with her. My stomach was in knots. She handed Lisa a piece of paper, which she placed in her pocket.

I had no idea if she accepted it to be polite or if she intended to use it. Even though this probably happened every night, it felt like I'd been sucker punched and had killed any desire I had to stay for the next set.

Even after Bea and I left, and I guess, Lisa had no idea we'd been there.

-

Lisa's exercise room was filled with the sound of punching. As I prepared for my sort-of-date with Danny, it occurred to me that the last time Lisa beat the crap out of the Everlast punching bag like that, it was the night of my date with Dr. Danger last summer. This felt like deja vu. I stood in the doorway, watching her attack the bag until she noticed me and stopped.

"What time are you leaving again?" she asked, out of breath.

"It will take about 45 minutes. I was just checking in to make sure you were ready to watch Bea."

She wiped the sweat from her brow. "Yeah. I'll shower and get downstairs before you leave."

"Thank you."

I nursed Bea while Lisa was taking a shower, just to make sure she had a full stomach before I left. She eventually fell asleep, so I put her in her crib before looking in the mirror one last time. Because the jazz festival was a laid-back affair, I wore a simple tank top with a denim hoodie and jeans.

Back downstairs, I waited for Lisa to give her some last-minute instructions. I was about to put a couple of bottles of pumped milk in the fridge when I heard her voice behind me.

"Is she sleeping?"

"Yup."

"So, what do I need to know?"

Lisa was leaning against the counter, looking stunning, when I turned around. A few strands of her wet hair were falling across her brow. He hadn't even bothered to put on a shirt, opting instead for a sports bra. My gaze was drawn down to her chiselled abs. Her thumbs were tangled in the belt loops around her waist. Her jeans were zipped up but unbuttoned at the top. I imagined myself licking a line straight down that happy trail. She was also barefoot.

Fuck. Me.

I needed to give her some instructions, but I'd forgotten them all. My mind had gone completely blank.

"I'm not stealing your words, Roseanne...but my eyes are up here."

"I know," I stated, feeling embarrassed.

She had a smug grin on her face. "So...answer me. What do I need to know while you're gone?"

"Um...I just pumped two bottles of milk. They're sitting in the door."

"I'm not going to drink them." She gave a wink and I let out a small grin.

"When she wakes up, she should have a bowl of rice cereal. If the two bottles aren't enough to keep her stomach full while I'm gone, this will help. I literally just fed her before she went down."

Her arms were crossed. "Alright...Is there anything else?"

"You should also change her diaper as soon as she awakens."

"I've got it."

I cocked my head. "Do you have any questions?"

"How late are you going to stay out?"

"Most likely not more than a few hours. I should be back by eight o'clock."

"Any more questions?" I asked when she didn't say anything else.

She was silent, but her gaze was fixed on mine. "Yes, I do," she finally admitted.

"Okay. What?"

"Why were you staring at me as if you wanted to eat me?"

"Are you serious right now?"

"Are you serious, Rosie?"

"I'm lost."

"Are you serious about going out with Danny Donkey when you'd rather be with me?" Lisa smirked.

"Who said I wouldn't rather be at home with you?"

"Your nipples."

Incredulously, I squinted my eyes. "My nipples?"

"Yes. I was watching them while you were looking at me, and they literally hardened before my eyes." She approached me slowly and then leant in. "You know that no part of you-body or mind-wants to be with him. You're doing this to fuck with me because you think I don't want you. You're doing this to make me jealous."

"That's not right. Not everything is about you."

"Not everything. But this...this is clearly about me."

"No."

"Bullshit. You were curious to see how far you could push me before I broke."

"Fine, if that's what you want to believe. In the meantime, you egotistical ass, I'm going to a jazz festival." I started walking away, not knowing where I was going because Danny was supposed to be here to pick me up.

She grabbed my waist and pulled me back. She flipped me around and pulled me closer to her, her eyes telling me I wasn't leaving until she damn well let me. Lisa then pushed me slowly towards the door, so that my back was now against it.

Her lips brushed against mine as she panted into my mouth. But she didn't say anything. I couldn't take it any longer because I needed to taste her. I pressed my lips into her while wrapping my hands around her head. We opened our mouths for each other, the sensation of her hot tongue swirling inside my mouth more incredible than the countless times I'd imagined it over a decade. As we kissed, I ran my fingers through her silky hair. Her mouth was dripping wet and hot, and her taste was addictive. There was no longer any notion of time.

She wedged herself between us by nudging my legs open with her knee. Her hot erection was pressing against my body. As we kissed, she took my hand and slid it down to her crotch so I could feel her.

"Fuck, Roseanne," she said over my lips. "You think I don't want you? Feel how much I don't want you."

I moaned against her mouth to confirm that I had felt it; it was almost halfway down her thigh. I was completely at her mercy due to a complete loss of restraint. Her kiss was unlike anything I'd ever experienced before. She kissed with all of her strength, as if the act itself was necessary for survival. If she kissed like this, I can only imagine what it was like to have sex with her.

The vibration of Danny's knocking on the door hit me in the back. Shamelessly, Lisa didn't flinch in the slightest. Instead, she kissed me more passionately and deeply. She made it difficult to want to stop.

"Just a minute!" I yelled, finally prying myself away from Lisa.

Her lips were still inches away from mine. She gave me a mischievous look because she knew that even though I was going out with Danny, I wouldn't be able to think about anything else.

"Have fun," she said, wriggling her brows.

She then turned around and walked up the stairs, disappearing.

Danny had no idea Lisa and I had been sucking our face just moments before he picked me up. Before opening the door, I checked my reflection in the mirror and blamed the delay on breastfeeding.

On our way to the jazz festival, which was held on the grounds of Fort Adams at the mouth of Newport Harbor, we stopped at McDonald's for takeout lattes.

Three stages were set up, each with its own jazz band. It was a beautiful afternoon with only a slight breeze. Panorama views of the Newport Bridge and the East Passage were available from the location.

I tried to concentrate on the scenery and music, but my thoughts were elsewhere. Lisa's kiss was still on my tongue, and I could still taste her. My panties were soaked. I wondered what it all meant and if things would change now.

A text message alerted me.

Lisa: Stop thinking about me.

Rosé: You are egotistical. You only kissed me because I was going out with Danny.

Lisa: You kissed me...technically.

Rosé: How is Bea?

Lisa: Changing the subject?

She then replied to my previous question by sending me a selfie of Bea and her. They were both sprawled out on the living room rug. Bea was smiling big. It was absolutely adorable.

Rosé : Looks like you guys are having a good time.

Lisa : We miss you. You should leave him at home and come hang out with us.

Rosé: To be honest, I'm a little scared to come home.

Lisa: I'm not going to bite. I guarantee it. Unless you specifically request it, in which case I will do it so gently that you will not feel any pain.

Rosé: I can't text anymore. It's rude.

Lisa: We'll talk later.

Rosé : About?

Lisa: I'm interested in the position.

Rosé : What position?

Lisa : Your casual fuck buddy.

Rosé : What???

Lisa: We'll discuss it later.

I didn't know what to say, so I hid my phone.

Danny rested his hand on my shoulder. "Is everything okay at home?"

No, not exactly.

"Yes. I just wanted to check in on Bea. Everything is fine." I smiled to him.

"Would you like to go out for an early dinner?"

Despite the fact that Lisa's text had managed to dampen my appetite, I said, "Sure. That would be great."

Danny and I ate dinner at the Brick Alley Pub after leaving the festival grounds. Throughout our meal, we talked nonstop. He mentioned his upcoming trip to Irvine to see his daughter. He glowed with pride whenever he spoke of Alyssa, and it occurred to me how fortunate she was to have a father who adored her; Bea wouldn't have had that. I could only hope that someone would step in for my daughter someday.

Despite the sexual game Lisa was suddenly playing, she gave me no assurance that she truly wanted to be with us long term. Despite the fact that she was so good with Bea, there was no sign that he was interested in being more than just her "aunt." Her statement that we should be "fuck buddies" didn't count. Lisa and I couldn't be together because she didn't want children in the long run.

After dinner, Danny drove me home. I didn't invite him in on purpose because I wasn't in the mood for Lisa's antics.

He persisted. "I'm hoping we'll be able to go out again soon."

"That would be fantastic," I said.

Despite my preoccupation with Lisa throughout the day, I thoroughly enjoyed Danny's company. He was intelligent, articulate, and an excellent listener.

Lisa was sitting on the couch watching television when I opened the door. Bea was in the crook of her arm, cradled.

"How was it?"

"It was actually a lot of fun. You'd enjoy the jazz festival. You should look into it. Tomorrow is the last day," I said as I sat down next to her on the couch.

"Good." She grinned, but it was a chastising grin.

I snatched Bea from her grasp and kissed her. "I've been missing you, Bea Bee."

"I'll get up so you can feed her privately. I'm guessing you're not hungry for dinner."

"No. Danny drove me to Brick Alley Pub."

Her face became gloomy. "Great."

Pots and pans clanged as Lisa prepared something for herself in the kitchen while I fed Bea. She fell asleep on my breast, so I put her in her crib upstairs. It was earlier than her usual bedtime, so I expected her to wake me up in the middle of the night.

Lisa appeared to have been waiting for me when I returned to the kitchen. She was styled in a grey hoodie that was zipped halfway up over her bare chest. She was pulling at her sleeves, looking tense.

"Rosie, we need to talk."

"Alright."

She raised her head to look me in the eyes. "I don't want you to date him again."

"You don't get to choose who I go out with."

"Well, I don't want you to date anyone."

"I'm not sure how you think you have the right to say that."

"Then hear me out."

"I'm listening."

"You stated that you don't want anything serious at the moment."

"Yeah, right."

"I don't either. I recently ended a long-term relationship. I really can't handle anything serious right now."

"So you think I'm the perfect candidate to screw around with? Don't you have enough options? How about that redhead that gave you her number the other night when you didn't even notice Bea and I standing right there."

Her expression turned angry. "What? You came to Starlight's that night?"

"Yes. You played Daughters. It was very touching."

"Why the fuck didn't you tell me you were there?"

"You were busy."

"You were all I could think about that entire night, Roseane. Every fucking song, I was thinking about you or Bea. That's the truth. I don't even remember that woman's name."

"Well, that's irrelevant I suppose. Get back to what you were saying...about wanting me to be your whore."

"It's not like that. AT ALL, Roseanne." Looking uncharacteristically nervous, she said, "I've been doing a lot of thinking lately. You've made it clear that you need someone to satisfy your needs. I don't want you fucking around with some random guy who doesn't care about you. Contrary to what you might think, I do care about you. So, I want to be the one to take care of it for you."

"Take care of it? You're making it sound like having sex with me is a surgical procedure."

"Far from it. And take care of it isn't the right term anyway. Technically I'd be fucking you into oblivion."

"I'm not going to be anyone's mercy fuck, Lisa"

"That's not what I'm saying." She pulled on her hair in frustration. "Fuck. Do you have any clue how badly I want you? I need this just as much as you."

"I'm sorry, but you're really confusing me. You care about me, but you don't want to be with me. You just want to fuck me. It just seems like an oxymoron."

"I want to give you what you need today...not tomorrow or ten years down the line. Today. It just so happens that what you need is also what I need. I need to satisfy this fucking itch that has been eating away at me for over a decade. I need to be with you on a physical level before I fucking explode. But I just can't put a label on everything right now. I can't make promises for the future because that would be irresponsible. There is too much at stake. I won't make a promise to that little girl only to let her down." She sighed and hugged herself.

"So, you're suggesting that we forget everything else, just start a physical relationship with no expectations."

"That was what you said you wanted with some random guy, right? Why not with me? It's a fuck of a lot safer."

"Because I don't think that's possible with you. I don't think I can compartmentalize years of feelings in order to have a casual sexual relationship with you. You matter too much to me. I will always want you in my life. If we have sex, we can never take that back. I would never be able to look at you the same."

"You'd never be able to walk the same."

"Can you be serious?"

"I am being serious." She smiled. "Okay...in all honesty, I want you to think about my proposition. I'm just asking you to consider living in the moment, having a little fun with me, taking things day by day."

"Take things day by day and then one day wake up and find you gone?"

"I'm not going anywhere anytime soon."

A part of me wanted to leap into her arms and take her up on her proposition right there on kitchen counter, but the logical part just couldn't agree to this. "I don't know."

"If there's anything I can do to help make your decision easier, let me know. Just think about it. You don't have to make a decision right now. Sleep on it. Or sleep on me. Whatever you decide." She started to walk toward the stairs.

"Where are you going?" I linked my brows.

"Upstairs. I'll leave the door open in case you decide there's something you'd like to watch later."

15. THE WITHSTAND

That night, I went straight to my room and didn't come out because I couldn't trust myself around her. Was she really serious? A small part of me wondered if she was just pulling my leg with that proposition. Maybe this was some grand plan to punish me for hurting her a decade ago... entice me to succumb to her sexual charms, then tell me it was all a joke

Tossing and turning, I weighed all the pros and cons and concluded that, while sex with her would be fantastic, it would only end in my being hurt. It would also jeopardise our second chance at friendship, which was still new and shaky.

At the same time, I was completely turned on, my panties soaked from the way she spoke to me. The mere thought of being with her was driving me nuts.

I must have dozed off somewhere in the middle of the night while ruminating. It was after 11 a.m. when I awoke the next morning. I hadn't slept that late in a long time.

My bedroom window's sheer white curtains were letting in the light. Was my last night's conversation with Lisa a dream? It occurred to me that Bea was missing from her crib.

I dashed downstairs to find Lisa, who was sitting in the living room.

"Where is Bea?" I inquired, somewhat nervously.

"She's right here. Look at this." Bea crawled towards her as she enticed her with a new stuffed animal. The squeak came from a long rainbow-colored stuffed caterpillar.

"Come on, Bumblebee," she encouraged her. God, I lover her nickname for Bea.

Bea was getting closer. It was her most impressive attempt at mobility yet.

"She's crawling up to you!"

"I know. We've been practising since the morning."

"Where did you get that toy?"

"I got it for her the other day from the downtown toy store."

"Did you come in here this morning and take her out of the crib?"

"No, Roseanne, she walked downstairs herself," she joked. "Of course not, duh. I peered in on you because you never sleep that late, and I wanted to make sure you didn't pass out from thinking about me last night."

"No, not quite. Despite the fact that you were on my mind."

"Anyway...She was just sitting in her crib, staring at me, as quiet as a mouse while you snored. So I took her downstairs so you could continue to sleep. We finished the pumped bottle you had in the fridge." She lowered her gaze to Bea. "She's now my breakfast buddy."

"Thank you for doing that."

"There's no problem."

Our gazes locked, and I felt compelled to break the ice. "Lisa, about last night..."

She abruptly rose from the couch. "Don't worry about it. I had crossed the line. I went a little crazy because I was jealous."

I was surprised at how quickly she'd changed her tune. "Really?"

"Yeah. I wasn't thinking in the right frame of mind."

"All right...then I'm glad we both agree."

"Well, I've got a lot of work to do. So..." She picked up Bea from the floor, briefly lifting her above her head. "I'll see you later, Bumblebee."

She then went back to her room and did not come out again for the rest of the afternoon.

I went about my day, cleaning the house and doing Bea's laundry, more dumbfounded than ever.

-

It was the beginning of September, and the weather on the island was starting to cool down. I officially informed the school department back in Providence a few weeks ago that I would not be returning to work this year. It was a difficult decision, but it was the best one for my daughter. My savings would see me through the next twelve months. In a year, I'd reassess my situation and decide whether to return to teaching or look for a work-from-home job.

When I heard a knock on the door, I quickly positioned my broom in the corner.

My heart nearly skipped a beat as I opened the door and saw a familiar leggy blonde with a pixie cut. "Winter. Oh, my God. This is unexpected."

"Surprise!" She leant in for a hug before taking a step back. "You look fantastic, Roseanne! Have you lost any weight? Isn't it normal for people to gain weight after having a baby?"

"I guess I was lucky because my daughter wouldn't let me eat or sleep for the first few months." Trying to mask my discomfort, I asked, "Is Lisa expecting you?"

"No. No, not at all. Is she up there? I noticed her car outside."

"Yeah. She's in her office... working."

Bea was playing in the Exersaucer when she noticed her. "She is beautiful. She has a striking resemblance to you. Can I get her out of this?"

"Sure."

As I watched Winter crouch down to see my daughter, I became uneasy.

What exactly was she doing here? Had she invited her? Was that why she abruptly changed her tune?

Jealousy washed over me like a flood.

Win supported Bea by lifting her up. "She has a wonderful scent. What did you use?"

"It's Dreft baby detergent, which I use on her clothes."

"Perhaps I should lend you some of my clothes to wash." She smells so clean and fresh."

I'd had enough of small talk. "What is it that has brought you here, Win?"

She sat on the couch, Bea on her lap, and said matter-of-factly, "I screwed up."

"What do you mean?"

"I fucked up everything with Lisa. I'd given everything I had to my job over the last year and nothing to her. I had taken her for granted. Did she tell you anything about why we broke up?"

"She just told me that she ended things when she returned to New York earlier this summer. She didn't go into much detail."

"It was a misunderstanding."

"How so?"

"She'd come to surprise me and found me having dinner with my co-star, Greg Nivens, at my apartment. Lisa jumped into a hasty conclusions. Greg had nothing going on. It had been arranged for a business meeting. Lisa and I had been having problems for a while before that, but I would never have cheated on her."

"So you've come to-"

"Get my girl back. Yes. I never stood up for her. I never tried to persuade her. I was so taken aback by how things turned out that I never gave much thought to my role in it all. It was almost entirely my fault. I still love her so much."

No.No.No.

This unanticipated and imminent threat was putting my true emotions to the test. I was terrified of losing her, terrified that she'd return to New York with Winter. My body stiffened in defence, as if it were preparing to go to war in a battle it would inevitably lose.

"Wow. I'm at a loss for words. I-"

Lisa's deep voice caught me off guard. "Winter. What are you doing here?"

She rose to her feet, still carrying Bea. "Hi."

Her gaze shifted to me briefly before returning to her. "Have you been here a long time?" she inquired.

"Just a few moments. I came all the way here because we need to talk. Do you want to go somewhere? How about going for a walk on the beach?"

My chest felt heavy, and I was nervously sweating.

Lisa gave me another quick glance before saying, "Let me get my jacket."

When the door closed behind them, all of the fear I'd been holding in was released in one swift breath, only to resurface in my gut.

I turned to face Bea and spoke to her as if she could understand. "I don't want her to leave."

She babbled and cooed as she smacked her hand against one of the squeaky toys attached to her playset.

"I'm afraid to be with her and afraid to be without her."

Drool dripped down her chin as she blew a couple of raspberries.

"You adore her, don't you?"

"Ba...Ba," she replied.

My heart pounded against my rib cage. "I know. Me, as well."

-

Lisa had been gone for nearly six hours. I was certain she wasn't going to return home.

When the key turned in the door around ten-thirty that night, I straightened up on the sofa, trying to appear casual so that it didn't appear that I'd been waiting for her return anxiously.

Lisa rubbed her eyes and tossed her coat against a chair. Before taking a seat next to me, she went to the kitchen to get a drink.

"Where is Winter?" I swallowed, afraid to ask.

She took a sip of her beer and then stared down at the bottle, twirling it in her hands mindlessly. "She's on her way back to New York right now. I drove her to the train station."

"I wasn't sure if you were going to return tonight."

She remained silent for a long time before looking me in the eyes. "Nothing happened, Roseanne."

"You don't owe me an explanation."

"I don't?" she said louder. "Are you kidding me?"

"What do you mean?"

"You seem to believe that I can't see right through you." When she arrived, I saw your expression. You were terrified. Why can't you just admit it? Why can't you admit that you're just as terrified of what's been going on between us as I am?"

I don't know.

"We took a walk on the beach...talked," she said when I didn't respond. Then I drove her to the train station."

"You were gone for such a long time. I just assumed..."

"That we were somewhere fucking? No. I drove around by myself for a while, just thinking."

"Ah, I see. How did you and Winter come to your decision?"

"She believes I ended it because I found her hanging out with that guy, but that is not the case. Before I even saw her having dinner with him, I'd gone to New York with the full intention of breaking things off."

"Did you explain it to her?"

"I couldn't possibly be completely honest about everything."

"What's the harm?"

"Because I'd have to admit things to her that I haven't even told you...and I didn't want to hurt her any further."

"Things such as..."

"Do you remember what I said about cheating?"

"That if you have the urge to cheat on someone, you should just break up with them?"

"Yeah. Last summer, I had the urge to cheat...with you...multiple times. I assumed that becoming a mother would cause me to see you in a different light, that it would make me less attracted to you, but that hasn't been the case. It's been the inverse. You've never been sexier to me. Even if nothing happens between us, my attraction to you is a sign that something is wrong between Win and me. If you're in a healthy relationship, you shouldn't covet someone else in that way. It's a sign that something is missing, even if you're not sure what it is. I don't believe in dragging things out if the outcome is already known in your mind."

"Is Winter okay?"

"Not really."

It hurt me a lot to know she was in pain. I felt bad for her and was still unsure what was going on with Lisa and me.

"What should we do now?" I questioned.

"I've already stated what I intend to do."

"I thought you said this morning that you decided it was a bad idea and that you didn't want to be with me anymore."

"I never said anything like that. What I meant was that the way I presented it to you was inappropriate. I was acting aggressively because I felt threatened, and I came on to you like a caveman. I never explicitly stated that I didn't want it, and you, for the record, didn't either."

"I stated my reservations..."

"And I understand what they're saying. I completely understand why you're hesitant to pursue a sexual relationship with me. The logical side of me agrees with you, but the illogical side of me doesn't care and is only thinking about lifting you over my face right now and making you come while you ride my mouth."

Those words smacked me between the thighs.

She continued, "The fact that you just squirmed in your seat demonstrates that you have an illogical side as well." Maybe our illogical sides should get together someday." She smiled as she leant into me. "But not tonight. You're not ready, despite your threats to find a fuck buddy. That would be equivalent to jumping from A to Z over all the letters of the alphabet."

"You and Bea have been watching way too much Sesame Street."

"Fuck. Maybe. Anyway, you're currently on level A. My dick is at level Z. And it's not the same. That was one of the things I discovered on my drive home tonight. That despite all your talk about hotel sex, you're still not there." She stood up. "I'll be right back."

She was holding something behind her back when she returned. "What was it that we used to do when we were younger when we were in a bad mood or didn't know what the fuck to do with ourselves?"

"We'd watch The Big Lebowski."

She held up the DVD from behind her. "Bingo."

"I can't believe you've kept that."

"Keep it on hand at all times."

"I'll make some popcorn," I dashed to the kitchen, relieved that the tension in the air had dissipated. She was right. I wasn't ready. I didn't want to lose her, but as much as I wanted her, I wasn't prepared for a sexual relationship with her or anyone else.

We sat in comfortable silence, watching a cult film that, in retrospect, was probably far too mature for our thirteen-year-old selves. But neither of us had parents who were watching what we were watching at the time. The opening scene, in which the main character's head is shoved into a toilet, brought back a flood of memories. We thought it was the greatest thing ever.

Lisa lay on her back, her head resting on my lap, halfway through the film. I did what felt natural at the time and massaged my hand through her silky strands of hair.

As she continued to watch the movie while I played with her hair, she let out a slight groan of delight.

When she turned to face me, I instinctively moved my hand away from her, remembering how she'd told me to stop last summer. "Why did you stop?" She figured it out on her own. "No way I'm telling you to stop this time, Roseanne. Please keep it up. It feels really good."

I kept at it for the better part of a half-hour.

When I asked, "What else did you figure out on your drive tonight?" my focus was no longer on the movie.

"I still love your moles." She raised her head to look at me. "I haven't figured it all out yet, but I know that for sure."

Oh my goodness, I'm terrible at deciding on a title hahahaha. Be safe ♡

16. The Trick-or-Treaters

We welcomed autumn and the changing colours of the leaves on the trees surrounding the island as September turned into October. We hadn't discussed sex or attempted to define our relationship in the month since the night we watched The Big Lebowski. But we were gradually getting closer. Bea was now seven months old and gaining personality by the day.

Lisa had travelled to New York for a brief visit at the end of September to meet with her music agent, who had arranged for a studio session to record some of her original songs for a demo. Overall, we were still taking things day by day, with no clear indication of when, or even if, she'd be returning to the city permanently.

This year, Halloween fell on a Saturday. We decided to take Bea to a pumpkin patch nearby. Lisa took a lot of pictures of me and my daughter in the midst of the sea of orange and hay. We also took a few selfies of the three of us. I knew I'd cherish those photos for the rest of my life. Lisa and I sipped hot cider while admiring the crisp air with a rosy-cheeked Bea, who was dressed warmly in a hat and mittens. Despite the fact that there are thousands of days in a lifetime, this was the kind of day you knew you'd never forget for the rest of your life.

The plan was to go out for a few hours, then come home and hand out candy while dressed up in our costumes.

Lisa went all out for Halloween, knowing that it was always my favourite holiday. She dropped Bea and me off at the house after the pumpkin patch before heading to the Christmas Tree Shops in nearby Middletown, where they sold a variety of seasonal Halloween items. By the time she returned with a slew of bags, it was late at night. She'd bought plenty of orange and black decorations, as well as candy packages and a bumblebee costume for Bea.

"The Christmas Tree Shops didn't have any suitable costumes for us, so I went to a couple of other places. That's why I'm late. I couldn't decide on yours, so I got more than one."

"Well, we'll see." I extended my arm. "Hand them over." One of bag was from Island Costumes, and the other came from... Eve and Adam. "Doesn't Adam and Eve sell adult novelty items?"

"Yeah. It was right next to the costume shop."As I squinted my eyes suspiciously, she flashed a wicked grin. I took out a one-piece black nylon Catwoman costume from the other bag first. It also included a mask.

"That's for tonight...for the trick-or-treaters," she said.

"What is the other one for?"

"For...whenever. All I thought was that you'd look good in it."

I grudgingly opened the Adam and Eve bag and took out a white sheer material with red accents. There were cross-shaped patches at the nipple area, and you could literally see right through the fabric.

As I read the tag, my eyes widened. "Nurse Feel Good?"

"It reminded me of the time you looked after me when I was sick." Her face was unusually flushed, as if she was embarrassed to give it to me.

"Y-you want me to wear this?"

She bit her lower lip. "Not right now."

I looked down at the tag once more. "Panties not included. I'm guessing it's because I'm not supposed to wear any?"

"Look...I know I may never actually get to see you in that. To be honest, I got really turned on in the store thinking about you. I had no choice but to buy it. Can't a dreamer dream?"

She was turning on thinking about me, and I was really turned on thinking about her turning on thinking about me.

I swallowed and cleared my throat. "What are you going to be?"

Winking, she said, "It's a surprise."

We had about an hour before the trick-or-treaters began to arrive. Lisa strung the orange lights along the window and placed some lit carved pumpkins along the steps outside. She turned off the house's main lights and lit candles. It was a mix of eerie, romantic, and cosy.

"I really missed Halloween living in the city," she said, ripping open bags and filling the bowl with candy. "There are no trick-or-treaters at the apartment."

I smiled inwardly as I noticed she'd bought extra Almond Joy candy bars from when we were kids.

"I'm going upstairs to dress Bea and put on my costume," I said.

"Alright. I'll go change right after you."

I went upstairs and put on the slinky black outfit that looked like it was spray painted on my body. I looked in the mirror after putting on the mask. Actually, it was quite sexy. It was no surprise she'd chosen it. The look was completed by my own knee-high black leather stiletto boots. Bea was standing in her crib, amused to see her mother dressed like this.

We went downstairs after she was dressed up as a furry bumblebee.

Lisa's eyes widened as she looked me over. "Wow. Look at yourself. I definitely chose the correct costume."

"It's not very frightening. More to sexy."

"Well, you're scaring the hell out of me." She wriggled her brows before grabbing Bea and kissing her on the cheek. "You're now officially a bumblebee, Bumblebee." Carrying her over to the window, she said. "Look at the lights, Bea. I put them up for you." She'd left with her, her voice barely audible as she whispered in Bea's ear while showing her the decorations. She led her outside to examine the carved pumpkins.

I just stood there watching them, wondering when we'd become a little family. Was there a specific time when we crossed over? As much as I tried to deny it as a self-protective mechanism, the last four months with Lisa had felt more like a family experience than anything else in my life had ever felt. It had happened, scary or not, and we were both unable to admit it to each other. It had just happened on its own, without any discussion. But, while Bea was my entire life for the next eighteen years, was Lisa just a houseguest? That was yet to be seen.

Lisa approached and handed her to me. "I'm going to change my clothes. I'll be right back."

Before Lisa returned, the first group of trick-or-treaters arrived. I grabbed the large bowl and headed to the door, Bea in one arm, to distribute the candy.

I felt the warmth of her body behind me as I waved them off.

"I'm back."

The sight of her nearly knocked the wind out of me when I turned around. Lisa was dressed entirely in black. She was supposed to be a member of the SWAT team. The shirt was covered by a short-sleeved black shirt and a black vest with the words SWAT written in white. She was dressed elegantly in black pants and heavy combat boots. It was one of the sexiest things I'd ever witnessed.

"Oh my..." My body was on fire beneath my tight spandex outfit.

"Do you enjoy it?"

"Yeah...I love it."

"They didn't have a lot of costumes in my size left. It had to be this or a clown. I didn't want to frighten Bea."

"This was...yeah...a good call."

"I'm glad you think so," she said softly against my neck.

We only had a few trick-or-treaters, but it was exciting every time someone knocked on the door. I was relieved that Roger was visiting his daughter in Irvine, so I didn't have to deal with any awkwardness between him and Lisa. If Roger had been home, he might have come in to say hello. We hadn't been out since the jazz festival. Lisa and I had grown apart since then.

It was almost time to turn off the lights. Cheri, the girl next door, had come in to see Bea in her costume. I glanced over at Lisa and Bea in the kitchen as I lingered at the door after saying my goodbyes to her. I had an epiphany as I watched her rock Bea to sleep. My heart was already invested, whether I avoided a sexual relationship with her or not. She belonged to me in my mind. So avoiding her physically out of fear meant missing out on something I desperately needed and wanted.

Whether or not we had sex, I'd be devastated if she left. I knew I couldn't let fear keep me from experiencing it any longer as I looked over at her in that sexy as hell SWAT uniform.

I approached them both and softly kissed Bea's head. When I looked up at her, she was already looking down at me, almost as if she knew exactly what I'd been thinking just seconds before. She cupped my entire face in her hand and drew me into her lips. It was the first time we'd kissed since just before my date with Roger. This kiss was different from the previous one; it was tender.

"Why don't you put her to bed?" she said gruffly over my lips, my entire body limp.

I just nodded. As I walked up the stairs, my legs felt shaky. I carefully removed Bea from her costume so as not to wake her and placed her in the crib in my room.

I looked over at the Adam and Eve bag taunting me on the bureau as I removed my Catwoman leotard.

Should I?

I considered her admission that she'd fantasised about me in it and decided to surprise her by wearing it. I wrapped the sheer material around my head. My swollen breasts were fully exposed, with only the red crosses barely concealing my nipples. It seriously looked obscenely hot; she was going to freak.

I was already wet just thinking about her reaction as I put on my own red thong. Tonight, I'd be able to touch her, taste her, and do all of the things I'd fantasised about. As I tiptoed down the hall, goosebumps covered my entire body.

Her door was only halfway open as she stood in her black shirt, staring out the window as the moonlight shone on her stunning silhouette. Lisa had been waiting for me.

She'd kept the black trousers from her SWAT outfit on. They hugged her round ass so tightly that it made my mouth water from the desire to bite it. I'd admired her beautiful body from afar many times before, but I knew this time was different.

"Hey," I said, causing her to turn around.

Lisa's breath caught in her throat as she examined me from head to toe, her hungry eyes soaking in every inch of me. "Fuck," she muttered to herself. "Holy shit. You've got it on." She approached slowly, then took my face in both of her palms. I was shivering with desperation. She slid her hands down my neck, over my breasts, and stopped at my navel. Her eyes seemed to be in a trance as she examined every inch of my body, which was completely exposed through the sheer fabric.

She briefly closed her eyes. When she opened them, she had the same expression of awe on her face. She acted as if she hadn't expected to see me still standing there. "No one has ever compared to you, Roseanne. You have to know that." Hearing her say that, my heart felt like it was going to burst.

Then, she dropped to her knees. She pushed me into her, her hands around my waist, kissing my navel and slowly swirling her tongue over my stomach. She lowered her mouth in soft kisses and stopped between my legs.

She slid her hand into the back of my thong and roughly gripped the material before slowly sliding it down my legs. "Fuck," she said as she stood up, holding my underwear. "They're soaked." She sniffed them slowly and exhaled a long breath before shaking her head slowly. "I can't wait to taste you."

She then pointed to her crotch. "Look at me." Her pants were barely holding her in, and her cock was so swollen that it appeared to be able to puncture the material. "I don't think I've ever been this excited about anything in my life." I've been waiting for this moment for what feels like my entire life. I never imagined it would happen. I'd like to savour it."

She took my hand in hers and led me to her bed. She sat down on the edge and lifted me onto her. My knees were wrapped around her thighs, and my bare pussy was straddling her pants' material, her erection straddling the material of her pants. When she looked up at me, her eyes were hazy. "Tell me about your darkest, deepest fantasy. I want to make it happen tonight."

When I hesitated, she said, "Let's play a little. Tell me exactly what you want. Don't be afraid; nothing is off-limits. Whatever you want."

I knew exactly what I wanted, what I'd fantasised about nearly every time I'd masturbated since last summer.

"I want you to stroke yourself like you did the day I was watching you, except this time I want you to do it while you're looking at me. I want to see how much you want me."

Her lips formed a smile. "I have a fucked-up confession."

"What?"

"That day, I was thinking of you. For a split second when you appeared at my door, I thought my mind was playing tricks on me, that I was imagining you."

"Oh Really?"

"I haven't been able to think of anything else for a long time." She pushed my body against her. "So your fantasy is to watch me jerk off to you, naughty girl?"

I took a swallow. "Yes."

"That is something that can be worked out. Three conditions though..."

"Okay."

"One...you're going to strip naked for me."

"Alright."

"Two...You'll help me."

"Alright. And three?"

"It ends with me inside of you. Tonight I need to fuck you. I can't keep waiting any longer."

I could no longer form coherent words, so I simply nodded and waited for her to move her body back against the headboard.

She slid her hand down her crotch and began firmly rubbing her cock through her pants. "You have the most amazing tits, Roseanne. Take that off so I can see them."

My breasts were tingling as a result of her commanding tone. I couldn't think of anything I wouldn't do for her right now. I sat atop her lower legs, slipping my spaghetti straps down. The material fell down but did not completely remove from my chest, giving her only a partial view.

"Such a tease," she gritted her teeth and clutched her dick even tighter. "Take it off."

I tossed the material aside, lifting it above my head. When I realised I was naked in front of her, I instinctively covered my breasts for a moment.

"Don't you dare," she warned, a sly smile on her face. "I need to see all of you."

Lisa slowly unzipped her pants, revealing her fully hard cock. As she looked up at me, she wrapped her fist around it and began to slowly pump it up and down. It was the most sensual experience I'd ever had.

"Is this what you wanted?" she asked, jerking herself hard as her gaze travelled over every inch of me.

As wetness trickled down my thigh, I nodded. She spoke in short bursts between laboured breaths. "You're so fucking beautiful, baby. So fucking beautiful."

I pressed up against her, turned on beyond belief by the way she looked at me as well as her words.

"I can feel your wetness against my legs. Keep rubbing yourself on me like that. I want to be covered in you," she said as she stroked herself more vigorously.

I rocked back and forth against her legs, licking my fingertips and circling them around my nipples before squeezing my breasts together.

"Shit. Keep doing that." She was covered in precum shaft to tip. It was thrilling to realise that I was the source of her arousal.

She came to a halt and lay back for a moment to catch her breath before saying simply, "Now, you touch me." I assumed she'd never ask. I reached over and wrapped my fingers around her thick girth, which felt hot and wet in my hands. It felt amazing to touch her. I jerked her slowly at first, then quickly, enjoying the sensation of her cum all over my hand. I stopped to lick my palm as she watched every movement of my tongue, wanting to taste her so badly. Then I swallowed as she fixed her gaze on me.

"Fuck that's hot," she exclaimed. She stopped me as I was about to lower my mouth down onto her to lick the fresh bead of moisture on her tip. "Don't do that. No, not yet. I'll be there in two seconds, and I want this to be the last.

"Okay." I smiled as I stroked her cock, enjoying the moans she let out as she fought to keep them in.

She eventually put her hand over mine and said, "I can't take it any longer. I have to taste you." She slid her body down beneath me, effortlessly lifting me over her mouth. I gasped, unprepared for the sudden sensation as she licked and sucked, alternately penetrating me with her tongue and lapping over my clit. She guided me over her mouth with her hands on my hips, her stifled sounds of pleasure vibrating through my core. She devoured me unreservedly and brutally. It was the most incredible sensation I'd ever felt.

Lisa stopped when she realised I was losing control. "As much as I want you to come on my face, I want us to come together inside you." She slid backwards and knelt above me. Her cock was ridiculously engorged. She kept jerking herself as she looked down into my eyes. She suddenly grabbed my face and began to kiss me passionately. As I landed on my back, she pushed her weight down on me. Her slick cock rubbed against my stomach as she kissed me with all her might.

"Why the fuck did we wait so long?" she asked, her lips against mine. I shook my head and pulled her hair, encouraging her to kiss me harder because I couldn't get enough of her taste.

I felt as if I was going to die if she didn't enter me right away. Lisa instinctively drew away from me and reached for the bedside table. As she ripped the condom package open with her teeth, I heard the crinkle of a wrapper. "I'm going to fuck you so hard, Rosie. I can't wait to hear how you sound when I make you come. Ready huh?"

I nodded in approval, biting my bottom lip. "Oh my God, yes."

Bea's frantic cry could be heard in the distance, coming from down the hall, as Lisa slid the condom on effortlessly.

We both froze, me with my legs wide open waiting for her and Lisa with her hand on her dick.

No.No.No, please!NOT. NOW.

We both remained motionless, as if not moving would bring it to a halt. That was just wishful thinking on my part. Lisa got up and slipped her underwear and pants back on when it became clear that we weren't going to get that lucky. "I'll go see how she's doing. Maybe she just needs to be changed."

"Are you sure?"

"Yeah. Stay exactly where you are... eagle spread Don't budge. Be right back."

Lisa paused in the restroom to wash her hands before proceeding down the hall.

I was too worked up to argue in my naked state, so I waited for her return with bated breath.

I could hear her voice from down the hall after a few minutes. "Roseanne!"

I jumped to my feet. "Is everything fine?"

"She's fine, but I need your help."

I raided Lisa's drawer for an outfit, then slipped one of her white t-shirts over my head and dashed down the hall.

As soon as I walked into the room, the air was filled with what smelled like a poop explosion. "We have a hazmat situation," Lisa said, holding Bea away from her with both hands. "She's covered in shit...up it's to the back of her neck."

Bea began to laugh, prompting Lisa to ask, "You think this is funny? How do you shit all the way up to your head? That's a rare talent, Bumblebee."

Despite the mini-disaster, she burst out laughing again, and we couldn't stop laughing with her.

"Okay," I said after I had calmed down. "This is what we're going to do. Just keep her in your arms. I'll get a plastic bag for her clothes and clean her as thoroughly as I can with wipes. After that, we'll take her to the tub."

Lisa stayed with Bea while I cleaned her up. While she was speaking to her, she was making me laugh. "It's no surprise you're smiling. Bumblebee, I'm sure you're feeling good right now. I'm calling the Guinness Book of World Records tomorrow to report the largest dump ever recorded."

Despite the fact that I knew she couldn't understand what she was saying, she responded to her as if she could. Lisa didn't care what she was saying; she just thought she was the funniest thing in the world.

I just threw her clothes in the downstairs trash can while Lisa stayed upstairs holding her out in the same position. We took her to the bathroom and plopped her in the tub, using the removable shower head to hose her down in an extra sudsy bath. When we were finished, she smelled like heaven. Lisa cradled her and I dried her feet while she was wrapped in a warm towel.

She gave me a look. "How did we get here from what was going on in the other room?"

I kissed her little toes. "It's kind of like the story of my life."

"You know, she's wide awake now." Lisa smiled.

"Well, that makes sense. I think I'll go feed her," I suggested.

"Yeah, as you should. Know what? I'd be surprised if she still had any-thing in her stomach after that." Lisa giggled and winked to Bea who's smiling to her.

Lisa accompanied me back to my room and rested her head on my shoulder as I nursed Bea. I hadn't bothered to cover myself in front of her for the first time. We all ended up falling asleep in my bed together.

Even though there was no sex that night, it was one of the most mem-orable nights of my life, not only because of what happened, but also because everything would change the next day.

17. THE Farewell

While I was making coffee in the kitchen, Lisa was still sleeping. It was a regular leisurely Sunday morning until I received a simple text message that turned my world upside down. I moved my gaze to Lisa's phone, which was charging on the kitchen counter.

Jisoo: Okay. When you've made your decision, give me a call.

Jisoo?

My heart began to race as I remembered that Jisoo was her ex-girlfriend and the only long-term relationship she'd had aside from Winter. What exactly did that imply? They'd been conversing? I hadn't given it a second thought about whether spying was acceptable or not; I needed to know. I read the two additional messages above it as I scrolled up.

Jisoo: Have you thought about it any further?

Lisa : Yeah. I need a little more time.

I started to feel a strong sense of dread. I believed that last night had marked a turning point in our relationship. Lisa had given me the impression that I could completely rely on her. It was as if someone had just dumped a bucket of icy water over my head to wake me up from a hallucination when I realised that she had been in contact with her ex and had been hiding something from me.

I became aware of the drizzle outside while gazing blankly out of the huge kitchen window. It would be a chilly, bare day. She walked downstairs without me even turning around. She kissed Bea, who was playing on the mat nearby, with a loud smack of her lips.

My entire body tensed up as she approached from behind me and pressed her morning wood on my ass while kissing my neck and said, "Good morning."

She could see by the look on my face when I turned around that something was wrong.

Her face became glum. "Rosie...talk to me."

I passed the desk and handed her her own phone instead of responding to her. What is it that you need extra time for?

Lisa blinked a few times while gazing down at it. "I was going to discuss something with you today. I didn't want to ruin Bea's first Halloween by doing so."

I had the impression that the walls were surrounding me. I regret putting my faith in any of this, I feel so foolish.

"Whoa. Hold on!" She got angry and her face started to get crimson. "What conclusion are you specifically drawing at this time?"

"It doesn't need a scientist, Lisa. You and your ex-girlfriend have begun exchanging texts. Trying to make a decision."

"That's right. There is something going on, but it has nothing to do with her. Nothing! She is an ex for a reason. You don't have to be concerned. You fucked me over last night, did you not see that?"

"Why else are you talking to her, then?"

She took a deep breath and ran her fingers through her hair to gather herself. "Oh sweet Rosie, Jisoo is Calvin Sprockett's tour manager."

"The singer Calvin Sprockett?"

"Yes!" She chuckled a little at my response. "The famous Grammy Award winner. That one." She shook her head and smiled to me.

"Okay...What is she talking about with you, then?"

"He will be on a five-month tour of North America and Europe. The artist who was meant to open for him has now unannouncedly entered rehab. Olivia and Steve Rollins, my agent, are close. We were dating when they met. Back then, Olivia served in a similar capacity to a manager for me. Anyway, I suppose Steve sent her a current tape of mine from the recording session in September, and she played it for Calvin. He asked her if I was interested in being the replacement opening act on the tour."

"Are you serious? God, oh God. That's a dream, Lisa!" I screamed in excitement.

It was odd to feel joy for her and like my entire world was falling apart at the same moment. The one thing I was certain of was that I would not let my fear prevent me from taking advantage of this once-in-a-lifetime opportunity.

"I'm sorry for not bringing it up earlier. Really, all I wanted yesterday was to be perfect. I swear to God I was going to tell you before the weekend was over."

I struggled to come up with something to say that wouldn't convey my anxiety. "Does he know that this is your first time on tour?"

Lisa gave a nod. "I honestly thought it was weird that he would take a chance on someone like me, but evidently I've since learned that Cal is renowned for showcasing up-and-coming talent on his tours. That was how Dave Aarons got his start."

"Really. Wow... and he selected you."

She gave a tentative smile. "Yeah."

"Your style fits him perfectly, too."

"I know. It fits well."

Despite my panic, pride also flooded my heart. I embraced her with my arm. "Holy crap. I'm so proud of you!" I continued, even though I felt like my world was imploding.

"I haven't accepted it yet, Roseanne."

I abruptly stepped back so I could see her in the eyes. "You'll do it, won't you?"

She grimaced. "I don't know,"

"You can't turn it down."

"I wanted to talk to you about it first,"

"What is there to talk about?"

"I'd be gone for five fucking months from you and Bea."

"You never really implied that your presence was permanent here to begin with. You've technically been living on borrowed time. You realise that, don't you?"

When she answered, "This would be different from my simply being in New York," she didn't directly answer my query. "I wouldn't be able to visit the island at will or anytime you need me or something. The tour never ends. They follow a strict routine. He enjoys performing two or three times in each city." She said again.

"Don't worry about me," I said. Even if I didn't want her to go, there was no way I was going to allow her to pass up this chance out of guilt. She would eventually grow bitter with Bea and me. The last thing I ever wanted was that.

"I don't need to worry about you? Do you even remember the state I found you in?"

"A lot has changed since then. Bea has grown a lot. She is sleeping better and is less reliant on me. Don't use me as a justification for passing up this chance. Five months will fly by quickly."

In reality, it seemed to last forever. In just five months, a lot might happen. In truth, in that same period of time, a lot had transpired between us. In that same amount of time, we had developed into our own special kind of family.

"You claim it will fly by now, but you'll feel it when there is no one around to relieve you when you want to leave the house or go shopping. If you don't call the asshat next door, you'll feel lonely at night. Roger will most doubt make the most of my absence."

She tried to be attempting to come up with every possible justification for why going was a bad idea.

"I do not want you to go, Lisa. It terrifies me to death, but I just know that if you don't, you'll live to regret it. With an offer like this, there isn't even a choice to be made."

She spent a long time staring at the ground and her shoes before finally saying, "You're right. If I don't do it, I'll always wonder what may have been. And I doubt I'll ever have another chance like it in my lifetime."

When I swallowed, my throat felt like sandpaper. "Well, then you have your answer."

Shit, murmured Lisa as she continued to squint. "This actually is taking place." She then made a timid turn to face me as if she still wanted me to try to talk her out of it.

"I'll still be here, and so will Bea."

"I'd be returning a month after her first birthday," she said. She turned to see Bea playing nearby. "I will miss it."

I asked, "When do you need to let Winter know by?" while trying to maintain my composure.

"Within the following few days at the latest."

I hesitated before asking, "Are you sure Winter wasn't right about her?"

"Why do you say that?"

"That means she wants to rekindle her relationship with you? Her efforts to secure your place on this tour look like a very generous gesture on her behalf."

"She has always been a big supporter for my music. Nothing else is happening there, Roseanne."

"Is she going to stay on the tour the entire time?"

"Yes. She manages it."

"Is she dating anyone right now?"

She hesitantly said, "I don't think so."

I felt a rush of adrenaline as jealousy set in. My cheeks got warm. "I see."

"I told you the story of my split from Jisoo. I wasn't the right one for her. It is done. The fact that she is on tour is irrelevant. Just don't think about that. It's a waste of energy."

"Okay. I'll try, but imagine your reaction if I embarked on a five-month bus journey with an ex. Even Roger next door is too much for you. You spent two years living with her. You can easily understand why it bothers me."

"Of course, I get it, but I can't stress enough that Jioo and I are over. Please don't worry about the fact that she's going on this tour."

"Alright. I'll try."

My heart weighted a thousand pounds, literally. I couldn't let her realise how heartbroken I was over her leaving. "Hey, is it okay if I take a quick jog on the beach?" I asked out of the blue. "Will you watch over Bea?"

"When did you start running?"

"I'd like to start."

She gave me a wary glance. "Yeah. Of course I'll keep an eye on her."

I quickly raced upstairs and as quickly as I could changed into my sports clothes.

Once outside, my heart could no longer keep up with how quickly my legs were moving. I was unable to resist the urge to flee the pain of realising she was leaving behind me. The thought that she wouldn't want to return to this routine existence on the island was more upsetting than her leaving. Lisa would be having a brand-new experience. A music tour would be filled with intrigue and temptation. No limitations.

The only thing worse than Lisa leaving would be if she stayed because of my fears, so I had to keep my fear hidden from her. I would know she was serious about us if we were able to endure her leaving. Up until that point, I had to live my life under the possibility that she would not return. The real test would be on this tour.

As I ran, the seashore air filled my throat. While dodging seagulls, the wind was so strong that sand was blowing into my mouth and into my eyes.

When I got back to the house, I paused just inside the door before going inside. Lisa had the radio on and was dancing around the kitchen with Bea. Every time Lisa quickly spun her around, she would chuckle. The music faded into the background, taking a backseat to the loud noise of the anxious thoughts passing through my mind.

It hit me that I wasn't going to be the only one devastated by her leaving. Bea had no clue she would be gone in a matter of days. She wouldn't even be able to understand why she left. My heart hurt for her, and Lisa wasn't even gone yet.

-

Time always moves the fastest when you want it to slow down.

Lisa discovered that she barely had a week and a half before she had to go to Minneapolis after accepting the tour job. Driving the Range Rover back to New York, she would then board a plane for Minnesota, where she would meet Calvin and the rest of the crew to begin the tour.

There wasn't much time to prepare because the other musician had left so abruptly. Lisa struck it lucky when the managers at her day job decided to give her an unpaid leave of absence after hearing about the circumstance. That helped because Lisa's president at the software company was a major Calvin Sprockett fan.

In my head, everything was falling apart even while everything was coming together on the exterior. I wanted so badly to just be thrilled for her-a part of me was. I was just unable to separate that aspect from my own melancholy and fear.

Even though we made the most of those last few days by spending time with Bea, our relationship was exceedingly stressful. I told Lisa over coffee one morning that I didn't believe it was a good idea for us to take things any further physically before she departed right after she made the decision to go on the tour. I told Lisa that would only make it harder for me to deal with her leaving. I used that as a big excuse. She may have seemed to comprehend, but I knew that deep down she recognised it for what it was: a lack of faith in her loyalty to me. Every night I went to my own room, and she didn't try to stop me.

I had to go to Providence to get my belongings out of storage two days before Lisa was supposed to leave. Since I wasn't working, I couldn't afford to keep it there any longer. I intended to give as much of it as I could while selling some of the smaller items during a yard sale in Newport. The majority of it was items I didn't need anymore. The husband of my friend, Jennie, met me with his truck and helped me in loading the majority of the items before she took them all to a Salvation Army store.

While I travelled to Providence, Lisa had remained in Newport with Bea. I was overcome with emotion over Lisa's impending departure throughout the duration of the entire trip back to the island. In my head, I could practically hear the time ticking. I imagined the last few months as a movie that was coming to a close. I had no doubt that Lisa would achieve unheard-of celebrity as a result of this exposure.

She was about to be swallowed up whole, and I really didn't think she knew what was coming. I knew how women reacted to Lisa because I had seen it happen in a smaller setting. That was poised to undergo a thousand-fold increase. She would never live the same life again. Neither would mine.

The beach home was surprisingly silent when I got back. The oven was baking something that smelled like tomato sauce. With a click of the stove light, I could see it was lasagna.

"Hello?" I yelled.

"We're upstairs!" I heard Lisa call out.

It sounded like it was raining inside of Lisa's room. Peaceful music was mingled with the sound. My heart almost stopped when I opened the door.

Lisa's bed had gone. Bea's white crib was placed in its place. There was a butter-yellow fluffy area rug on the ground. Slowly moving stars with lights were projected onto the ceiling. A contraption on the desk was producing the sounds of nature. There was a framed photo of Anne Geddes hanging on the wall. It featured a sleeping child decked out in bumblebee garb.

I put my mouthpiece down. "How...when...did you..."

She had Bea in her arms. "She needed a separate space. Bumblebee is growing, so she can't stay in your bed with you indefinitely. It's now. It was the ideal moment to surprise you before I departed that you were in Providence today."

Bea moved her tiny head and stretched her neck to follow the movement of the stars as she was mesmerised by them on the ceiling.

I grinned. "She really loves those, huh?"

"I knew she would. I occasionally take her up on the deck when she stays up late with me. We look up at the stars together." Her words pinched at my heart, "Perhaps she'll look at these and think of me while I'm away."

"I never knew you did that with her." I looked around the space in awe of the transformation. "Where are all of your things?"

"I broke down my bed and temporarily placed it in the corner of my office."

It didn't set well with me that she was leaving the bedroom and giving it to Bea since it seemed so definitive. I overreacted when I tried to interpret the message.

In fear, my heart began to race. "You won't be returning," I said. It was not what I intended to say out. I swear to god, I was so stupid.

"What?"

"You gave up your room since you were sure you wouldn't return. You'll disappear and rise to fame. Even though you'll come visit, you know you won't be living here any longer."

It seemed as though all of my anxieties acquired a voice overnight. I honestly hadn't intended to lay everything on the table in that manner. It all just came out after a long, stressful day.

Lisa was speechless at first. When she finally spoke, her voice almost sounded hostile. "That's what you think?"

"I don't know. I suppose that I'm just thinking aloud."

"She shouldn't be sleeping in your fucking room, so I made this nursery. She deserves a nice space of her own. Before I even knew about the tour, I had already begun to plan something. Over the previous month, I gradually gathered all of this stuff and stashed it away in my closet." She pulled a stack of receipts out of the bureau drawer, hurled them obnoxiously into the air. The floor was covered in a shower of white slippers. "Look at the dates on these. They're from weeks ago."

I felt very stupid. "I'm sorry. I've just been stressed about you going. I was trying not to let it show, and I guess it finally caught up with me."

"You think I'm trying to separate myself from you? The moment I told you about the tour, you were the one who immediately erected a huge wall. If I had my way, I would want nothing more than to sleep in your fucking bed tonight-inside of you-because I'm leaving in less than two days. Two fucking days, Roseanne! Instead of enjoying each other, you've been shutting me out. I'm respecting your wishes and not pushing anything because I know my leaving is hard enough for you, but fuck!"

Feeling ashamed, I said, "I'm sorry for overreacting. I made this about more than the nursery. The room is beautiful. Really."

Lisa put Bea in her crib and slammed the door behind her saying, "I'm going to go check on the dinner." I looked up at the stars on the ceiling, deeply regretting my loss of composure. The sound machine had switched to a medley of thunder and lightning. It accurately captured the atmosphere.

The meal that night was quiet. Since she no longer had a bedroom, Lisa slept on the couch. I didn't sleep at all.

-

Lisa would be gone tomorrow.

I needed to fix things before she left, or I would regret it. I thought I would use Bea's peaceful nap time in her new nursery as an opportunity to speak with her.

The corner of Lisa's office was filled with a mountain of black luggage. Even just seeing that made me miserable.

She was punching the punching bag in the gym room, and I could hear it as I moved down the hallway.

She hit the bag with more force than I had ever seen her use while I stood in the doorway and watched. Lisa was completely in a zone and either hadn't noticed me or pretended not to.

"Lisa."

She kept going. She was wearing earbuds, so I wasn't sure if she could hear me. The music was playing loudly through them.

"Lisa," I repeated louder.

She struck the bag harder as she continued to ignore me.

"Lalisa Manoban!" I yelled.

This time, she gave me a fleeting glance before continuing to punch. That proved she was blatantly ignoring me.

I lingered in the doorway watching her for a few minutes till she finally stopped since I was unwilling to leave this circumstance no matter how terrible it was. She looked down at the ground while gasping for air, but said nothing as she leaned against the punching bag and gripped it. She finally spoke after an extended period of silence.

"And I haven't even left yet, I'm losing you." She looked at me. "That is not worth this tour."

"You must go. You won't lose me. I just don't know how to handle it."

A stream of sweat trickled down the length of her glistening chest as she walked toward me but stopped short of touching me. The combination of the scent of her flesh and cologne acted as a stark reminder of how much I had been deluding myself about my sexual restraint.

"I can understand that. Absolutely reasonable," she said.

"Uh what?"

"All of your concerns. If it were you going on the tour, I would have the same sentiments. This scene is not amusing. I get why you're scared."

Knowing that she thought my concern was justified didn't exactly make me feel better.

"It's not that you don't trust me right now," she said, "but you worry that environment would somehow change me and cause me to desire different things than I desire right now."

"Yes. That's exactly right. Why are you so upset with me about it if you understand my fear?"

"It's more like...frustrated. Because everything is moving so quickly, I don't have much time left to fix this before I leave. We must have faith that the goal we have been pursuing is more important than anything insane life may throw our way in the ensuing five months. Because I never want to let you or Bea down, I'm also afraid, Rosie." She said softly by the end of the words and I don't know what hurts but it hurts. It just happened. The look of fear in her eyes was unprecedented, and the uncertainty in them made me uneasy.

"Let me down?"

"Yes. Bea is growing fond of me. Even if she won't recall these recent months, she is simply growing older and will begin to comprehend more as time goes on. There is no game here. I know that. I would rather die than hurt her."

She wasn't stating it directly, but I interpreted her statement to mean that she wasn't sure whether she wanted a child, which suggested that she might not have been sure about us. It pained me to know that she still held doubts, given how phenomenal she was with Bea.

And with me.

This tour was making Lisa do things she never would have otherwise done, like leave us and take a step back to consider the responsibility she unintentionally took on when she opted to travel to Newport last summer one month earlier than planned, anticipating an empty house. That day, she undoubtedly received much more than she had anticipated. Since then, she has been our strength. I didn't want to lose her, but she needed this time apart to decide what she really wanted.

I knew that I truly wanted her. I also knew that I loved her enough to let her go. I vowed to stop pushing guilt.

This trip was actually a blessing in disguise because it would allow her time to think about what her true calling was. If we weren't strong enough to endure this, I didn't want Bea to get closer to her. Now, Bea's heart needed to be safeguarded more than my own.

I reluctantly told Lisa what I had realised. "Perhaps taking this break is necessary. It will help you realise what you really want out of life."

I was taken aback when she said, "You know what? That's right."

She agreed with me, and I felt a little queasy. At the same time, I promised to be courageous and let everything unfold naturally. I wouldn't act stupidly and sabotage anything one way or the other, because I loved her. Very much. Even if it wasn't possible for Bea and me to be a part of her happiness, I wanted the best for her.

The cosmos had previously demonstrated that it had predetermined plans for me that were out of my control. Bea was living proof of it. I had to have faith that something greater than us was in control and that this most recent difficulty was necessary. It would either split us apart or make us stronger than ever, that much I was certain of.

I'd know the answer within five months.

--

All day long, it rained.

Bea refused to sleep in her new crib that night, as if she sensed something was awry. It led me to believe that it was very feasible for babies to possess a sixth sense. She has enjoyed sleeping in the nursery and observing the stars ever since Lisa redecorated it. But tonight-Lisa's last night-Bea only quieted in the safety of my arms. intuition, perhaps. She couldn't fall asleep like me, so I allowed her to lie next to me in bed.

As midnight approached, I was more dejected as insomnia continued to prevail.

Lisa knocked softly. "Are you still awake, Rosie?"

"Yeah. Come in."

She entered and lay down on my bed next to us, repositioning the covers. "I can't sleep,"

"Are you nervous?" I queried.

"Scared as hell is more like it."

"About what specifically?"

She laughed sarcastically once. "Everything. I'm worried she won't remember me if I leave you alone. scared she will remember me-remember that I left. I'm afraid to mess up when I perform in front of thousands of people. You name it. I'm worried about it."

"You shouldn't be worried about performing. You're going to knock them out cold."

She got Bea from next to me and put her on her chest despite my assurance. Bea's breathing began to stabilise.

It broke my heart when she softly kissed her head and whispered in her ear, "I'm sorry, Bumblebee."

My mood had been all over the place throughout the day, alternating between feeling sorry for myself and Bea, to feeling proud and excited for her. In this particular intimate moment, I felt compelled not as her lover-but as her friend-to help her understand that she deserved this opportunity that she'd worked her entire life for. She had nothing to be sorry for. That was how I knew I truly loved her, because in the eleventh hour, all I wanted was to take away her guilt and make her feel good, regardless of how much her leaving hurt.

"Grandma would be so proud of you, Lisa. She always used to tell me that she believed you were destined for greatness. When you go out there, don't even think about how many people are watching, just sing for her, sing to grandma...do this for her."

"She'd be pleased with how you turned out, too, Patch...all you've undertaken. The mother you've become despite how shitty your own mother was. Grandma would be so damn proud. I'm so damn proud."

With Bea now fast asleep on her chest, Lisa leaned in to kiss me. She began to devour my mouth, firm but tenderly.

We kissed for several minutes, careful not to wake Bea.

She spoke into my mouth, "I want to make love to you so badly right now. But at the same time, I get why you think that would make tomorrow even harder. I don't know if I could ever walk out of here after that."

"I don't think Bea would allow it right now anyway. She looks too comfortable."

She looked down at Bea and smiled. "You're probably right." She turned to me, her brown eyes luminescent in the darkness. "Promise me a few things."

"Okay."

"Promise me that we'll video chat at least every other day."

"Sure. That'll be easy."

"Promise me that if you get lonely, you'll call me any time-day or night."

"I will. What else?"

"Promise me that we won't keep anything important from each other and that we'll always be honest with each other."

That one made me feel a little queasy as I started pondering what things she anticipated having to be honest with me about.

"Okay. I promise." I swallowed. "Anything else?"

"No. I just want to sleep next to you and Bea tonight. Is that okay?"

"Of course." I took her hand. "It's going to be okay, Lisa. We'll be okay."

She smiled and whispered, "Yeah."

Lisa placed Bea between the two of us. As she lay in the middle, Lisa and I looked into each other's eyes until sleep finally claimed us.

-

When I woke up the next morning, panic hit me for a brief moment because Lisa was gone from the bed. Looking at the clock, I calmed down, realizing it was only 9AM. She wasn't scheduled to leave until around noon.

The smell of her signature coffee brewing wafted up the stairwell and immediately made me sad. It would be the last time I would smell her coffee fusion for a long time.

Feeling my eyes getting watery, I took my sweet time before going downstairs, hoping to regain my composure before then. I did some mindless things: cleaned the bedroom, threw a load of laundry in, anything than to have her see me break down. Bea was watching me from her Exersaucer as I ran around my room like a maniac.

Lisa walked in as I was vacuuming my rug. I wouldn't look up at her as I moved the vacuum back and forth.

"Roseanne."

I pushed it along the carpet faster.

"Roseanne!" she yelled.

I finally looked at her. She must have seen the sadness in my eyes because her expression slowly darkened. I just stared at her as the vacuum continued to run, even though I'd stopped moving it. A teardrop fell down my cheek, and I knew I had officially lost my ability to hide my feelings.

She slowly approached and shut off the vacuum, her hand lingering over mine which was still gripping the handle.

"I've been waiting to have coffee with you," she said. "I need to have breakfast with you and Bea one last time before I leave. It's my favorite thing in the world."

I wiped my eyes. "Okay."

"It's fucking okay to be sad. Stop trying to hide it from me. I won't hide it, either." Her voice cracked a little. "I'm so fucking sad right now, Roseanne. Leaving you guys is the last thing I want to do right now. But time is running out. Don't waste it hiding from me."

She was right.

Sniffling, I nodded. "Let's go have coffee."

Lisa ifted Bea into her arms as she closed her eyes tightly and breathed in her scent as if she wanted to burn it into memory. When she pulled back, she lifted her up into the air as Bea looked down at her. "Are you my Bumblebee?"

She smiled at Lisa, and if that didn't feel like a knife to the heart, I didn't know what did. My emotions were all over the place again. A part of me was still selfishly angry at Lisa.

How could you leave us?

Why haven't you told me you love me?

Why haven't you told Bea you love her?

You don't love us.

A bigger part was angry at myself for even having those kinds of thoughts again. I was coming to realize that it wasn't so much the fact that she was leaving that bothered me as it was the fact that she was leaving me so unsure about where things really stood with us.

She treated me as if she loved me, but even when we were acting like a family, she'd never defined our relationship, never even labeled me as her girlfriend.

As Lisa prepared the mugs of coffee like she always did, I followed every move she made and couldn't help but wonder what the next time I'd watch her make coffee would be like.

When she handed me my cup, I put on the best smile I could. I didn't want her to leave thinking of my sad face. Just as I was trying like hell to put on a happy facade, her own expression turned sullen.

"What is it, Lisa?"

"I just feel helpless. If you need anything, I told Tom you might call him from time to time. I left his number on the fridge. He said anytime day or night, don't hesitate. Call him instead of that tool next door, please. I also installed a new alarm system." She waved a hand, leading me to the door. "Come on, I'll show you how to use it."

Everything she was saying was muffled as my eyes followed her fingers, hands, and lips as she explained how to maneuver the alarm control pad. Her voice was fading into the background, losing the battle with my accumulating panic.

Lisa took notice and stopped talking. "You know what? I'll email you the instructions." She stared at me for a bit before pulling me into an embrace. She held me for what seemed like several minutes, slowly rubbing my back. There wasn't anything we could do to slow down time.

I watched from the window as Lisa loaded her luggage into the back of the Range Rover.

When she came back inside, we took a quick but quiet walk on the beach with Bea. At one point, I stayed behind as Lisa took Bea closer to the shore. She whispered something in her ear. That made me curious, but I never asked her what she'd said to Bea.

Once we returned to the house, it was time for Lisa to leave. The morning had flown by way too fast; it almost seemed unfair.

Trying to suppress my tears, I said, "I can't believe this moment is finally here."

Miraculously, I was able to keep the crying at bay because, mostly, I was in shock. The best thing I could do for her right now was to reassure her that I would support her while she experienced this new chapter, let her know that I would be there for her in the very way we started-as a friend.

I returned her own sentiments from earlier. "The same goes for you, Lisa. If you need me, or you get lonely, or maybe you're feeling doubtful, you call me day or night. I'll be here."

Lisa was still holding Bea as she placed her forehead on mine and simply said, "Thank you." We stayed like that for a while with Bea sandwiched in the middle of us.

Still wanting to avoid breaking out in tears, I forced myself away. "You'd better go. You'll miss your flight."

She kissed Bea's head gently then said, "I'll call you when I land in Minneapolis."

Bea and I stood in the doorway, watching as she walked away. She got in the car and started it but didn't move. She looked over at us as we continued to wait. Bea was reaching out her hand to her and babbling; she obviously had no clue what was going on.

Why wasn't she moving?

She suddenly got out of the car, slamming the door. My heartbeat accelerated with each step she took toward me. Before I could ask her whether she'd forgotten something, her hand wrapped around the back of my head, pulling me into her. She opened her mouth wide over mine, plunging her tongue inside and twirling it around at an almost desperate pace as she groaned into my mouth. She tasted like coffee and a flavor all her own. This was not the time to be getting aroused, but I couldn't help my body's reaction.

When she forced herself back, her eyes were hazy, filled with just as much confusion as passion. I had to once again remind myself of the old adage of setting someone free, that if they come back they're yours; if they don't, they never were.

Please come back to me.

She said nothing else as she walked back to the car, started it and this time...drove off.

18. THE HEART-ATTACKED

Blind faith.

That was the only thing that got me through Lisa's first month of absence. Even though I couldn't be there to witness it myself, I somehow had to persuade myself to believe in her decisions and deeds.

She gave us a call every night. Sometimes, it would be during what she referred to as her relaxation time around 8PM, right before their 9PM performances. Sometimes it would be during her break for lunch or dinner. She had described to me how her daily schedule was tightly packed with sound checks and rehearsals at each new location. The only free time was just after the show, and by then she was either dragged along to afterparties or was simply worn out.

The band would all check into a hotel if they spent more than one night in the same city. They would travel through the night and spend the night on the bus if they had to go somewhere else the following day.

There were two buses: one for Lisa and the rest of the crew and one for Calvin and the main band. Each bus slept roughly twelve people, according to Lisa. I never asked her which bus Jisoo slept in, because I was afraid of the answer.

So, Blind faith again yalls.

Okay, so even though I decided to put my trust in her, I still managed to find a tiny window into their world that would assuage my paranoid moments. It appeared on Jisoo's Instagram profile.

I looked up Jisoo's profile on Winter's page back when she was still residing at the beach home and used to complain about Jisoo commenting on all of Lisa's postings. Even before Lisa left, I periodically stalked her online. She started posting photos from the tour every day. Many of them were merely scenic images, such as the sunrise as they reached a new city from the bus or whatever the band and crew happened to be eating at the time. Backstage photos of Calvin and his band were also included.

I opened Instagram one night while Bea was napping. Jisoo shared a photo of Lisa on stage while performing.

It was just a typical picture of her leaning into the microphone, the spotlight pouring down on her lovely face, which was framed by that shadow at five o'clock. I yearned to be there and watch her perform on the large stage. I saw the hashtags as I lowered my gaze.

#LadiesKiller#LalisaManoban #UsedToTapThat #ExesOfInstagram #Hotgirl#CuteCat#LikeForLike#FollowMe

Even though some of the hastag bothered me, I resisted bringing it up to her or seeming like a jealous girlfriend-especially since she had never referred to me as such.

I was startled by a knock on the door. I closed the laptop.

Who would be coming by this late?

Thank goodness, Lisa had also installed a peephole in my door before she travelled, in addition to the alarm system.

A woman standing there shivering had long brown hair. I opened the door since she seemed innocent enough.

"Hello, can I help you?"

"Hi." She smiled. "Roseanne, right?"

"Yes."

"I wanted to introduce myself. My name is Hailey. The blue home next door is where I live."

"Oh. Did Roger move?"

"No. Actually, I'm her wife."

Wife?

"Oh. I thought he was-"

"Divorced?" She grinned.

"Yeah."

"Technically, he is. When he recently visited our daughter in Irvine, we were able to make reconciliation. The visit, which was meant to last one week, ended up lasting three. In the end, he brought Alyssa and me back here."

I was shocked to hear this news and I muttered, "Wow. I was clueless. That is fantastic." I waved my hand. "My god, where have I left my manners? Come in. Come in." I chuckled.

She wiped her feet and muttered, "Thank you," before going inside. "Our daughter is currently asleep, but I'd also like for you to meet her. She just turned 8 years old."

"Bea, my daughter, is likewise sound asleep. She will turn nine months soon."

"Roger said you had a child."

"I've also heard a lot about Alyssa."

"Roger also said that he and you were good friends."

"In case you were curious, we're just friends."

She was unsure. "It's all right if it was more. At the time, we weren't together"

"No. It wouldn't be right. That is, not for me, at least. I'd be curious to know. I know how it feels to have those kinds of questions when you care about someone."

She had a relieved expression on her face. "Well, I appreciate your clarification. If I said I hadn't wondered, I'd be lying."

"Actually, I'm kind of in love with my roommate. Currently, she is on tour. A musician. I fully understand jealousy."

She sat down after bringing a chair up. "Oh man. You want to talk about it?"

"Do you drink tea?"

"I do. I'd love some."

And just like that, Hailey and I grew closer that evening. She was willing to assist me with Bea if I ever needed it after I told her about my relationship with Lisa in the past.

She said that Alyssa would like watching Bea with her. I was grateful that there was never anything between Roger and me since it would have been freaking awkward.

I have to admit that when she initially appeared, I felt even more alone after learning that Roger had returned with his wife. But that self-centered notion was rapidly overtaken by the joy of a newly formed female companionship, which was sorely absent in my life.

-

I frequently hung around with Hailey. She exhorted me to venture out more and try new things. I began using the daycare at the gym and enrolled in a Mommy and Me class with Bea so that I could workout a few times a week. With Lisa gone, I was doing the best I could to establish a new routine.

Daylight hours were somewhat tolerable but nights were the hardest. I always felt the most alone in the nights when Bea was asleep and Lisa was working.

One late night, near midnight, a text message came.

Lisa: We're in Boise. Before tonight's performance, a crew member who is from here brought his baby into the bus. It only made me miss Bea more.

Rosie: We also miss you.

Lisa: In a few weeks, the tour will make a stop in Worcester, Massachusetts. What are the chances that you'll come see me?

That was only a little more than an hour's drive away. It would be the closest and only tour stop anywhere near Newport for the remainder of her time away.

Rosie: I don't think Bea would enjoy the noise and environment. But maybe I can track down a babysitter.

Although I knew Hailey could monitor Bea for me, I purposely kept her information from Lisa for my own use. Her jealousy of Roger was something I quite loved. It was the one advantage I was now holding. I so made the decision to keep my information of their reconciliation to myself for the time being.

Lisa: I agree. She would find it to be too crazy and loud.

Rosie: I'll work on it.

Lisa: Sadly, it's just one night. When the show is over, the bus leaves for Philly.

Rosie: Fingers crossed I can make it.

Lisa: It's not just Bea I miss.

My heart raced.

Rosie: I also miss you.

Lisa: Sweet dreams.

Rosie : XO

Since it was unclear whether I would be able to secure a babysitter in order to see Lisa in Massachusetts, she'd sent me a laminated backstage pass that would allow me exclusive access in the event something came through at the last minute.

She said that she wasn't sure whether or not she'd be there to meet me when I arrived. In the event that she was mid-sound check-or, depending on how late I arrived-mid-performance, having the card would be a safer bet.

Hailey was the only babysitter I had, so I wouldn't know until the very last minute if I could make it. She had a crucial appointment in Boston that day and was unable to reschedule it. She wasn't sure if she'd return in time, depending on traffic.

On the day of the concert, I was starting to feel really impatient. Bea had a cold, so I had played with the notion of taking her up there during the day, but that was no longer an option. It wasn't a smart idea to take her out in the cold and to a crowded place like that; she might get pneumonia.

By the time evening rolled around, Hailey called from the road to say that she'd gotten stuck in traffic and hadn't even made it out of Boston's Ted Williams Tunnel yet. If I were lucky enough to arrive at the show at all, I would have missed the beginning by that moment. I was honestly heartbroken. Throughout the entire tour, I only had one opportunity to see Lisa. It didn't look fair.

Nevertheless, I had dressed myself anyhow, keeping my hopes alive. I appeared less like a stay-at-home mother and more like a lingerie model when I wore a short, tight satin blue dress with accents of black lace.

In the event that I got to see her tonight, I wanted to knock her socks off. After all, I was battling for her attention against a sea of models and groupies. I felt twitchy as I applied my matte purple lipstick and curled my hair into long, loose tendrils. Though I had a sneaking suspicion that my efforts had been in futile, I needed to be ready to go the moment Hailey returned. It was obvious that I would have to miss her performance when the timer rang eight no matter what happened.

Just before she had to report to the stage at eight forty-five, Lisa called me.

"No luck?" She asked.

"I'm truly sorry. She hasn't arrived yet, despite how desperately I wanted it to work. I have no chance of arriving in time tonight." I was sobbing but kept my composure because crying would have caused my mascara to run down my face.

"Fuck, Rosie. I'm not gonna lie. This is a major disappointment. I was looking forward to seeing you so much. It helped me get through this week. Of course, I understand though. Bea is put first. Always. Kiss her for me. I wish she were feeling better."

She let out a deep sigh of frustration as we continued to speak, and our silence made it clear how disappointed we were.

I heard a man's voice before Lisa said, "Shit. They have called me."

"Okay. Enjoy the show."

"I'll be thinking of you the whole time." The telephone abruptly disconnected before I could answer.

After fifteen minutes, a frenzied knock on the door was heard. I heard Hailey panting as soon as I opened it. "Go. Go, Rosie!"

"It might already be too late. The show will be over when I get there."

"Yes. But before they take off, you'll get to see her, right?"

"I think so. I'm not sure exactly when the bus leaves for the next city."

"Don't waste time talking to me. Just tell me where Bea is."

"She's sleeping. I left a long note with instructions on the counter."

"I've got it." She waved me off. "Go get your woman, Roseanne!"

Blowing her a kiss, I said, "I owe you big time. I appreciate this."

I hadn't travelled by car at night on a highway in a while. As I sped along I-95, the beginnings of a panic attack started to set in. I managed to prevent my terror from turning into a full-blown attack by attempting to keep my attention on Lisa rather than the cars zooming past me. I had no idea where I was heading, so the GPS acted as my co-pilot. My knowledge of this region of Massachusetts was nonexistent.

As I neared, sweat started to infiltrate my body. Despite the fact that it was cold outside, I put on the air conditioner to help me relax. What did I do? The show had ended. I hadn't sent her a text.

I tried to convince myself that I was doing it to surprise her, but part of me secretly wanted to experience life when she wasn't expecting me.

Parking in the large lot outside of the venue, I wrapped my arms around myself. I left the house so quickly that I forgot my coat. Running to a thick chain-link fence that divided the VIP section from the parking lot, I arrived wearing the same high-heeled boots I'd used for my Catwoman costume.

Just inside the gate, two black tour buses with tinted windows were parked. Standing at the entrance was a security with a headset on. Nearby, swarms of women gathered in anticipation of possibly catching a peek of the artists.

I spoke to the guard, presented my unique badge, and could see my breath in the darkness. "Is the show over?"

"Almost. Calvin is currently doing the last set."

"Where can I find Lisa? Lalisa Manoban? She gave me this access card."

"Lisa is in Bus Two. On the right one."

As I walked through the gravel lot to the bus, my heart was thumping against my chest.

I let the door open. I was surprised to see that nobody was inside. I thought that until sounds coming from the back bedroom disproved it.

The sides of the bus held a number of coffin-shaped beds, but Lisa had indicated that the back of each bus had a master suite.

Each night, she swapped with the crew as to who got to sleep in it.

As I walked up to the locked wooden door, a knot started to form in my throat. From behind it, a woman's moaning noise could be heard.

Lisa was in this, according to the guard.

I had to know.

I had to open it. I had to see it with my own eyes.

My faith may have been deaf, but it was about to receive a rude awakening.

I turned the doorknob slowly and pushed it open a little. All I could make out was a dark hair mane. She lay flat, being ridden by a woman. Jisoo seemed to be there, but I wasn't sure. Any woman may have been the one.

Whoever it was didn't matter. They didn't notice me. Bile was rising and my stomach was turning. I had to stop looking. I just couldn't.

My legs trembled when I got off the bus. Too shocked to cry, I walked in a daze as numbness consumed me. I couldn't see clearly. With each step off the bus, I had the sensation that my heart was slowly breaking. Was I a fool to believe she would hold off? That she could resist the overwhelming temptation that was presented to her every day? She never promised anything, and there was excellent reason for that.

Roseanne, you're an idiot. A fucking foolish.

I would have expected to be crying, but for some reason, the shock seemed to freeze my tear ducts. My eyes felt dry, icy, and incapable of producing any tears.

A text message came through, then my phone rang.

Lisa : I truly missed you this evening.

19. THE SENSATION

What?

She's fucking with someone else, how could she be texting me?

My nerves went through an emotional roller coaster as a result of the flow of adrenaline through me.

Rosie: Are you on the bus?

Lisa: No. Getting a drink at Dave and Buster's across the street from the venue. How does Bea feel?

It wasn't her.

She didn't fuck that bus-bound chick! Oh god. I'm so... God.

I clenched my chest and let out the breath that had before seemed to be imprisoned inside and smothering me. Euphoria surged through me like a tranquillizer pistol, it was so intense.

Rosie: Still has a cold. I'm here, so she's with my friend Hailey. in front of your bus.

Lisa : Holy fuck! Don't move. I'm going back now.

I waited outside in the chilly air for at at least five minutes while rubbing my hands over my arms. The two individuals who had been making out inside the bus abruptly got out. The man was attractive, but he wasn't Lisa. Additionally, I was able to confirm that the participant was not Jisoo.

I despise myself for being this way.

Suddenly, a group of females gathered around the entryway. The guard could be heard saying, "Back. Back! Pass her by!"

I suddenly noticed Lisa pierce through the crowd of people. She entered through the mesh fence and started hurriedly scanning the area before focusing on me.

She approached me and encircled me in her arms as the chaos around us appeared to fade. I was so close to melting into her. She had a scent that was a cross between cologne, cigarettes, and beer. I wanted to take a bath in it because it was so enticing. I yearned to be covered in her.

She leaned in and whispered in my ear, "You're cold as ice.

"Just hold me. Keep me warm."

"I really need to do more than hold you right now." She pulled back to take me in, giving my outfit a once over. "Fuck," she growled. "Don't take this the wrong way, but why do you look like a whore?"

"I was dressing for the occasion. Too much?"

"God no. Just what I needed, thank you. Just the fact that you were waiting for me in public while dressed like that irritates me. The fucking guys around here are worse than the girls. Anyone mess with you?"

"No." Looking down at myself, I said, "I'm sorry if it's too much. I just figured I had to compete with all those groupies."

"Don't be sorry. Rosie, you need not contend with anyone. Never did you." Time seemed to stop when she placed her forehead against mine. "All I could think of while I was singing tonight was how much I wished you were here."

"When you texted, I was numbing my sorrows at the bar. I still can't believe you made it." She inhaled deeply while touching my neck's flesh. "I'm already as hard as a rock from the smell of you. We need to go somewhere to be alone. There isn't much time left before the buses leave."

"Where can we go?"

She touched my cheeks with her hands. "Fuck. All I want to do is bring you along on the bus and stay up with you till the sun rises over the next city."

"I would really enjoy that. I apologise for not being the type of girl who could just accompany you on tour."

"You have bigger things to be taking care of. By the way, you sure this friend watching Bea is someone you can trust?"

"Yes. If not, I wouldn't be here."

Her hand was on my shoulders. "Stay right here. Let me just go check what time we're leaving Massachusetts."

Lisa sprinted to the other tour bus, and I waited. She seemed worried when she came back. "There are two hours left till the buses depart for Philadelphia. I would introduce you to the band, but I really don't want to waste your time listening to them chat."

"What shall we do?"

"They just told me there's a small hotel down the road. If you'd like, we can go there on our own. We can stay here if that's what you like, but then we'd have to socialize."

"Being alone sounds good to me."

Lisa stroked my face with her thumb. "Wise choice."

I gave her the keys, and she used my car to take us to the hotel. She gripped my hand firmly and didn't let go the entire ride. She once gave me a seductive side glance. "God, you look so good."

I joked, "Even though I look like a cheap groupie?"

"Especially because you look like a cheap groupie." She chuckled. After briefly looking back at the road, she lowered her voice. "I wasn't expecting how lonesome this tour would be. I'm even more aware of it after seeing you."

As soon as we arrived at the hotel, Lisa checked us in and got our key cards. She had to report back to the bus in exactly one hour and forty-five minutes.

Despite the darkness of the space, neither of us lit a light. The door clicked shut behind us, and I waited for her to take the initiative, unsure of what was supposed to be happening here.

She approached me carefully and placed her chest against mine. "Jesus. Your chest is thumping. Are you afraid of being by yourself with me or something?" She rubbed my neck and said, "Maybe you should be, the way I'm feeling right now."

I remained silent, just staring at her before my gaze fell to the ground because I was too afraid to confess what was actually bothering me and because I didn't want to ruin the moment.

She took hold of my chin. "Look at me, I haven't been with anyone else, Rosie, in case there was any doubt in your mind," she remarked as soon as our eyes met. "Nobody else is what I want. I sincerely hope you don't, too."

"How did you know what I was just thinking?"

"I suppose I just hear you that way. I sensed you need that assurance. I don't want you to continue to be curious about that." She kissed me on the forehead. "Now that we've cleared everything up, I do need to be completely open and honest with you about something."

The lump in my throat was swallowed. "Okay."

"I somehow believed I could go five months without having sex, but the truth is...I'm feeling more like an animal in heat than a celibate monk."

I chuckled. "Oh, really?" My voice became solemn. "Maybe I can help. Tell me what you need."

She muttered, "Confession," over my lips. "You know, I didn't really bring you here so we could talk."

I kissed her. "Confession. I didn't exactly dress like a dirty groupie so you could sing to me."

Her mouth curled into a sardonic smile while touching against me. She quickly grabbed my face in her hands before completely sucking it up with her lips. We were both desperately trying to taste one another when a choked groan from me emerged into her starved mouth. When she kissed me, she always grabbed my face in a controlled manner, which I enjoyed. There was no sign of trepidation or caution this time, unlike any previous time we had been together. She was blatantly taking what she wanted, and I was completely giving it to her. Nothing was off limits as we both completely surrendered to what our bodies need. This would have been like a dream come true if not for the fact that she was departing in an hour. But we were aware that our time was limited.

She gripped my ass, pushed me up against her erection, and gave me a passionate kiss as her hands slowly moved down my back. She softly released my bottom lip after sucking it. "Last chance to stop me."

"Make every second count," I said in between kisses. "For the next hour, my body is yours, Manoban."

"I only had to wait decade to hear you say that." The discussion came to an end there. Lisa pushed me through the window by slamming her chest into mine with an iron fist. She started kissing me so hard that the suction made my lips pain while I had my back to the glass.

My hands developed a will of their own and were anxious to explore her. I threaded my fingers through her hair, rubbed my palms down her chest, gripped her ass. I was so overwhelmed that I wanted to touch every inch of her at once.

"It's going to be a while before we get to do this again. She fisted my hair and tilted my head back as she murmured, "We need to make it last". She gently kissed the back of my neck. She reached up my dress, grabbed my panties, and said, "Don't ever forget that I respect the heck out of you."

"Why do you say that?"

"Because I'm about to fuck you full of disrespect." She ripped my underwear off, the elastic burning my thighs from the friction.

My pussy was already wet and ready for whatever she had in mind. Whereas before she had gently kissed down my throat, now she was sucking hard on the skin at the base of my neck. I felt two of her fingers slip inside of my opening. Her mouth stilled on my neck the moment that they were fully deep inside me. She said something unintelligible as she shook her head slowly in ecstasy before suddenly flipping me around so that I was facing the glass.

She pulled his fingers out and almost immediately I felt the burn of her cock replacing them as she sunk into me. "Damn!" She muttered.

I hadn't expected her to take me so soon. From the sound she let out when she was all the way inside of me, I don't think even she expected to lose control so fast.

It felt painfully pleasurable as my skin stretched to open for her. Lisa's cock was thick. I'd always admired its girth, but it was another experience altogether to actually feel how completely she filled me-skin to skin. She hadn't put a condom on, which surprised me. I was too weak to question it, enjoying the raw sensation too much to think about anything else. But I'd come prepared.

"Please tell me you're on the pill. I've never done it like this before, but I don't think I can stop either way. It feels too damn good."

I'd never seem her lose control like this.

"I am. I just started taking it. Don't worry."

"Thank fuck." Her muscles seemed to relax.

As she moved in and out of me, she lifted my dress over my head before throwing the frock aside. There was something so sexy about being completely naked while she was still fully clothed. Her pants were hanging halfway down her legs, and her belt buckle clanked as she pounded into me.

I could see our reflection in the window. She was looking down at my ass the entire time, mesmerized as she watched our bodies joined together. She wouldn't take her eyes off of it. Her palm was firmly planted on my ass cheek to guide the movements of her thrusts, her nails inadvertently digging into my skin.

She began to suck on her finger, and before I could wonder what she was doing, I felt it inside of my ass as she continued to penetrate me with her cock at the same time. No one had ever done that to me before, and while her finger there felt foreign, the pleasure derived from the double penetration was incredible.

She pushed it inside slowly until it was all the way in. I let out a long breath.

"You like that, huh? When we have more time, we'll try it the other way around. I want to fuck that ass so badly. But we need time for that."

I simply moaned in agreement, too turned on by what she was doing to form words.

She pulled her finger out. She was now holding onto my ass with both hands, spreading it apart with her thumbs as she fucked me harder and faster.

"I love the way your ass jiggles when I'm pounding into it." She slapped me. "Fucking beautiful."

My muscles tightened every time she'd open his mouth. I'd always loved to be talked to during sex, but her dirty, gravelly voice was the sexiest I'd ever heard. Every single time she'd speak, my muscles would spasm.

"Tighten against my cock like that again."

I clenched around her.

"Goddamn, that feels good," she growled. "I want you to do that when I'm coming inside you."

I wanted her to spank me again. I never imagined the pressure of her hand would feel so good; but it did.

What was happening to me?

My voice was throaty when I said, "Slap my ass again."

And I shy.

God.

But she obliged, and when she struck me this time, the sting of her hand was perfect.

Everything about this experience was unlike anything I'd ever felt before from the skin to skin contact, to the forceful way she fucked me. She'd broken through a barrier of pleasure that I didn't know I was capable of feeling. I didn't know how I was going to live without this now that I knew what it was like.

I could feel her body trembling at my back. "I need to come. Tell me when you're close," she said into my ear.

I watched her face in the reflection and now, instead of looking down, she was looking straight at my face.

"I'm coming," I said as I tightened my muscles like she'd wanted.

"Wait. Oh God, Roseanne. That feels...oh shit...I'm coming," she groaned out then muttered low, "Yeah, baby. I'm coming. So good. So fucking good."

Warm cum filled me as I continued to squeeze around her cock. Lisa stayed inside of me, fucking me slowly long after she came, kissing my back softly.

"Shit. I don't know what that is that you do when you tense your pussy around me, but I'm going to be jerking off to it for the next four months."

"What was that we just did?" I asked facetiously. "That didn't feel like just sex. That was far too incredible."

"That was a decade's worth of frustration barreling out of me, baby."

"You're so good, Lisa. It was worth the wait."

She slowly pulled out of me and turned me around, planting a firm kiss on my lips. "We have forty minutes."

"What are we gonna do?"

"I need you again."

My eyes widened. "Can you go again so soon?"

"With you? I could go all night. No one's ever made me lose control like that. That's how it should feel every single damn time, like it's all that matters in the world. I couldn't give a shit if the world is crumbling around me when I'm inside of you."

We smiled at each other, and the streetlights from outside shined into her beautiful brown eyes. Forty minutes wasn't long enough. To squelch the dread creeping in, I took off her shirt and began to kiss her chest softly.

"This time is gonna be different, okay?" she said.

I simply nodded, anxiously awaiting her direction. She stripped out of her underwear, and I could see her dick was still gloriously hard, glistening with arousal.

"Lie down, Roseanne."

Admiring her chiseled body, I lay on the bed and backed up against the headboard.

When she turned on the small desk lamp, I asked, "What are you doing?"

"I want to look at you for a while. Is that okay?"

I nodded. "Y-yes."

"Spread your legs apart," she demanded.

Lisa kneeled at the foot of the bed as she took in the sight of me.

"So sexy...seeing you wide open like that with my cum dripping out of you. God Roseanne." she breathed out as she started to jerk herself off. She looked down at her engorged shaft. "I'm ready to go again. This is fucking crazy."

"We don't have a lot of time. I need you inside of me again."

"Touch yourself for a little bit."

I positioned my fingertips at my clit and began to circle them around. The room was so quiet except for the slick sound of her cock moving against her hand.

"Open wider, Roseanne."

Spreading my knees further apart, I had to curb the need to come.

"You ready?" she asked.

"Yes," I whispered.

This time when she sunk into me, it was slow and controlled. She stopped when she was fully inside and just stayed there without moving for a while.

"How the fuck am I going to be able to leave you after this?"

When she picked up the pace again, it felt better than ever, not only because of the pressure of her weight on top of me but because we were both fully naked, our skin rubbing together. The room was cold, but the heat of her body warmed me.

I held onto her ass, pushing her deeper into me as she circled her hips. Her breathing matched the rhythm of her movements. When my orgasm suddenly rolled through me, she must have been able to feel it, because she also came without warning, grunting loudly in my ear. There was no sweeter sound that the noises she made when she came.

She collapsed over me and said, "Thank you for giving this to me. It's the only thing that's gonna get me through the rest of this time away."

Looking at the time shown on my phone, I felt sick. We had ten minutes before we had to drive back to the bus. It was odd to feel sated and scared at the same time. She'd left my body completely satisfied, yet my heart was still yearning for more. It just wanted to hear those three words so desperately.

-

When we arrived to her bus, I gripped her black jacket, unable to let her go. After what we'd just done, my attachment to her was stronger than ever. It felt more impossible to let her go now than it ever had before.

"I want you to meet the crew before we leave."

Although I wasn't feeling very social, I said, "Okay."

Lisa brought me inside the bus. A bunch of guys were sitting around eating pieces of a gigantic apple pie that looked like it was from Costco. It smelled like a mixture of coffee and beer. Lisa went down the line, introducing me to each crew member. They were all super nice and down to earth. I didn't have a chance to meet Calvin Sprockett, since she was on the other bus.

A few minutes later, the one person I'd dreaded meeting the most finally made her appearance.

"Is everyone accounted for?" Jisoo asked, holding a walkie talkie.

Lisa looked at me and whispered, "That's Jisoo."

She didn't realize I'd already known what she looked like from my stalking. I was starting to feel nauseous, and it only got worse with each step she took toward us. With luxurious dark hair and a megawatt smile, she was even prettier than her pictures.

I fucking hated her.

"I see we have an extra passenger?"Jisoo said.

Seeming to lose my ability to speak, I smiled like a fool without saying anything.

"Jisoo, this is my girlfriend, Roseanne," Lisa said.

Girlfriend.

The fear inside of me began to slowly evaporate.

She hadn't said the "L" word, but she'd finally given me the validation that I so desperately needed, especially now with her leaving again.

Jisoo hadn't seemed too surprised. "It's nice to finally meet you, Roseanne."

"Likewise." I smiled.

"Are you coming with us to Philly?" she asked.

"No. I have a baby girl at home, so I'm not able to travel."

"That's right. Lisa showed me her picture."

It further calmed me to know that she'd also spoken to her about Bea.

"Well, it was nice meeting you," Jisoo said before giving Lisa a slight look of warning. "Buses are leaving in five."

Waiting for her to get out of earshot, I said, "So, that's Jisoo..."

"Yep."

"She sleeps on the other bus?"

"Yeah. The tour manager goes on the main bus." She smiled, examining my expression and seeming amused at my transparent relief.

She nudged at my dress, and my nipples immediately perked up. "Let's get you a jacket," Lisa said. "Then I'm gonna tell the driver to hold up while I accompany you to the car. I don't want you walking alone."

Lisa retrieved one of her black hoodies and held it open for me. I zipped it up, loving the smell of her cologne that saturated it. She led me by the hand across the VIP lot to the regular parking area.

Lisa gazed into my eyes as we stopped in front of my car. She held me tightly as she buried her nose in my hair. "You're lucky we don't have any more time. I'd take you right against this car."

"I'd let you."

"Thank you for tonight, Rosie. You were amazing. I'm gonna fucking miss you so much."

I spoke against her chest. "Can I ask you something?"

"Yeah..."

"When did you decide I was your girlfriend?"

She looked up at the sky and hesitated as if she had to really ponder it. Her answer wasn't what I was expecting. "The matinee show of El Amor Duele at the little red theater circa 2005. I wasn't even paying attention to the movie. You were really into it. I was really into you. You didn't realize I was staring at you the whole time. You were so enthralled with the movie that you didn't even notice that you'd finished your popcorn. You kept shoveling it into your mouth. Without your knowing, I replaced your empty bucket with my full one. You just kept eating. I decided at that moment that whether you knew it or not, you were my girlfriend. I kept telling myself...that after the show, I was finally gonna make you aware of that fact, too."

"What happened?"

She shrugged her shoulders. "I chickened out." We both laughed and could see our breaths colliding in the cold air. Lisa looked down at her phone. "Shit. They're texting me to hurry up. I have to go."

"Alright Lis."

She pulled me into her as tightly as she could and planted one final kiss on my lips. "I'm gonna miss you so much. Thank you again for coming." She wriggled her brows. "And for coming again. And for letting me come." As I giggled against her lips, she said, "You were so amazing."

"Call me tomorrow."

"Be careful driving home."

"Okay."

She lingered then said, "It's never been that way for me, never felt that way with anyone else."

Hearing that was great.

"Neither do I,"

Our fingers remained entwined until the force of her stepping away naturally tore them apart.

Over the parking lot, Lisa ran.

I got inside my car and started the heater. I continued to idle until the two buses departed and vanished from view.

Later that evening, while I was returning to the beach home, my phone rang with a text from Lisa.

Lisa: All that time I was furious with you. I may have been banging fucking you instead. What a dumbass.

And I just smiled stupidly there. Cheesy.

20. THE PANIC

The days leading up to the holidays were the most difficult ones without Lisa. Bea's first Christmas would be this year, and we would be celebrating it without her.

Lisa's journey has reached the West. She wouldn't have any time to slip away to go home because she would be playing two gigs in Los Angeles, one on Christmas Eve and one on Christmas Day. The band would only stay in the US for another week after those shows before departing for Europe, where the tour would continue until they came back to the US in the spring. Just imagining how much travelling she was doing exhausted me.

Lisa deserves some credit, though. She had kept her promise to skype with us every other day. Even though I eagerly anticipated our conversations, I found it more difficult to be apart from her. The new recollection of our time spent together in Massachusetts faded as the days passed. With every day that went by, the assurance that night had provided me was gradually being replaced by anxiety and insecurity once more. While I trusted her more after we'd made love, she still hadn't told me she loved me. In my mind, that meant that nothing was set in stone. That made for one paranoid girlfriend, especially when you consider the fact that she would be gone for more than a dozen further weeks.

Two days remained until Christmas. I received an invitation from Roger and Hailey to attend their ugly sweater party with Bea. Lisa had called earlier to say they'd just arrived in California. I was appreciative of the distraction the party would provide. It would keep me from pouting in front of the Christmas tree at the beach house, at least for a few of hours.

I had purchased a hideous red sweater with tiny Christmas lights sewed onto the front at a nearby thrift shop. Even better, I was able to find Bea an ugly Christmas sweater onesie online. Thus, we were all prepared for the celebration.

I wrapped Bea in a blanket and went across the street to the neighbours' house, which was decorated with colourful lights because it was bitterly cold outside. Out front, an inflatable snowman was being blown by the wind. It wasn't ideal to live by the lake in the dead of winter.

Since I didn't have any extra hands, I used my foot to knock on their door while carrying a few freshly baked sugar cookies.

Roger let the door open. "Roseanne, you made it! Hailey didn't have any idea that you would show up."

I gave him the platter of cookies and added, "I wouldn't miss it. Hailey is in the kitchen, right?"

"She is. The first person here is you."

"Figures." I smiled. "I commute the least distance."

Roger's words abruptly halted me as I turned to go see Hailey. "Hey, Roseanne."

"Yes?"

"We really haven't had an opportunity to communicate since Hailey came back. I've always felt a little weird about holding back on telling you about our reconciliation."

"You didn't have to explain anything to me. I've previously told her that nothing has changed between us."

"I'm sure you did. The friendship between you two makes me very happy. And I also want you to know that at the moment I really needed your friendship, I was sincerely appreciative of it."

"I'm very thrilled for you guys."

"Thank you." He paused. "What about you?"

"What about me?"

Roger tilted his head. "Are you happy?"

"I am. Just a little lonely with Lisa gone."

"You know, you used to tell me that there was nothing going on between the two of you..."

"At the time, there wasn't. I'd always had feelings for her, though."

"She's coming back, right? After the tour?"

"Yes."

"Is that what she wants to do with her life? Be a touring musician? Live on the road?"

"I'm not sure if that's how it's always going to be. She works in software sales, but that's not her dream. Music is her dream. This was a once in a lifetime opportunity, so she had to take it."

"Who's she on tour with again?"

"Calvin Sprockett."

"Wow. Yeah. That's pretty big stuff."

"It is."

After a bit of awkward silence, Roger asked, "Are any of those guys still married?"

"You mean Calvin and his band?"

"Yeah..."

I had to think about it. "Now that you mention it...I don't think they are."

Roger hung up my coat as he said, "I suppose marriage doesn't really mesh with sex, drugs and rock 'n roll. Not to mention constantly traveling. You know, things had never been harder for me than when I was physically away from Hailey and Alyssa. I don't know too much about Lisa, but it seems like she's very fond of Bea. If she wants to be a "father" to her, absenteeism really doesn't work.

I figured that out the hard way, and that was without the additional complication of fame."

"I don't think she's figured out whether she wants kids."

"Well, don't you think it's time she did, if she wants to be with you?" Roger must have sensed that he was stressing me out. "I'm sorry, Roseanne. I'm just looking out for you."

"I appreciate that. But I'm just looking for eggnog tonight, nothing more complicated than that, alright?"

Closing his eyes briefly in understanding, he chuckled and said, "You got it. Let me grab some for you."

Through the muffled laughter of their guests, who were dressed in a rainbow of ugly sweaters, my thoughts kept me distracted. Even though my conversation with Roger had long ended, I'd spent the remainder of the party pondering everything he'd said.

It was nothing I didn't already worry about, but hearing the concern come from someone else-someone who understood the long-term responsibilities of fatherhood-was eye-opening.

--//--

Back at the house later that night, I rocked Bea to sleep in front of the tree to the sounds of a children's choir CD of Christmas carols. Earlier in the week, I'd wrapped some presents and placed them under the tree. They were all for Bea and included a small box that Lisa had shipped to her to be opened on Christmas morning.

I didn't need anything this year; Bea was my Christmas gift. She was the greatest gift from God and had taught me more about unconditional love than anyone or anything else ever had. She'd given me a purpose. I kissed her head softly, vowing to always be there for her no matter what happened with Lisa. I vowed to be the type of mother that I never had.

Still in my Christmas sweater, I placed a sleeping Bea in her crib, taking a moment to look around and admire Lisa's handiwork in the nursery.

Back in my room, I couldn't sleep. I'd just nodded off when my phone chimed, waking me up.

Lisa : Hey, you asleep?

Rosé: Wide awake now.

Lisa: Will you call me? I don't know if Bea is near you and don't want to wake her.

She picked up on the first ring after I dialed her.

"Hey, beautiful."

"Hi."

Lisa's voice sounded sleepy. "I woke you, didn't I?"

"Yes, but it's okay. I'd rather speak to you than sleep. Where are you?"

"I'm at the hotel in Los Angeles. We're off the buses till Christmas night."

"That must be a nice change, getting to sleep in a real bed."

"It only reminds me that you're not here with me."

"I wish I were."

"It's really bugging me that I can't be with you guys for Christmas."

"I don't understand why they don't give you Christmas off."

"Calvin's always done Christmas shows. It's sort of his tradition. It sucks. You'd think none of these people have families. I feel bad for the crew members with kids."

"It doesn't really ever end, does it?"

Lisa sounded confused by my comment. "What in particular?"

"I mean, this tour will end. But the life of a musician never really does."

"It's not like I won't have a choice in the matter. I don't have to go anywhere or do anything I don't want to."

"Yes, but after this tour, so many more people will know who you are. The opportunities will start coming, and fame will be addicting. That was the point of all this, right? To grow your music career? Are you really going back to your software job, like none of this ever happened? What exactly is going to happen?"

"I don't know. I haven't thought that far. I just want to come home to you first. That's all I want. I won't be going away again anytime soon after that."

"But you might be going away again at some point. This isn't just a one-time thing, right? It never really ends."

"Why all of the worrying all of a sudden, Roseanne?"

"I don't know. I guess I have too much time alone to think."

"I'm sorry. But the truth is, I just don't have all the answers tonight. I can only tell you what I'm feeling right now, and that's that I don't want to be here and would give anything to be home for Christmas with you and Bea."

Rubbing my tired eyes, I said, "Alright. I'm sorry. It's late, and you must be tired."

"Don't ever be sorry for talking to me about how you feel. Remember, you promised to be honest with me if something is bothering you."

"I know."

Just when my nerves had started to calm down, it sounded like there was a knock at her door.

"Hang on," she said.

My heartbeat started to accelerate when I heard a woman's voice in the background.

I couldn't make out what she was saying but could hear Lisa say, "No, thanks. I appreciate it, but no." She paused. "Alright. Good night." I could hear the door click shut.

She returned to the phone. "Sorry."

"Who was that?"

"Someone wanted to know if I was interested in a massage."

"Massage?"

"Yes. Calvin sometimes hires people to give massages. He must have sent someone up here to ask if I wanted one."

The eggnog from earlier was starting to come up on me. "So it was just a random girl coming into your room to give you a massage?"

"Rosie...I didn't ask for one, nor did I want one. I sent her away. I can't help it if someone knocks on my door."

"Have you ever had one?"

Her tone was angry. "No!"

"I can't handle this."

"I get why a strange woman coming to my hotel room door would piss you off, alright? But you either trust me, or you don't. Trust is a black or white issue. There is no such thing as trusting someone a little. It's either there, or it isn't. Fuck. I thought you trusted me."

"I do! I never said I didn't trust you. It's just...that lifestyle makes me uncomfortable. And I'm lonely. I don't know if this is the kind of life I want."

"What exactly are you saying?"

"I don't know." I said, my voice barely audible.

There was a long moment of silence as I listened to her breathing. Then, she finally spoke, "I can't even see the faces of the people in the audience.

When I'm singing, I'm singing to you, counting down the days till I come home. Wouldn't that just be a fucking hoot if there was nothing left to come home to."

Why haven't you told me you loved me?

I'd really pissed her off. I needed to end the call before I said something further that I'd regret.

"You have two big shows coming up. You can't afford to get all stressed out. I'm sorry for causing a fight."

"I'm sorry, too."

"I'm gonna try to get some sleep."

"Alright," she said.

"Good night."

"Good night."

After we hung up, I had a hard time falling back to sleep. Ending the call on bad terms made me feel like shit. I thought I couldn't feel any worse.

The events of the following morning would make the previous night's argument seem vastly insignificant.

Call it mother's intuition.

Something woke me up, even though it was quiet. The clock showed nearly 4AM.

A few minutes later, I was trying to get back to sleep when I heard what I thought was light wheezing coming over the baby monitor.

I got out of bed so quickly out of panic that I felt dizzy. I nearly tripped over my own feet as I ran down the hallway to Bea's room. It felt like my heart was in my mouth.

They were the longest, scariest minutes of my life even yet it all seemed to be occurring so quickly. Bea was gasping for air and her tiny eyes were desperately staring up at me. Though she tried to cough, she was choking.

I struggled to recall the procedures from the baby CPR course I had taken in Providence as my thoughts raced.

I supported her head by turning her face over my forearm while holding her jaw with one hand. Five times between her shoulder blades, I whacked her on the back. Nothing came out as she continued to have trouble breathing.

I quickly thrust two fingers down in the centre of her chest while she was facing up. Still, the thing wouldn't move. She and I hurried to my room, where I grabbed my phone and called 911. Since Bea stopped responding, I was having trouble breathing myself, so I couldn't even recall what I'd said to the operator.

As the dispatcher directed me, I alternated between chest compressions and back blows. The object finally flew out of her mouth, and I realized it was one of the small bulbs from my sweater. It must have fallen into her crib.

Bea had passed out during the bulb's removal.

The next thing I knew, sirens were blaring. I ran downstairs with her to let them in. Men stormed the room. They began performing CPR on my baby girl.

I watched helplessly, frozen by fear, as my entire existence hung in the balance. It was the same as if I had been unconscious.

It felt as though I had awoken from the grave when one of the EMTs pointed out that she was breathing again. As they placed her on a stretcher and told me to board the ambulance, tears flowing down my face prevented me from seeing clearly. Because she'd been unconscious for so long, she needed to be taken to the hospital for treatment and to ensure that there wasn't any brain damage or internal injuries.

I sat next to her in the ambulance while one of the men held an oxygen mask over her face while I was still wearing my sleep sweatpants and having no coat.

I typed out a string of choppy texts to Lisa because I was too shaken to speak.

Bea is alive.

Choked on a tiny decoration.

Got it out.

EMTs performed CPR.

In ambulance heading to hospital.

I'm frightened.

Within seconds, my phone rang. In Los Angeles, it had to be one thirty in the morning.

Lisa's voice trembled. "Rosie? I got your message. Oh God. I-Is she alright?"

"I don't know. She's conscious and breathing. I just don't know if there was any other damage."

"Can you see her? Is she with you?"

"Yes. She's got an oxygen mask over her face, but her eyes are open. I think she's scared."

I heard rustling then she said, "I'm getting on the next flight out there."

Still in shock, I was silent.

Her voice seemed to be fading into the distance. "Rosie? Are you there? Hang in there, baby. She's going to be okay. She will."

"Okay," I whispered through my tears.

"Where are they taking her?"

"Hasbro Children's Hospital in Providence."

"Call me as soon as you know anything."

"Alright."

"Be strong, sweetheart. Please."

21. The Relief

The first few hours of waiting with Bea in the intensive care unit were agonising and genuinely the most terrifying of my life.

They had her hooked up to an IV and were giving her oxygen. In order to rule out internal traumas and neurological issues, the doctors performed a number of tests. Apparently, after respiratory failure, there could actually be delayed brain injury that wasn't apparent right away. It would be a while before all of the results came in.

With no clear prognosis, my silent prayers were non-stop. I begged God to spare my baby from any serious harm. It was challenging to determine Bea's true condition because she was sleeping a lot and undoubtedly felt fatigued from the ordeal.

I had to be thankful for both the fact that she was able to open her eyes and the fact that she was still alive and breathing. Thank God I woke up at that time on a whim. The situation may have turned out very differently if I had arrived in her room even a minute later. I was unable to bear to think about it at all. There was clearly someone keeping an eye on us last night. I had to keep praying and concentrating on the fact that she was still alive until I had answers.

I was still standing by Bea's side at this point in the morning. I was afraid to even go to the bathroom so as not to miss the doctor coming in with information. Finally, a nice nurse made me go get something to drink and use the restroom. She assured me that nothing would occur while I was away and promised to watch Bea.I started crying as I entered the restroom next to the nurse's station.

Finally losing it, I was overwhelmed with guilt. None of this would have occurred if not for that foolish shirt and my carelessness. How could I have left her crib unchecked before putting her to sleep? I forced myself to gather myself and put up a brave face before going back to my daughter. She was perceptive, and I couldn't let my worry show.

Shortly after I settled in at Bea's bedside, the doctor entered.

"Roseanne..."

I got to my feet while feeling the weight of my anxious, heavy heart. "Yes?"

"We got to know the results of the examinations done on the woman's inside health. Apart from a minor rib fracture that will mend on its own, there are no internal wounds. Her neurological evaluation also appears to be good, but I want to keep an eye on it the following day before we think about releasing her. We're planning to transfer her to a regular room on one of the main floors since I no longer believe she needs to be in the intensive care unit.

I had a tremendous wave of relief. "Doctor, thank you. Thank you. I could hug you. Can I hug you?" I hugged him when he nervously nodded. I truly appreciate it.

"It might have been quite serious. All too frequently, this exact same incident has a different ending. choking on grapes, hot dogs, or small toys by babies or toddlers. You're very lucky."

I texted Lisa once the doctor was out of the room.

"I thank God! She will be well, according to the doctor. But they want to keep an eye on her for at least the next 24 hours. I'm so happy right now!"

There was no response.

We were soon transferred to a new room on the third level. Bea was lying in her new bed, her eyes open, and she looked puzzled as she peered up at the ceiling's panels of fluorescent lighting. She didn't seem as cheerful as usual, but she did seem alert. She was undoubtedly baffled as to why she was even in this place.

I was instructed that I could hold her one more. They advised me to feed her even though she had been receiving vitamins and fluids through an IV. She had just received more formula than breastmilk, but I still decided to nurse her since I thought it would make her feel better. I was relieved that she was eating with no problem.

Every minute that went by gave me more assurance that my baby would be alright.

She had to be.

Bea's vital signs were checked by Shelly, the nurse, after I put her back in her bed. I was practically blind to him standing there since I was so preoccupied with everything Shelly was doing.

Lisa was in the doorway, her chest rising and falling as she took in the sight of Bea lying in the hospital bed. I hadn't heard from her in a while and wasn't sure if she had been able to catch a flight, even though she had indicated she was boarding a flight. Her eyes were red, and her hair was a mess. She appeared practically strung out and ragged, but she was still wonderfully attractive.

My heart jumped. "Lisa."

She remained silent and kept her gaze fixed on Bea as she slowly made her way nearer the bed. She appeared as though she was in disbelief when she saw Bea lying there, looking so frail. "Is she okay?"

"We think so, yes. You didn't get my texts?"She shook her head while keeping her gaze fixed on Bea.

"No, my phone died while I was in the flight. I arrived right here after boarding the earliest available flight from LAX."

Shelly gave her a glance. "Are you her...?"

"Yes, I'm Bea's parents too." Lisa added as she extended her hand to massage Bea's cheek. Her response surprised me. Chills ran through me when she looked at me and repeated, "Yes, I am."

Her red eyes glistened with emotion as she returned her sight to Bea. I had never seen Lisa cry in the entire time I had known her. On the seat opposite Bea, she took a seat.

When Shelly saw Lisa crying, she responded, "I'll give you some privacy."

Lisa dipped her face into the bed and gave Bea a quick kiss on the cheek as the door shut behind her. I waited for her to speak although I was still equally as shocked and moved by her telling me that she was her parents. The words did not come right away. She simply stared at Bea, the initial shock slowly giving way to admiration and relief. I knew she noticed that Bea wasn't her normal self. It was hard not to see it. Bea would have been smiling or giggling at her by now. Instead, she was merely awake but quiet. I hoped it was just because she hadn't seen Lisa in a while and not a sign of something more serious.

"I love you, Bumblebee. I'm sorry it's taken me this long to tell you." Lisa wiped her eyes then turned to me.

"I've never been more scared in my life, Roseanne. I was afraid something would happen to her before I could get here, that I'd never see her smile again, that I'd never have a chance to tell her how much I want to be her father. The whole flight here, I prayed to God, bargained with him, that if she turned out to be okay, I wouldn't let another second go by without telling her I loved her. The thing is...even without my saying it...she already thinks I'm her Daddy. I know I'm not her biological parents, but she doesn't know that. Blood doesn't make someone a parents anyway. What makes me her parents is that she chose me. She owned me from the moment she first smiled at me. And while that used to scare the shit out of me, I couldn't imagine life without her now."

"I thought you didn't want kids."

"So did I. Maybe I didn't want some generic imagined kids. But I want her." She repeated in a whisper, "I want her."

Now, I was crying, too. "She loves you, too, you know. Very much."

"I'm the only father she's ever known now. And she thinks I left without explanation. That kills me every day."

"What's happening with the tour?"

"Well, they're without an opening act now for the Christmas shows in L.A., but Calvin understands my situation. They're gonna wing it. They all know how much Bea means to me. They said they would make due for the next few shows if need be. I'm not going back until I'm sure she's okay and home."

Our attention turned to Bea when she suddenly started to babble.

Lisa teased, "Hey, you have something to say for yourself?" She smiled at her for a bit before turning to me. "Is it okay to hold her, or is it better not to?"

"They told me I could take her out. It's okay. Just don't toss her up into the air or anything."

Lisa slowly lifted her out of the bed and cradled her in Lisa's arms. "You scared the crap out of me, Miss Bee. You sure this wasn't a ploy to get me home for Christmas? If so, job well-done."

It had completely skipped my mind that tonight was Christmas Eve; we'd be spending her first Christmas in the hospital.

Tilting my head, I admired the two of them together. I'd always felt their connection but worried that Lisa would never truly give into it. I felt so happy for Bea, that this wonderful guy wanted to be her father. I knew no matter what happened between Lisa and me, she would always be there for her.

When Bea fell asleep in his arms, I told Lisa the full story of what happened as best I could remember it.

Bea was still asleep when he returned her to the bed and asked, "When was the last time you ate, Roseanne?"

"Sometime yesterday."

"I'm gonna go get us some food and coffee while she's sleeping."

"That would be great."

With Lisa gone and Bea asleep, my tired mind went into overdrive. It was getting dark outside the hospital windows. Left alone with too much time to think, I started to push guilt on myself for allowing this to happen. I had one job, and that was to take care of my daughter and keep her safe; I couldn't even do that.

When Lisa returned, she was carrying a paper bag of food and a small Christmas tree that probably came from a pharmacy.

I must have looked like a wreck because she dropped everything and came over to me. "What's wrong?"

"This is my fault. I should have checked her crib before I left the room."

"It was an accident. That damn bulb fell off your sweater. You didn't see it happen."

"I know, but I can't help feeling like if I'd just done something differently..."

"What are you talking about? You saved her life."

"Yes. But only because I was lucky enough to wake up when I did. I can't even imagine what today would be like if I hadn't."

"Don't think about that. God was with her. She's okay. She'll be okay. It wasn't your fault."

"I just can't help feeling like a horrible mother."

"Listen to me. Remember that night we stayed up the whole night talking at the beach house that first summer? You told me you felt like teaching wasn't what you were meant to do, that there was something else out there you'd be better at?"

"Yes."

"I'll never forget coming home unexpectedly this past summer to find you and Bea there. You were disorganised and in that screwed-up state. I had never seen somebody give of themselves so completely for the sake of another person. There is never a time during the day when you don't prioritise her. You don't consider taking a break for yourself, your own mental health. Sometimes I'd watch you feed her and wish I'd had a mother like you-but not to get a taste of your tits." She smiled then continued, "But because of your maternal nature. I always thought you were pretty amazing when we were kids, but that's nothing compared to how I see you now. So don't you dare, Park Roseanne. You have no right to refer to yourself as a terrible mother. What was that thing you were supposed to do but couldn't figure out? It was to take care of that tiny girl as a mother. Your calling is that. And you're working really hard."

I was so appreciative of her assurance, which essentially talked me down from a mental cliff, that I closed my eyes and took a big breath. "I'm grateful,"

She approached the bags and handed me a Chipotle burrito bowl and a Dunkin Donuts iced coffee. Eat right away so she doesn't wake up.

After we had done eating, Lisa plugged the tiny tree into a wall socket in the room's corner. After we had done eating, Lisa plugged the tiny tree into a wall socket in the room's corner. Under the circumstances, this was the best Christmas Eve was going to get.

We experienced a small Christmas miracle when Bea finally awoke. Lisa was looking down at Bea when she finally smiled for the first time since the choking incident. The greatest gift imaginable was given to us.

"Merry Christmas, Bumblebee," Lisa said. The air was filled with a sense of relaxation. Even though it was only one of many smiles, it was nevertheless significant. It indicated to us that she would be alright.

Lisa opened Pandora on her phone and listened to holiday music until it was time to go to bed. We positioned a cot on either side of Bea's bed using two that the hospital brought in.

It was after midnight. After her excursion, Lisa was worn out and fell asleep next Bea. I was still unable to unwind sufficiently to close my eyes. Until we got back home, I wouldn't be content.

Both of them fell asleep, so I fooled about on my phone for a while, reading back through the text thread with Lisa to check exactly what I had texted her from the ambulance. Because I was under so much pressure, I am not sure what I penned during those terrible times. That's when I realised she had sent me a text earlier in the evening, but I had missed it because of everything that had happened with Bea.

Lisa : I don't like fighting with you. I love you. In case there was any doubt.

The message was sent just before 4 AM. I had first woken up at that very moment just before Bea began to wheeze. I had assumed that my sudden awakening was a random occurrence, but the SMS must have been what jolted me out of sleep.

My heart felt like it was going to burst out of my chest as I turned to see Lisa sleeping soundly across from me. Not because she said the three words

I had been waiting to hear from her. I wouldn't have woken up had it not been for that text.

I didn't save Bea's life.

Lisa did.

22. THE BEGINNING

Christmas Day.

After the doctors had ruled out any brain injury, we were happy to bring her home. A really white Christmas had even begun to fall while travelling from Providence to Newport.

Lisa would spend a couple of days with us before joining the tour in London to begin the European leg. This was stolen time, therefore I wouldn't allow myself to be upset about her leaving just yet.

We gathered with Bea around the tree on Christmas Eve and assisted her in opening her gifts. I waited till last to open the tiny box Lisa had previously mailed. When we arrived there, Lisa watched me rip open the tape and took off the copious amount of bubble wrap as I did so nervously.

A little wooden guitar was within, and it was positioned vertically atop a cylindrical base. Additionally, the bottom opened and could be used to store tiny items. An intricately painted black and yellow bumblebee was perched on the instrument. It was created to appear as though the bee had just touched down on the instrument. I gave it to Lisa, who wound the bottom. A song that I wasn't familiar with started to gently revolve around the guitar.

She said, "I have a friend name Justin Henderson, who makes custom music boxes back in New York. I requested Justin to create one for her, our Bea. The bee stands for the fact that she is constantly by my side, wherever I am."

I was so deeply moved that I paid close attention to the song, but even after many seconds of listening, I couldn't recognize it. "Which song is that? It's amazing."

"I'm writing something, and this is the melody. It might be programmed into the box by Justin. The lyrics, though, are still something I'm working on."

"That is freaking fantastic. You could not have gotten her a more considerate present than this and you got some cool friends. Seems like everyone loves you."

"It's merely something to help me feel as though I'm with her even when I'm not, and yeah I'm thankful for them." Bea watched the guitar spin hypnotically as Lisa stared down at Bea. "What do you get for someone you can never repay...for all she's taught you, all she's given you?" Lisa regarded for a while before asking.

"I believe it's a fairly great gift that you're taking on the role of becoming her other parents," I said.

Lisa gave Bea a head kiss. "I own that gift completely."

I grinned at them both and posed a query I'd been considering ever since she returned home. "What changed?"

"What are you saying?" She looked confused.

"Before you left, it seemed as though you were still unclear of your future involvement in her life. What changed?"

She briefly fixed her gaze on the music box before turning to face me. "I never questioned her, only if I was deserving of her love. I didn't want to let down someone who meant a great deal to me. But being apart from her made me feel...that she had already blended with me. Despite my fears of being inadequate, she was already my daughter in all relevant respects. I was able to observe that much more clearly after moving away."

I had earlier told Lisa about my realisation regarding the timing of her text. She insisted that I should get all the credit for saving Bea's life and she would not accept responsibility for doing so. I had avoided talking about the main point of her text until now.

I put my head against her shoulder, feeling absolutely thrilled to have her here with us, even for a little time. "I love you, Lisa. You see, I had become fixated on the fact that you hadn't yet addressed me with those three words. Hearing you tell me you loved me meant so lot to me. It didn't surprise me when you eventually did-in that text-because I knew it in my heart. I've learned from you that words don't describe love. It's a series of actions. You've proven your love for me by the way you treat me, the way you view me, and most importantly, by how much you love my daughter as your own."

"I love you both so much," she said as she kissed me on my forehead. "That evening, I came to the absurd conclusion that I should have said those words. However, the reality is that I hadn't exactly recently fallen in love with you, so telling my friends about it almost felt forced. It is a situation that this feeling has existed for a long time. I've always loved you. I may have tried to hate you at times, but even then, my love for you never wavered."

"Even I never stopped loving you. I made a mistake by assuming that because you didn't express your love for me, you didn't."

She moved her eyebrows. "You know of the adage, never assume anything...."

"Yeah like you. Never assume a woman like you likely end up seeing anal in a porno theatre?" I laughed.

"Good girl, That is correct." She chuckled.

Since Bea's ordeal started, I have not slept, and I was rapidly running out of patience. We three went to bed early for the night. I simply wasn't prepared to put Bea back to sleep alone in the crib tonight. She slept between Lisa and I-her parents. I think I could adjust to that.

The day after Christmas was our last day with her. Then Lisa would depart from us once more by flying from New York to London.

Being awakened by the aroma of Lisa's coffee fusion brewing in the kitchen was like waking up from a dream.

Bea was still sleeping when I went downstairs and snuck up behind her, looping my arms underneath her. My nightgown allowed my braless chest to rub into her wide back. We both looked out at the arctic waves crashing on the icy sea. Summer was already making me long for it, not just for the warm weather, but also because Lisa would be staying with us by then.

She turned around and gave me a hungry kiss on the mouth. My anxiety regarding Bea had subsided by this point, and my desire for sex was gradually returning to normal. Lisa's hair was sticking up in all directions, and her coffee-coated sweet smell covered me from full body.

She gave my face a nice sniff, and I felt wetness between my legs. I inhaled deeply, loving the smell of her combined with the aroma of the steaming coffee, and pressed my body onto her erection.

That was saying something because I wanted her more than I wanted my morning coffee. It would be difficult to get through the coming months without her, but at least I now understood where we stood. She pulled back from kissing me and stroked my face as if she had something on her mind.

She said, "I have a few questions for you."

"Okay..."

"I was thinking that... I would love for you and Bea to attend the final performance in the spring. It won't be too far for you to travel as it will be in New York. If you don't want to drive, I can arrange for a flight for you. Then, we can all ride home in my car together. Before it's finished, it would be good if you could at least catch me performing on the main stage. How do you feel? If it's too noisy, we could get noise-cancelling headphones for her."

"I wouldn't trade it for anything. I've been considering how I ought to at least catch one of your tour dates. New York is a perfect place."

"Good. I'll do all the preparations."

"Okay and what is the other question?"

"Before she wakes up, what are the chances that I could fuck you raw on that counter?"

I was hesitant. I desperately desired her, but my cycle had just started this morning. On the day of my cycle when I was the heavy, I was never at ease doing the act.

"I want that so badly right now, but..."

A look of disappointment crossed her face. "What?"

"I stabbed myself...pretty heavily." Smiled and bitting my bottom lip because I felt bad.

She rolled her eyes shut in frustration and muttered, "Shit. I really need you right now." Before turning to face me, she first glanced me up and down. "If you don't mind, I don't mind too. I'm going to stab you so hard that you won't even notice the second wound."

I simply couldn't, despite my best efforts.

I tugged on the edge of her jeans to get a better look at the incredibly solid erection hidden inside. "I've got a better idea."

"Oh, yeah?"

I knelt down and began to slowly untie the string on her navy pyjamas.

The only resistance Lisa offered was a sly chuckle as she remarked, "Or... we could do this," as she leaned her elbows back against the counter. "Fuck. Yeah."

I added, "I've always wanted to go down on you." Admiring the sharp V of her lower abdomen and the small line of hair that ran down the centre. "Remember when we left the porno theatre? Although I was unable to have you at the time, I daydreamed about sucking you off the entire night."

Her touch was on my hair. "That night is one I'll never forget. Watching you become hot during the movie was so unbearably hot. Nothing would have made me happier than to haul you up on top of me and fuck that adorable pink pussy there in the tiny red theatre. That night, I wanted you so much it hurt to think about it. As much as I want you right now."

When I removed her cock, her breathing became laboured. I gave it a wide opening and my lips were around it. She uttered a heated, throaty sound, and when my tongue began to circle about her crown, she was already wet.

She gasped, "Holy fuck! That's great oh god. Nothing like it, Roseanne, your lips on my cock. This feels like a dream."

As I licked and ran my palm along her shaft, she tasted warm and salty. She grabbed the back of my hair to control the bob of my mouth over her cock.

I eventually started inhaling her as deeply as I could without suffocating. I sneaked a glimpse up at her reaction as she murmured, "Oh, you evil bitch," as I purposefully tightened the back of my throat around her cock. "That is so freaking good." I kept performing the same motion. Her eyes were clenched so firmly that she appeared to have entered another realm in her imagination.

As she abruptly bucked her hips and came down hard on my throat, my own groans reverberated over her cock. She tugged at my hair and moaned,

"Shit. Take it all, baby." I gulped down the hot bursts of cum that were flying down my throat, saying "Take it all."

As I sucked in every last drop, I cast a sultry glance up at her.

When all that was left was her panting, she exclaimed, "Fuck. You didn't hold back. I've always known you loved your coffee with cream, but damn. It was sweltering to see how much you took pleasure in it." She adjusted her pants as she exhaled deeply. "I already want to do it again. Is this some sort of ruse to keep me here? Because it just might fucking work."

"Really? If that's the case, my mouth is ready."

"Oh sweetheart, before I leave, we'll surely do that again. That was truly astounding. Where the hell did you learn to suck like that" She quickly shook her head. "Never mind. I don't really want to know anyway." She exclaimed, "What the hell did I do to deserve that anyway?" as she wiped the corners of my lips.

"You saved my daughter's life. So, you deserve to get the biggest blow job of your life." I smiled.

She pressed up against me. "Run to the beach right away, and jump in the water."

I narrowed my vision. "Why?"

"I can save you that way. Perhaps you'll let me to blow that ass later."

That afternoon, Lisa tried for an unprecedented amount of time to get Bea to say "Mommy."

She generally spoke incoherently. She was also capable of saying "Bye bye."

I saw the two of them as Lisa set Bea down on the couch and asked her to repeat what she had said as I stood in the kitchen.

"Mom-my."

She blew a raspberry and giggled.

"You silly girl. Say Mom-my."

Bea paused for a bit then said, "Ma-ma," before cracking up. Lisa tickled her belly with her nose, and she fell into a laughing fit.

Wiping the kitchen counter, I was in stitches watching all of this go down. Either I was raising a Mama's girl, or she was one hell of a little comedian.

23. THE redamancy

The three months after Christmas were tedious.

Around the time she turned one on March 15th, Bea began to walk. Lisa was furious that she had missed to celebrate her first steps as well as her birthday. Throughout our Skype conversations, she kept trying in vain to persuade her to say Mom or Mommy.

Those were difficult weeks, but I was able to get through them by knowing for sure that she would return to us. Getting to finally see her in concert at the end of it all was the cherry on top.

Finally, the group had returned to this side of the water. The last performances took place in New York City, Maine, and Nova Scotia.

Finally, the long-awaited Manhattan show's opening weekend had arrived. Lisa had bought tickets for Bea and I to take a flight to New York. Then we would head straight to a hotel close to the music location. We wouldn't get to see Lisa until after her concert that night because the band's return trip from Maine on Saturday afternoon would cut it close to show time.

On the little commuter flight from Providence to La Guardia, Bea was excellent. I had brought a polka-dot umbrella stroller and just one small carry-on for the two of us.

Steve, Lisa's manager, was kind enough to meet us up at the airport when we landed and take us to the hotel. We had to pass through Times Square.

Bea was in astonishment as she observed the bright colours flashing and activity around her. Undoubtedly, it was sensory overload for both of us. For so long, I had been confined to my home on the island that I had almost forgotten what city life was like.

The hotel was only a few steps away from the event space. The three of us would stay here for the night following the performance and stay in the city tomorrow before returning to the island.

I started to feel uneasy after we were checked into our hotel room. I was always so moved when I saw Lisa perform, but to see her on a big stage for the first time would be incredibly moving.

Bea would be up way past her bedtime tonight, so I sat down next to her in the plush hotel bed and tried to convince her to take a nap. Before we packed up and went to the venue, she was able to sleep for an hour.

The wait to enter the concert hall was a mile long when we got there. I got shivers as I stared at the illuminated sign that read,

"Calvin Sprockett, featuring Lalisa Manoban."

I'm so proud—more than I could describe it.

We were able to bypass the regular line and enter the VIP area. An usher then led the way to our seats, which were in the middle of the third row.

Bea looked so damn cute as she sat on my lap as she wore enormous noise-canceling headphones. In them, she appeared to be a little martian. She had thankfully been a well-behaved baby despite the weeping she had done during the first three months of her existence, so I figured she would be able to sit through the entire concert without messing up.

My heart beat fastly when the lights went down and the spotlight descended on her. The clatter of enthusiasm was all-consuming. Even though Lisa had claimed that it was always too dark for her to see faces, I caught a glimpse of her for a brief time just before the first song started. I almost melted into my seat from the force of her amplified voice, bowing low.

It was always so thrilling to hear her rich, soulful voice on the very first note.

I held Bea firmly and listened to her sing song after song that I had never heard before while we rocked back and forth. I was unaware that she didn't play any covers on this tour; she solely sang original songs. I felt as though I had missed so much by not having heard the majority of these tunes. I'd occasionally close my eyes and appreciate the sound waves that her guitar strings sent through me as I processed all of the lyrics.

For the first forty minutes, I just sat there in awe of her; the way she could captivate large crowds using nothing more than her lovely voice, a guitar, and a microphone hence her ability to play the instrument with lightning-quick precision and to alter her voice according to the music.

I knew we were getting close to the conclusion because Lisa had told that this opening performance was only approximately 45 minutes long.

She said over the microphone, "Tonight is special for multiple reasons, not just because this marks the end of our tour, but also because we're here in my second favourite town in the world, New York. This was my home up until recently. My new home is on an island with the love of my life and my daughter. I've been away from them for a while, but after tonight, I get to go home. But my daughter's presence is the main factor making tonight special. Bea, I appreciate you teaching me that sometimes what our souls most desire is also what we fear the most. This last song is one I finally finished. Because I wrote it for her because it was so meaningful to me, it took me a while. It goes by the name "Bea-u-tiful Girl."

The opening tune of the song that was pre-programmed within the music box she had created was immediately recognisable to me.

She then began to sing, at which point I was a goner.

Her lyrics went:

Bea-u-tiful Girl,

Thank you for helping me see,The way life was meant to be.With every one of your cries,

A part of my heart dies.But you'll smile at me and then,Put it back together again.

Bea-u-tiful Girl,I didn't make you, but you were made for me.

Bea-u-tiful Girl,Thank you for helping me see,The way life was meant to be.

An angel in disguise,Is reflected in the eyes,Of a little Bumblebee.Thank you for choosing me.

Bea-u-tiful Girl,I didn't make you, but you were made for me.

Bea-u-tiful Girl,Thank you for helping me see,The way life was meant to be.

There was a standing ovation for Lisa when the song was over. Tears of happiness were hurting my eyes. She impacted me on so many levels when she wrote that song for Bea. I wished so much that my darling Bea, could understand the words.

As they briefly shut down the stage to prepare for Calvin, Lisa vanished from view. I was meant to have access to backstage with my badge, but we hadn't talked about the technicalities. I debated whether to try to return there right once, wait for a text from her, or even watch part of Calvin's performance.

I got Bea and myself out of the seat and walked down the length of the centre aisle to the door, eager to see her and tell her how much I loved the song. We were taken to the backstage entrance by an usher. There was a big security guard waiting for me.

"Is there a badge on you?"

I flashed it and replied, "Yes. This is Lalisa Manoban's daughter, and I'm her girlfriend."

She gave the badge another long look before stepping aside and pointing behind her. "In this direction. She can be found in dressing room 4."

I was astonished to see Lisa wasn't there by herself when the door was just partially open. I instantly stepped to the side, listening to their chat without being observed.

"I hope it's okay for me to come here," she said. "I just had to see you when I heard you were playing in town. I contacted Steve, and he gave me a backstage pass."

"Of course, I have no problem. It's great to see you again, Winter."

It wasn't like it used to be, despite the fact that a little jealousy had crept in. My assurance that she felt the same way about me suddenly overcame my uneasiness. Nevertheless, considering all of my memories of Lisa and Winter together, it was always going to be hard for me to think about them.

"Lisa, I just need to talk to you. To be quite honest..., I'm startled when Steve informs me that you are now dating Rosie. And after that, the song you sung"

"I apologise, Win. I ought to have been the one to break the news to you. Since I had already hurt you, I didn't want to do it again."

"So, apparently...you did want children, but just not....mine?"

"I didn't expect to fall in love with that baby girl."

"But you did see falling in love with her mother coming a mile away. You seemed to hate her when we were living together. It certainly wasn't hate, was it? I should've been aware. Except for those who care excessively, no one behaves that way toward others."

"I kept it inside, so there was no way you could have known. It was challenging back then. In the beginning, I struggled with my feelings for her. I genuinely did. I wanted our relationship to be successful. I didn't think I'd end up with Roseanne. However, the hatred I felt for her came from other deeply ingrained emotions that I was unable to suppress. It was quite challenging." Lisa explained.

After a brief awkward pause, she asked, "Were you with her at any point when we were together?"

"No. Nothing happened till after we broke up. I didn't mean to hurt you, but it seems like I did nonetheless. I'm terribly sorry for that. You're a beautiful person, inside and out. I shall always remember our time together with pleasure. I wish you luck in finding someone deserving of you."

I made the decision to leave so they could conclude their conversation in peace after hearing Winter start to cry. Since I was the last person she probably wanted to see when she emerged from her dressing room, my heart truly broke for her.

I went back to the lobby and texted Lisa to tell her to let us know when to come backstage. I got Bea's stroller while we waited because they had generously been holding it for me behind the ticket counter. I watched Winter go across the foyer and through the rotating doors from my vantage point in the corner.

My phone rang shortly after that and it was Lisa texting.

Lisa : Backstage, please.

She first didn't pay attention to us. She had her back to us. I paused to gaze at her round, chiselled behind. Lisa turned around when Bea shouted with delight.

I got her out of the stroller and held onto her hands as she staggered toward Lisa on shaky legs.

Lisa welcomed her with wide arms as she crouched down. "Oh My Bumblebee! You're walking, holy God!" When she saw Bea wearing her noise-canceling headphones, she appeared amused. I had forgotten to remove them. "Those objects are larger than you are." She planted a messy kiss on her cheek before standing up to kiss me.

She was so horny, as shown by the desperate groan she sent out into my mouth. I started to get a bit wet just imagining what might occur later tonight after Bea went to sleep. I'd ordered a crib to be sent up to our room so that Lisa and I could have the bed. I wished it would succeed.

"You were incredible. That song—"

"Did you enjoy it?"

"I loved it!" I looked at her face and asked, "Are you alright?"

"Winter was here. She attended the show and heard the song. She was given a pass by Steve, and when she saw me in this room, she questioned me about us." She needed to be honest with me, and I appreciated that.

"I know."

"You know?"

"Yeah. We were in front of the door. I briefly overheard the conversation before leaving to give you some privacy."

"Wow."

"There is no need for an explanation. It is what it is. And I am aware of what she is experiencing. I understand what it feels like to lose someone you love. I'm just so happy to have you in my life right now." I hesitated. I had a lot I wanted to tell her. Proud was not enough to express how I felt after watching her perform tonight. "Now that I've seen you perform on a large platform, it is clearer than ever how much you were destined to lead this life. You are not only incredibly skilled, but you also have a wonderful personality. I don't want you to ever give up on this out of guilt. You'll never need to make a decision. We'll be there for you at all times."

She gave Bea a lift before giving me another kiss. "Considering how difficult it has been for me to be away, you are fantastic for expressing that. I used to believe that I wanted celebrity, but this experience has shown me that, for me, it's really all about the music. The rest, I don't think I actually want it in the long run. I wouldn't swap this experience for anything, but I'd think about it if the right chance came up. It is not acceptable for me to spend so much time away from my family. I don't want it at all." My face was cradled in her hands after a little pause. "Music would not exist without you. All of the things you live for may be expressed through music, which is a mirror of your enthusiasm. I breathe for you. You are my heart. You're my music...you and Bea."

"I love you so much."

She reached for her coat. "Let's leave right away."

"What? No wild after party? What kind of rockstar are you?"

"What do you mean? I'm wild." She chuckled. "I'm returning to my hotel room with two girlfriends." She winked.

24. EPILOGUE

Pov: Lalisa Manoban.

Never in a million fucking years did I think that my life would be like this- in this way.

If you had asked my pussy-whipped fifteen-year-old self where she envisioned herself in ten years, she undoubtedly would have replied, "On an island somewhere with Patch."

That is still exactly how I would respond now, so I guess some things never change. Then, it would have seemed like a pipe dream, but today, it was a reality for me.

Watching Roseanne playing with Bea down at the shoreline, I thought about the evolution of the roles she'd played in my life.

The mysterious girl with the eye patch.

The best friend.

The teenage fantasy.

The girl who stole my heart then broke it and took it with her when she ran away.

The estranged friend.

The forbidden roommate.

The girlfriend.

The mother of my babies.

She had never been sexier than she was right now, carrying my own baby-our baby. When Roseanne was four months pregnant, she had just begun to show, mainly in her tits and ass, which was perfectly great with me.

A few months after I returned from the trip and on July 26th of last year, I had proposed to her. We were supposed to get married exactly a year from that day, but I changed my mind and chose to propose on that day. It was significant since 0726 was the last set of numbers on my barcode tattoo, which was meant to stand for the day she left me ten years prior. I was committed to changing how those numbers were seen. Now, that date-today-would always be the day she became my wife.

We wanted a simple beach wedding with just the three of us, not a lavish reception. We would spend the morning by the beach, have a wedding on the beach at dusk, and then have a clam bake with Rosé's favourite seafood-dirty-grab crabs and lobster.

We were going to let Roger next door to marry us because it turned out that he had ordained himself to officiate a ceremony for a friend of his years earlier. Ironically, despite the fact that I still regularly busted Roger Podger's balls, he had grown to be a good buddy of mine.

As Bea ran in my direction, a group of gulls dispersed. Her dress was saturated as she handed me a seashell. "Mommy! Blue! "

"What do you have for me, Bella Manoban?"

"We're looking for something old, something new, something borrowed, and something blue for the ceremony later," Rosé said as she dusted sand from her skirt. "We found this blue shell."

I gave it back to her and she grinned, "That's perfect, Bumblebee."

"We have to figure out the rest," Rosé said as she took something out of her pocket and handed it to Bea. "We have something brand-new, but it's really for you, not for me. Give it to Mommy, Bea."

I was given a little box by my daughter. Inside was a guitar pick with the words "Thank you for picking me."

I hugged her and said, "Thank you for picking me, sweetheart. I really love this."

I was going to legally adopt Bea after the wedding. She was now two years old and even more devoted to me. Thankfully, Shawn, that asswipe, voluntarily gave up his parenting authority.

Life was good. I continued to work my software job and played at Sandy's a couple times a week. I had already rejected down a chance to tour with a different, lesser-known musician. Even though being a travelling musician was exciting, the drawbacks outweighed the advantages. I didn't want to lose any special opportunities to spend time with my family. I was mistaken when I thought that music was my life.

My girls are my life.

"Hm so...we have something brand-new and something blue, all right. We just need something old and borrowed right now," I said.

I felt Rosé's arm around my neck. "I was thinking of looking through some of Grandma's old things in the safe area. Since we moved in, I haven't looked through it. We could probably get something old there." I moved from my sand-based position. "Let's get moving."

We all three took a stroll back to the house. Roseanne's plain white strapless dress was hanging off the mantle in the main room. It made me giddy simply looking at it, knowing that tonight, she would officially become Roseanne Manoban. The paper, however, was irrelevant. For as long as I could remember, she had been mine. I gave her a long look as she fiddled with the safe. Knowing she was pregnant with my baby did things to me. Knowing that I was to blame for her changing body's sumptuous shape, sparked a primordial reaction in me.

My need for sex was out of this world, but happily she shared my enthusiasm. I was eagerly anticipating tonight's wedding night. For the first time ever, Bea would spend the night with Hailey and Roger. I had grand plans to make the most of Roseanne and the vacant house.

Behind a picture in the kitchen wall was where the locker was hidden. She finally succeeded in unlocking it. We looked through the contents when I moved closer to her.

There were a few documents, a few pieces of jewellery, and numerous pictures inside.

I put a vintage-looking rhinestone barrette in Rosé's hair and tucked some hair behind her ear with it. "Beautiful" I briefly caught a glimpsc of Bea and little Patch in her face, the two young girls I had fell in love with.

Rosé started looking through the pictures, some of which were of her mother and grandfather. Before she lifted a Polaroid, her hand briefly stopped moving. Even in the digital age, grandma loved to capture images with analogue cameras.

Roseanne and I were in this particular photo when we were about ten and eleven years old. The picture was taken from back as we were seated on Grandma's steps. Rosé was resting her head on my shoulder while I was carrying my first guitar.

The bottom had the following written in blue pen by Grandma: The way it was meant to be.

She handed me the picture, which I took to look at it more thoroughly. "Wow."

"This is proof, Lisa. She gave us this house because she was sure it would reunite us. She hoped that when we did discover this photo, it would serve as a reminder of how pointless our estrangement had been. She probably didn't have faith that we would find our way back to each other on our own. She wanted to send us a message." She gazed at it. "Check this out. How priceless. Look at all the years we wasted."

I remarked, "It happened the way it was meant to."

"You think so?"

"Yes. Think about it. We wouldn't have had as much angry sex without all of that bottled up rage," I grinned. "That tiny child in your belly may not have been anything we could have created." We found out recently that our baby was a girl. She was going to be called Melody.

I continued, "I know this is strange for me to say, seeing as though I don't want to think about you and that asswipe, Shawn, but if we hadn't separated, Bea wouldn't be here. So, no...I wouldn't change anything in the past. Never."

I took another look at the writing on the picture.

The way it was meant to be.

I grabbed a pencil from the counter and finished the phrase by inserting a small letter S.

The way it was meant to Bea.

I then take out another piece of paper and begin writing on it. It appeared to be:

To Rosie, my future wife;

Life or death doesn't matter, the only thing I wanted is to be with you and marry you. I'd like to resolve this with you. I want all of my poetry or song to be about you. I want my future to be filled with ours. I want you to have all my years.

I want to argue, make up, and be close to you. I want to go grocery shopping, build a home, and share silence with you. I want to trace stars, reach dreams, and share victories with you.

I'll love you forever, and even after forever. I'll love you a moment longer, even after time does not exist anymore.

-From Lisa.

As soon as I add the dot to the end of the word, I look at Rosé with so much-so much love. Then I folded the paper and attached it to our childhood photos on it. Soon, when Bea and her sister have grown up, we will open this locker again-we hope to see it there once more.

A proof of my love for their mother.

And of course, my love for them as well.

With a light touch she turned my face to hers. Then her hands settled on my chest like a bird's wings at rest. Our faces were very close. It felt to me as though my whole life was held in the balance of that moment.

I held her face with both hands and forced her to look directly at me, still shivering beneath her touch. "I'm in love with you. I love you"

Our fingers are entwined as we lie there for a while-just breathing and feel each other's warmth.